One Day In The Promised Land

Ryan Greenp

Text Copyright © Ryan Greenpike

All Rights Reserved

Table of Contents

The Hens Part 1 : Packing

The Dealer Part 1 : Arrival

The Reps Part 1 : Welcome To Wonderland

The Journalist Part 1 : Bit Early For All This

The Resort Manager Part 1 : San An In The Morning

The Bouncer Part 1 : A New Toy

The Stags Part 1 : London

The Resort Manager Part 2 : Breakfast By The Beach

The Reps Part 2 : Perfect Party Planning and Preparation

The Bouncer Part 2 : Croissant Show

The Stags Part 2 : Stansted

The Journalist Part 2 : Pikes

The Hens Part 2 : Bora Boring

The Dealer Part 2 : Delegation

The Resort Manager Part 3 : Meeting

The Thief Part 1 : Commuting

The Shop Girl Part 1 : Daytime Dullness

The Holidaymakers Part 1 : Arrival

The Bouncer Part 3 : Sunset

The Thief Part 2 : Sunset Vibes

The Reps Part 3 : Boat Trip

The Resort Manager Part 4 : Super-sleuthing

The Stags Part 3 : Hotel Playa Sol

The Dealer Part 3 : Collection

The PR Part 1 : Fishing

The Hens Part 3 : Dinner

The Journalist Part 3 : Dinner

The Shop Girl Part 2 : Star Signs

The Thief Part 3 : Clocking On

The Holidaymakers Part 2 : A Drink At The Rock Bar

The Bouncer Part 4 : A Fight and A Lost Phone

The Reps Part 4 : Best Laid Plans

The Stags Part 4 : The West End

The Thief Part 4 : Clocking Off

The Bouncer 5 : Rough Justice

The Holiday Makers Part 3 : A Bit of Good Luck

The Dealer 4 : Delivery

The Hens Part 4 : Cream

The Stags Part 5 : Amnesia

The Reps Part 5 : Reckoning

The Resort Manager 5 : Caught In The Act

The Shop Girl Part 3 : Gunfight At The OK Corrall

The PR Part 2 : Casting A Line

The Journalist Part 4 : West End Girls

The Dealer Part 5 : Search and Rescue

The Holiday Makers Part 4 : Dancing In The Disco, Bumper To Bumper

The Stags Part 6 : San Rafael

The Shop Girl Part 4 – Disco Bombshell

The PR Part 3 : Biting

The Journalist Part 5 : Exit Strategy

The Holiday Makers Part 5 : Escape To Victory

The Dealer Part 6 : Going For A Dip

The Shop Girl Part 5 : Rave-elation

The PR Part 4 : Reeling

The Hens Part 5 : Starting Again

Epilogue

Acknowledgements

The Hens Part 1 : Packing

The baggage carousel splutters into life and the parade of suitcases begins snaking its way through the hall. Mine is a little pink number, which you'd think would be easy to spot, but no way – at least 30% of the bags spilling onto the carousel are pink. Mind you, my one has a distinctive red wine coloured stain on it.

Except it's not red wine. It's my blood.

It ended up there last night when my fiancée said goodbye in his own inimitable style. He's usually quite careful, but I ran into a door trying to get out of the room, and got a nasty nosebleed for my trouble. Although that pales into insignificance next to the beating I received. No hits to the face though. He's far too clever for that. Mainly body blows and hair pulling. He's such a lovely man. And he's mine. And I'm his. In nearly every conceivable way.

I knew when he got home that I was in for a long night. I can always tell from the sound his keys make when he throws them on the table by the door. If it's a gentle spill of metal on the table, I might just get bullied a bit; if they land with a crash, then I'm more than likely going to be hit. The noise they made last night sounded like a dustbin lid in a hailstorm. It's a great early warning system.

He was back late, just after ten. He'd sent me a text about five saying to have dinner ready for eight. And it was. I'd left it under another plate in the kitchen, so it wouldn't dry out too much. It must've been less than ten seconds after he'd got through the door, that I heard swearing, exaggerated retching and the sound of a plate being thrown on the floor. I felt my stomach constrict with every heavy stomp on the stairs, before all the air rushed out of my chest as he barged into the bedroom.

"What the fuck was that shit supposed to be? Are you trying to poison me?"

"It was chicken and pasta, Paul. And no, I'm not trying to poison you."

"Don't be fucking smart with me, Vicky. I'm not in the fucking mood." His eyes took in the suitcase on the bed. "What are you doing?"

"I'm packing for your sister's hen," I said. My tone of voice was apologetic. He snorted derisively. I pressed on with something placatory.

"I'm sorry you didn't like your dinner. Give me ten minutes and I'll come down and make you a sandwich."

He then went over to the suitcase and poured the contents on the bed. I had anticipated this, so the clothes I knew he wouldn't approve of were hidden in the washing machine in a Sainsbury's bag. But he still found fault with nearly everything in the bag. I'm only going for a day and a night, so there wasn't much in there. He first held aloft my solitary pair of semi-sexy knickers, holding them up to the light like they would reveal some sort of secret when illuminated.

"These are like fucking dental floss. Why the fuck would you want to wear these? You'll look like a slut, what with your arse all hanging out of this cheese-wire. And let's face it Vicky, it's not exactly a nice arse."

"They're comfortable, Paul, and no-one's going to see them."

"Yeah, right. I know what Ibiza is like. And I know what my sister and her mates are like. Fucking slappers, the lot of them."

Next up is a long sleeved, rather snug dress. That got thrown over me, humiliatingly draping itself over my face.

"Why are you taking that? You'll look like a fucking slag. And you're too fat. Are you going out there on the pull? Is that what it is? At least tell me if that's what you want to do. You owe me that."

"No, Paul, I don't want anyone else but you. And please don't call me that."

He then proceeded to work his way through everything in there – my hair straighteners: "you're only going for one night, why do you need these"; my one-piece, extremely un-revealing swimming costume: "you'll look like a beached whale in this"; even my dowdy just-above-the-knee skirt: "sluttish". His suitcase biopsy was only the start of the humiliation. I went downstairs to make him a bacon sandwich. Just as I'd turned the rashers and laid them in the bottom of the pan, he came storming downstairs with the suitcase – apparently there was a packet of condoms in the zip-up pocket inside.

"What the FUCK are these doing in there?" He said, throwing the small cardboard box across the kitchen at me. It bounced off my head and landed next to the pan.

"I don't know. I borrowed the suitcase off Debbie yesterday. They must be hers." I said calmly, working on keeping the quiver out of my voice. I did borrow the suitcase. And the condoms are nothing to do with me. But my explanation wasn't going to make any difference to anything. I was due a kicking anyway for daring to be out from under his control for less than 48 hours. My heart sank into my stomach and my pulse began to race.

It happened fast, it always does, especially when I remember it later on. The first salvo involved being clumped around the head with the empty suitcase. Not particularly painful, but enough to throw me off balance and onto the floor. He then tossed the suitcase behind him and grabbed my hair, bending my neck back and leaning into me and shouting. He called me every misogynistic, foul mouthed and disgusting name under the sun you can think of, and probably a few more. He then pulled me up off my knees and shoved me towards the cooker before booting me in the arse. It was then that I ran out of the room, tripping over on my way and cracking my face into the door. The suitcase broke my fall. I wish I could say it ended there, but it didn't. It continued into the front room, until he had satisfied his rage. And then he ate his sandwich. The bacon was perfectly cooked by the time he'd finished. The worst part was later. When, as he so sweetly put it, we "made up".

Luckily this morning, I left before he woke up. I grabbed the case of decoy clothes, then the real ones from the washing machine, and hopped in the waiting cab before he could get up and start again. I left him a note on the table, telling him I love him and with instructions for how he could heat up his dinner, which was already cooked and in the fridge. As I got in the cab, I sent him a text, again telling him I love him. He needs to be told I love him. A lot. All the time. I got a reply a few minutes later. "Sorry we rowed last night. Sometimes I just lose it a bit. But it's only because I love you so much."

Quite.

I turn my attention back to the baggage carousel. There it is. Debbie's pink bag. I grab it as it goes past, wincing at the pain in my ribs, and hoist it onto a trolley. The girls grab theirs and soon enough we're through passport control and outside in the stifling heat waiting for a cab. There are four of us. Me, Sharon, Kelly and Keeley – Paul's sister. We used to be a very tight group of mates when we were younger, but over the last few years, different career and life trajectories (and one possessive fiancée) have all played their part in knocking a wedge between us. The camaraderie and closeness once there now seems forced. Well, it does to me at least. The banter is snippy and sly, not funny and affectionate like it used to be. I don't really care about their lives, and I know they don't care about mine.

They all know Paul is rough with me, but they never bring it up; they never ask me if I'm ok. I'm not sure exactly how much they know, but I've heard enough moronic comments coming from them about how passionate he seems and how sweet that is. Idiots. How sweet is this broken rib I'm nursing? How sweet is the aching in my scalp where he nearly ripped my hair out? How sweet is it that my bruised coccyx makes sitting down agonising? Not fucking very, I can tell you. His sister is the worst. She was the one that introduced us. She must have known what he was like. Over the last seven years she's witnessed every belittling Christmas meal, every birthday slanging match and the gradual whittling away of my self-esteem by that life-sucking bastard. And has she ever said anything to him by way a chastisement or to me by way of support? Has she fuck. But then again, she's the only reason I've been allowed on this trip. So maybe there are some thanks due.

The Dealer Part 1 : Arrival

My innards lurch as the plane crashes back down to earth. I've never been a fan of flying. When you factor in the contents of my stomach, and the fact that I *really* need a shit, you go some way to understanding what an ordeal this is. As we shudder to a halt by the terminal and the seatbelt lights ping on, the entire aircraft gets up in unison and everyone starts clamouring for the exit. I try and make myself as unnoticeable as possible, and assiduously avoid making eye contact with the group of boisterous lads in front of me, all wearing matching T-shirts and already well lagered-up. They look like trouble, but that could work to my advantage. As long as they remain in front of me, it's much more likely airport security will pull them in for a check rather than me.

It's when I'm stood in the queue at passport control that the first serious pang hits me. I think for a moment I'm going to go right there, but I steel myself as a battle of wills between my colon and my mind takes place. My mind wins. The wave passes and I get to the front. The pig glances at my passport and waves me through. I march straight out of the baggage hall, past the bog and out of the terminal. The heat hits me like a baseball bat as the exit doors part before me. The rise in temperature makes the brownie I'm baking even more eager to break out. I wince as a rivulet of sweat trickles down the small of my back in down my arse crack, taunting me. Luckily the cab queue is short and I'm soon on my way to Charlie and Eddie's.

It takes about 15 minutes to get to their villa, which is up a hill off the side of the main motorway on the island. The cab drops me off outside the big white security gate and I press the buzzer and shove my face into the camera. The lock clicks and I step through the small side gate and begin the three minute walk up to the house. Another gut-wrenching twinge hits me and I find myself having to stop and clench my sphincter closed. Again, the pain subsides and I reach the house. I go down the side to the terrace that runs round to the back. It overlooks a lush, landscaped garden with a dazzling swimming pool at the bottom. Beyond that, the sea makes its presence known by the sound of its waves breaking over the rocks on the other side of the high security fence.

Charlie and Eddie are sitting on these massive sofas next to an equally large glass coffee table. Charlie's got his head stuck in the Sun, and Eddie's eyes are glued to Georgie Thompson's cleavage on Sky Sports News. I approach and wait for them to acknowledge my presence. After about 20 seconds, Charlie lowers his paper. He clocks my stance, which clearly gives it away that I need a dump, and I need one rather urgently.

"You alright there, Rocky?"

"Er, do I look alright? I need a shit. Badly."

This causes them to burst out laughing. Ha ha fucking ha. They eventually relent, and Charlie turns to Eddie and motions towards the kitchen.

"Fetch him the kettle and a sieve."

Eddie comes back moments later holding an orange colander and a bin bag.

"Can't find the sieve, so use this. Bin it afterwards when you get back to town. And make sure you get me a replacement from the Eroski before tomorrow. I always have pasta on Fridays."

"Cheers Eddie."

I turn and waddle into the house to the bog.

"Leave the door unlocked – I'll bring the kettle when it's boiled."

I crab-walk down an air-conditioned hallway and into their luxurious bathroom. I lift both the toilet lid and seat up, and position the colander in the bowl. I put the seat down and in one fluid motion, I tear the buttons on my jeans apart, shove them and my pants down and land my arse on the lav.

I savour what is about to happen for a couple of seconds and then I drop my guts. It sounds like an avalanche. Some passes easily, some needs a little squeeze, but the overriding feeling of relief I feel when emptied is palpable. I almost float off the toilet. I hear Eddie's footsteps approach, and he walks in without knocking, carrying a steaming kettle. He puts it on the floor and leaves me to it. Half-way down the corridor I hear him shout:

"Don't forget to wipe your arse."

I don't, and put the soiled bog roll in the bin bag, before getting up and pulling up my strides. I reach down for the kettle and slowly pour it over the contents of the colander. The torrent of water washes away the faeces fast, revealing four, slender, waxy, cellophane logs about 3 inches long and just under an inch thick. I empty the kettle over them, swirling the colander around, and then scoop them out and chuck them in the sink under the hot tap. A poke around in the cupboard finds some disinfectant, and I squirt a load into the sink and give the cellophane and wax covered eggs a good clean, before drying them off and sticking them in my pocket. I tie up the bin bag and head back downstairs.

"Well, give 'em here then." Charlie opens with when I walk back onto the terrace.

I fish them out of my pocket and put them on the table. Eddie picks up a knife and slices one open from top to bottom with the dexterity you would expect from a surgeon. He peels off the outer layer of wax and cling-film without causing any damage to the tightly rolled baggie inside. He unfurls it and sticks the tip of the knife into the 100 or so grams of cocaine it contains, and brings a small mountain up to his nose. It vanishes in a sniff and he leans backwards onto the sofa, exhaling theatrically. He swings back up like a Weeble and announces that it's "lovely stuff."

Charlie picks up one of the packages and throws it at me.

"Go and start knocking that out down Bossa this afternoon. There's four ounces in there, so that's at least 200 grams once you've stepped on it. You can come down the club later and sling some out there as well. Bring us back 10 large by Monday."

"No probs. Any chance of a lift into town?"

"Yeah, I've gotta go and see Roger anyway. Do you want anything, Eddie?"

"Nah, I'm good." Eddie replies as he sticks the knife back into the bag. He looks up at me as he remembers something. "Oh yeah. Passport."

He clicks his fingers impatiently as I hand it over. I leave the terrace and half jog to catch up Charlie who is already opening the big metal garage door. His motor is one of the flashiest I've ever seen. A fucking Lamborghini Diablo. Old school style. We speed off down the winding track that leads to the main road, every bump and loose stone ricocheting off the underside of the car. Because we're so low on the ground, the noise is intensified and makes the drive feel even more of a rollercoaster than it usually does. I fucking love it. We emerge onto the main San An-Ibiza Town motorway from a tiny slip road hidden behind a road sign. Blink and you'd miss it. The car pelts down the concrete highway, past San Raf and towards Ibiza Town.

We bomb past Amnesia, where they're getting ready for Cream tonight, and approach the turn off for the road to PDB. We take the corner of the roundabout fast, and I push against the g-force as we come out of the bend and speed past the Coca-Cola factory. It's a rush. I look over at Charlie and see he's enjoying himself even more than me. I grin as he gives it some more on the accelerator and we hurtle onto the motorway proper. Almost immediately, we slow down and take the exit up to the Tapa Tapa roundabout and head towards the coast.

About five minutes walk from PDB, Charlie pulls into a hotel car park and kills the engine. He turns in his seat and, to my surprise, begins to tell me that I'm doing a good job and they're happy with me. This isn't the kind of appraisal one usually gets in this firm. Usually motivational pep talks are, er, a little bit more Neanderthal. Charlie winds up his fluffing of me with some extra work for the evening.

"I'm going to need you for something a bit more demanding later on tonight," he says softly. He's always more menacing when he's quiet. "Go with Perry to pick up something from a friend of ours in Ibiza Town. Then you're going to drop it off to someone, then get over to the club as soon as. He'll pick you up at about 2am. Be sober and dress smart. Now, fuck off and get busy slinging that gear out."

He's such a charmer. I hop out and start walking back to my flat near the beach. That's sweet about tonight. Definitely constitutes some sort of promotion. Seeing as I'm "contracted" to this pair of crooks, I might as well do the best I can and try to enjoy the trappings of a successful and villainous lifestyle. The flash cars, the Goodfellas-style way we enter clubs, the birds, the constant VIP service. It ain't all bad.

The Reps Part 1 : Welcome To Wonderland

Ah, Thursday morning at Hotel Tropicana. Let me take you to a place where membership's a smiling face. And 59 Euros per person, per night. Not much rubbing shoulders with the stars, mind, although I can see George Michael dressed as an airline pilot over there with his mate Andrew. And coming up behind them are Pepsi and Shirley. Hold on a minute. What the fuck is going on here? And what the fuck is that beeping noise? I look around and realise I'm actually stood in the car park at Pikes. Eh? This is a tad confusing. I'm sure I went home last night. And what is my bed doing over there? In fact my whole bedroom is here, sandwiched between a white Golf convertible and a jeep. This is weird. I'm feeling knackered anyway, so I decide it's probably best to go and lie down and try and make sense of this strange situation I find myself in.

As soon as the back of my head disappears into the soft pillow, I feel myself falling and jolt myself back upright. I blink a few times, and shake the dream out of my head. I slowly come round and hear Wham!'s finest tune blaring out of my radio alarm clock. That makes sense. I'm glad I'm not having dreams about George Michael dressed as a pilot of my own accord. I lean over and grab my phone, mashing my thumb on its face in order to stop the electronic birdsong. Then I turn down the radio a bit. Out here, it's smart to have two alarms. I know I've entered the world of the fully awake when I realise how hanging I feel. I close my eyes and let my brain defrag to the point where it's of some use to me.

I feel myself to see if I'm in one piece. I am. Nothing seems to be broken. I ache all over though and my head is banging like a rusty gate in a force 10 gale. Not as banging as last night was though, but it's still scoring pretty high on the bang-o-meter. But what a fucking scream we had. We ended up in the VIP at Pacha for Subliminal. We'd got chatting to some crazy dude in Grial beforehand, turned out he had a table booked in the club so we tagged along with him and his mates. We drank all their booze and sniffed all their gak. Lovely stuff. Nice bunch of lads. Proper mental though – one of them was blatantly doing lines off the table and got us all chucked out – still, rock'n'roll and all that.

I check out the time. Shit. Better get moving soon. I look at my phone and see a few missed calls from my team leader, Amy. We were reps together last year, and shared a flat and spent most of the summer getting wrecked together. But this year she's been promoted and isn't handling the transition from colleague (+friend) to boss (+friend) well at all. She's become a bit of a bitch. Which is a shame, because I know she's actually super cool underneath. I know she has to act in a different way now she has a different role, but she's overcompensating for her lack of experience by becoming a ball-busting bastard.

A text arrives, from her, asking me to ring her back ASAP. Fuck that. I have an inkling of what she's calling about, but I'm not going through this shit again. This company is getting on my tits with their out of touch attitude and obtuse way of doing things. All I need to do is avoid Amy until later, when hopefully she'll be fucking off to Mallorca on a jolly with the other managers, and it'll all be fine. I've got a lot on today, but if it all goes well, which it will, I'm going to be making them all a lot of money and giving their waning credibility a shot in the arm. And I can well do without her nagging this afternoon, giving me shit about what I plan for this evening. I can just see her now, after the fact, patting me on the back and praising my ingenuity.

Tonight, I am throwing the party to end all parties. I've marketed it to my guests as being a secret party in a secret location, which it pretty much is. The bosses are unaware of what I'm doing, although I suspect Amy has twigged. And only a select few on the team know where I'm doing it.

On one of my recent drug-fuelled adventures out in the campo, I came across a little clearing formed around a natural bowl not far from Bennirass. You can get to it by following a dirt track across some old Ibicencan's huge back garden, or more interestingly, via a tunnel in the rock that opens out onto a little cave in the cliffs by the sea. It looks fucking magic. There's a shack in the clearing that I'm stocking with a rude soundsystem, as well as a generator to power it. I've also gained permission from the land-owner to use the place – due to the rather incestuous nature of the natives, it turns out he's the cousin of an old geezer who runs a Spanish bar I frequent back in San An, and he put in a word for me. I've hired a boat to get us there in style, also decked out with a pretty thermonuclear rig. There will be dancers, people on stilts, fire-eaters, tons of booze, torches, decorations and a couple of sick DJs to get the party rocking. I conservatively estimate that about 150 people will come, but because of the cloak and dagger way I've had to do this, I've not sold any pre-sale tickets – everyone will pay on the door. Or on the boat, as it were. So I'm taking a bit of a risk, especially as I've already forked out cash from my liquidation for it. If I get 150 people at 30 Euros each, coupled with the amount we'll get from selling our own grog, we should see a return of a few grand. I hope. Or it could all go to shit and I'll be on a plane home tomorrow.

The thing is though, I've been given express orders by the powers that be not to do anything like this. I suggested it at a meeting at the start of the season and they shot me down straight away. The bosses are scared of any new ideas, so it immediately had a nice soggy blanket tossed on it. Clueless cunts. So I'm doing the only thing I can in this situation: I'm ignoring them and doing it anyway. And when I come back later with a fat bag of money for them, they can just shut it, suck my balls and start counting the cash. And I'll be a hero. Either that or they'll sack me out of spite. Ha.

So, anyway, today is going to be well busy.

I've got to get over to the venue and get everything ready this afternoon then come back here to collect the guests by 10 o'clock. I look at my phone again. It's just gone 1.30 – which is much later than I had hoped to get up, so I should really get a move on, but fuck it –

I've planned this one thoroughly enough and can afford another fifteen minutes in bed. I reset the alarm on my phone for 1.50, and lie back. I momentarily drift off and start to dream about being on a boat somewhere on a river, surrounded by jungle. I have a feeling of being hunted. Hopefully not by George Michael and Andrew Ridgeley though. Almost immediately the alarm drags me back into the real world. Time for me to face the day. I vault out of bed, do a nice big stretch and roar "Uggadugga" at myself in the mirror.

I drape my towel over my shoulder, yank open the door to my room and stick the kettle on. Having one of these is a rarity out here – I had to pinch this one from the managers' flat upstairs. I make a brew and have a quick shit, shower and shave and skip back to my room and throw my clothes on. My phone rings, and surprise, surprise, it's Amy again. Christ, she must really be pissed off. I drop the call, hoping she gets the message and gets off my back for a bit. I grab my stuff, finish off my cuppa and get out the door. Jody's going to be my number two today, but there's a couple of things I need to take care of in the hotel before we get cracking.

I canter across the road from my apartment block and into the hotel. I enter the lobby and enjoy the silence. At this time of day, it's positively peaceful; a stark contrast to the usual drunken and drugged-up hubbub that comes later. Over in the corner, Ash is setting up a welcome meeting. An obviously very hung-over Kirstie stumbles around behind him, struggling with a huge saucepan full of Don Simon and slopping most of it on the floor. Haha. She was in a right two and eight last night, well trolleyed. I seem to remember her dancing on the table when we got home with her shirt tied round her neck. She was singing about it being a makeshift cape to the tune of Spandau Ballet's 'Gold'. Priceless. It was one of those nights.

I get into the office to check my emails on the big dinosaur of a desktop that lives in there. There is a confirmation one from Artemis, the bloke from the titty-bar who has sorted the dancers. I've fronted cash from my liquidation to pay for it, so I'm mildly annoyed that it's shown up in the group inbox and potentially exposed my subterfuge. Shit. Amy might have seen it and that's why she's having an epi. Or maybe someone's grassed me up and let on that I'm putting on this shindig anyway. Or maybe she's seen one of the flyers I did knocking around, although I thought I'd left the flyer drop until late enough to minimise my chances of detection. I hit every room in the hotel with one last night just after she left, and paid a couple of workers to flyer the strip, beach and West End. And there are a couple of receipts knocking around as well that might let on. Oh, well, can't do anything about that now. On a positive note, there's also an email from the landowner that found its way into my personal inbox, saying that it's fine for us to hold a private party on his property. It's not legally binding obviously, but it might save me a headache if the pigs show up and kick off. If they can find us, that is. I print it off and delete the incriminating emails, then shut down the computer and head off to meet Jody in the lobby.

Kirstie is sat at the reps' desk, having abandoned Ash to do the welcome meeting by himself. I can hear his patter booming out from the other side of the lobby, telling the package holiday makers how they can save money buying their club tickets off him, and spouting the rest of the bollocks that we do in order to squeeze as much cash out of them as possible.

I pootle over to Kirstie and perch on the stool next to her. She's on her laptop, looking at various capes on some website. She's so engrossed she doesn't even register my arrival. In my peripheral vision, I see a group of girls walk past, and get a pang of fear. One of them I shagged the other day. I went up to her room to introduce myself and tell them about the hotel, seeing as they were late arrivals and hadn't attended a welcome meeting. And, well, you know how these things are. Flirting quickly escalated – her mates were out at the shops, before you think I was lucky enough to be involved in an orgy – and we ended up doing it on the balcony. Brilliant. But she's been a bit full-on whenever we've met since then, and I want to avoid her, so I duck under the desk and keep out of sight until I can see the reflection of her back receding in the glass wall behind the desk. I spring back up like a jack-in-the-box, and am greeted with a puzzled and perplexed looking Kirstie.

"I don't know if what you did just then was normal behaviour, Sean, because I'm still so wrecked from last night. But can I just ask why you crawled under the desk?"

"Avoidance tactics, Kirstie. Avoidance tactics. Anyway, have you found a nice cape yet?"

"I've found lots of nice capes. Too many, I think. I can't wear them all. I need to be harder on myself." She gasps, with a little more drama than necessary. I sometimes wonder about the girl and her obsessions. But she's very entertaining. A group of lads come up to the desk and enquire about some tickets for Cream. I tell them about this evening's shindig, and they say they'll come along to that as well. One of them furtively leans in to me and asks me if I can get him some coke.

"Mate, I wouldn't even bother. There are loads of people offering it round the West End and the seafront, but to be honest, it's all shit. You can't get good coke for love nor money here. It's all cut to fuck before it even gets to Ibiza. If you like, I can sell you this packet of sugar here," I say, holding up a sachet that came with Kirstie's cup of coffee. "It'll probably get you more buzzing than any of the ching on the island. I'd recommend you stick to the pills and booze, mate."

He looks disappointed and heads off to join his mates. I hate it when guests ask me for drugs. It goes against every entrepreneurial bone in my body to turn them down. I could make a fortune serving up to these guys, but I don't want to lose my job over something like that. Short term financial gain does not outweigh the long term benefits of not being sacked from a job that I'm actually pretty good at and enables me to have the time of my life. And the possibility of being buggered senseless by some hairy Juan in jail isn't one that turns me on too much as well. But, fuck me, it's hard saying no to these guys.

I see Jody coming through the doors and slide off the stool and bid farewell to Kirstie, who half croaks/half squeaks a goodbye at me. We meet in the middle of the lobby and high-five each other. We're on our second season out here together, and are both fully aware that in years to come we'll look back on these summers as the best days of our lives. And believe we're making the most of it. It'd be a crime not to.

We exit the hotel in a flurry of excitement and stop off at the shop on the way to the car to buy a couple of litre bottles of orange Aquarius. We stand by the counter and down them. They barely touch the sides, so I go back to the fridge and grab a couple of the pre-made iced coffee cartons. I know the caffeine will help us accomplish our missions, which include sneaking the hotel's back-up sound-system down to the shack, setting up the rig, getting the bar ready, doing the decorations and banners, and then going to the supermarket for the booze to stock it. We've got all afternoon to do it, so it should be easy. We leave the hotel grounds just as Amy pulls into the car park, but she doesn't see us. I jab Jody in the ribs and we stifle giggles as we duck out the other way and take the long way round.

"Not someone we need to see right now, don't you reckon?" I say, showing off my mastery of the skill of stating the obvious. Jody responds by wagging his finger at me in mock nag and making a repetitive honking noise.

"Do you think she's rumbled you then?" he says once he's finished his impression of her.

"Maybe. There was an email from the stripper guy in the group inbox, and I had a bunch of missed calls from her this morning, so I reckon she knows something. But fuck it, if this works I'll be her favourite person in the world."

We walk round to the car, and have a brief post-mortem of last night's antics.

"You were well cunted last night," Jody opens with a sage observation. "And you were making an awful noise on the balcony when you got back."

"Was I? I can't even remember getting home this morning. I'm glad I managed to get more than couple of hours' kip though. Tonight is going to be epic," I state. "I just need to shake off this hangover."

Jody brings up another couple of incidences from last night that were up until now unremembered. Apparently we went to the Bay after the club to drop some girls off, and in the cab I was speaking in tongues. The only time I was coherent was when scolding the cabbie for trying to "mug me off." I then accused him of being my best mate. Oh dear. I can see why I didn't want to remember all that. Embarrassing and clichéd is not my style. Still, I allow myself a guilty smirk at a night well had, although I'm mildly annoyed with myself that I got on it last night of all nights. I know I can throw a party with my arms tied behind my back and my eyes closed, but still, it doesn't help that I'm still a little bit fucked. But I can deal with it.

We get to my car, a dirty blue Volvo estate I drove over in April, and head round to the loading bay at the back of the hotel to pick up the sound-system. We cram four fuck-off loud speakers, an amplifier, speaker stands, two CDJs and a DJM 800 (with all attendant cables) into the back and are soon heading off through town to the road that leads up towards Benirras.

The Journalist Part 1 : Bit Early For All This

My alarm explodes into life. It sounds like someone is fucking my ears with a pneumatic drill. Shit. I've got to go to work. I only got into bed an hour and a half ago. Well, I say got *into*, but I'm on top of the covers and fully clothed. I feel like I'm coming down with something, but I know it's just the booze and drugs from last night's unexpected shenanigans exacting their toll. I roll on to the floor and drag myself out of my clothes and into the shower. I'm flying out to Ibiza to write a piece on one of the clubs out there today and meeting my snapper at Liverpool Street in less than an hour, so I need to move. Unfortunately, also tagging along on the trip is my boss, who is a cretin of the highest order. His presence threatens to ruin what should otherwise be an excellent jolly. I love trips like this. Although I must admit, after 5 years of working at the mag, I've started to feel a bit jaded by it. I've had a blast, but it's hardly Pulitzer Prize winning stuff. I know I can't do this forever. But I mustn't grumble. It's still the best job in the world.

    I finish in the bathroom and go thought to the kitchen and drain all the remaining liquids in the fridge – half a can of coke and an inch of concentrated orange juice. I shove a couple of tee-shirts and my Dictaphone in my bag – I decide against taking my proper laptop – and pack my little netbook instead. The cab arrives and beeps its horn, and I stumble out of the flat and hop in the back seat. It takes less than

20 minutes to get to Liverpool Street. Giles the Snapper is already waiting when I get there. He looks nearly as rough as I do.

"Morning nob-head. You look I how feel." I croak at him.

"Yeah, and you look even worse than I feel. And believe me, I feel fucking hanging."

I've been working with Giles for the last three years. Not only is he a brilliant photographer, he's fearless, funny and extremely persuasive – he seems to have the power to make anyone do anything he likes, just by pointing a camera at them. Makes my job a million times easier when I have an instigator like him in tow.

He hands me a hip flask and tells me it'll take the edge off. I have a long swig and gasp as the brandy sears through the fur that coats the inside of my mouth and throat.

"Agh. Uggadugga," I half burp, half wheeze to him. He takes a sip himself, and we go and grab a couple of cans of reasonably priced coke from the shop and head over to the Stansted Express.

The first few carriages are full of kids off to the White Isle and other exotic locations for their holidays in the sun. The hubbub of the various groups needles my lingering headache a bit, so we plot near the front of the train, where it's practically deserted. Giles stows his gear on the rack above, and I drop mine into the seat next to me. The train splutters into life and we ease out of Liverpool Street. We fly through east London towards Tottenham and then Essex, and soon enough we pull into Stansted. As we get onto the platform, I fish out my mobile and tell Giles to hold on while I call Kevin.

"Why on earth are you calling that nob?"

"He's coming with us."

"Oh fucking hell. Great. I've done trips with this twat before. All he wants to do is sit in his hotel room sniffing coke on his own."

"Here's hoping. I want to have some fun on this trip and if he's holed up in the room the whole time, then he's not cramping our style."

I get through to the snivelling bastard. He's already at the airport, so I tell him we'll meet him in the pub in the main terminal building. We head up the ramp and enter the booking hall. It's heaving, full of hopeful holidaymakers on their way to sunny climes for a week of shagging, fighting and boozing.

We fight our way through the throng to the grubby pub and find Kevin sat on his own at one of the tables near the back. We go through the motions of pretending to be happy to see each other. The faux camaraderie is a see-through as a wet T-shirt in one of the competitions I expect you see down San An. I dump my bag and go and get a round in.

The bar is brightly lit and loud, and threatens to bring my hangover back to the surface, so after I deliver the drinks to the table I skulk over to the McDonalds and grab a couple of double cheeseburgers. The high concentration of essential sugars, salts, fats, porkiness and stodge will bolster me. I order two and the dude chucks them in a bag. I clutch the warm brown package lovingly as I go back to the pub.

I flop down in the chair and fish one out. It doesn't even touch the sides, and I slosh it down with the rest of my jar, before releasing a low growl of a burp. My stomach rumbles, and I can feel my internal game of intestinal Tetris freeing up pockets of air as the much needed food absorbs the remnants of hangover inside me.

Giles fetches some more drinks from the bar. I notice Kevin is drinking coke, while we're on the pints.

"Not getting involved, are we?" I quip, motioning to his drink. Kevin casts me a disapproving look.

"We're not all as hard-core as you, Jack," he sneers. "Some of us have to remain professional."

Is he having a laugh or is this his snide attempt at banter? I can't quite decide. He's clearly having a dig, but in my less than 100% state, a tentacle of paranoia slides over me and pierces my chest. Twat. He can talk anyway. He's renowned for going on trips and jollies and not being able to handle his booze and drugs. More than once have I had to write his features for him when he's come back empty-handed. I've written some amazing stories about places I've never been to and things I've never done, with the only information available pried from Kevin's Swiss-cheese mind over a fag on the office roof the day after he's got back. Unprofessional? Well, he'd know. At least when I go off and do a story, I come back with the piece regardless of how twatted I get. And this story will be no different.

"Of course. That's why I'm having a drink, I'm being utterly professional by experiencing this exactly the way any of our readers would want to. I'm putting my health on the line in the name of true investigative journalism. I should win an award for this."

We laugh and the tension eases. The conversation turns to our plan of attack for Ibiza. We're on the island for just 24 hours, so for us to get what we need for the story, we need a flimsy itinerary of sorts. The club that's flying us out there obviously is the priority, but we'll need some action shots from the beach and the West End first – preferably with birds frolicking around with their tops off. Then we'll hit the club, get the required shots of me pissing around, and take as many drugs as we can and cause some havoc. Fucking lovely. The actual club night is cheesy as fuck, but with me covering the words, and Giles covering the visuals, we'll come back with a suitably raucous story, like we always do. I'm feeling happy and confident about it going smoothly when Kevin's mouth flaps open and the following words spill out:

"Oh yeah, and there's going to be those girls off Big Brother there as well. We're doing a glamour shoot with them, so I want you to do the interview with them when we're at the club. We need to keep them sweet because their PR gets most of the reality stars."

"Are you joking? Those fucking idiots?" This is bollocks. I hate having to talk to these chumps.

"Yeah. Have you got a problem with that?"

"Yeah, I've got a problem with us featuring morons like that. Not only are they as thick as pig-shit, they're hardly worthwhile for the mag. The only thing remarkable about them is their tendency to shun clothing whenever a camera is about."

"Exactly. Perfect for us."

This pair of oxygen-thieves have featured in this year's BB. Their 'thing' was to lie around wearing no clothes and bitch about the other housemates. And they've assumed that's enough to guarantee them some level of stardom. And the sad truth is, it has. This bothers me. If you get your tits out on telly, that's an achievement? That it's not hard work and using your brain that's going to make you a success, it's actually the opposite that will make you rich and famous? But that's how it works now. The need for content to fill magazines, websites and millions of TV channels makes stars out of anyone. Doing these kinds of interviews makes me feel like a fucking hypocrite. I want to scream at the top of my lungs "You're making the human race stupider", but I know I wouldn't be heard. My voice would be drowned out by the babble of a million talking heads reminiscing on E4 about the 100 Greatest Nails In The Coffin Of Anything Resembling Culture. Presented by thingy off Celebrity Love Island.

I really need a new job. I'm not usually this angry.

We go through the security checks and I leave Giles and Kevin while I go to WH Smiths and grab a copy of the Times, the Sun and the Guardian, as well as a couple of bottles of coke and some sweets.

The sugar will keep me going until I can have a disco nap on the plane. There's a group of hens playing silly buggers with a dildo in the queue in front of me. One of them is incredibly cute, but given the way she's carrying herself, she seems too self-conscious to acknowledge it. She catches my eye so I smile at her and she looks away as if she's done something wrong. I pay up and go outside to check out the TV screens for boarding details. Our flight switches from "wait in lounge" to "go to gate" and I go and find Kevin and Giles. We get on the monorail and glide round to the gate. We get on the plane and take the very back seats, so we'll be the first off when we get to Ibiza. The plane fills up swiftly in front of us, and we're soon bombing and rattling our way down the runway.

As the ground falls away from us, a cheer goes up from the majority of the plane. The buzz is infectious and excitement ousts hung-over as the predominant feeling in my stomach. I crack the lid off one of the bottles of coke and drain half of it in one go. I aim the resulting jet of belch-air at Giles and he gags and elbows me in the shoulder. Kevin is already trying to sleep, leaning up against the window with the shutter down.

Once we reach cruising altitude, I get the sweets out and stick a wad made of about six fruit gums in my mouth. I flip open my notebook and start writing some notes and jotting down a few questions for the reality birds interview later on. I start off by writing the kinds of questions I want to ask but never will, generally pertaining to the decline of society and the role of reality television in its demise. I then write a load of inoffensive yet extremely left-field ones. I hate interviewing these kinds of celebs. Invariably they are either too young or too thick to have anything interesting to say, so it falls to me to dig out the turd polish and make their inane monosyllabic mutterings interesting. I'll do this by asking them a series of absurd questions which are entertaining enough in themselves, so that their brainless replies are entirely unnecessary. I toy with the idea of writing a scathing attack on the current state of popular culture and reality media. Ha. Yeah, like they would ever have the balls to publish that.

The trolley dolly comes round offering drinks, and I take great pleasure in leaning over Giles and jabbing Kevin hard in the ribs. He jumps awake, and before he can snap off a complaint, I enthusiastically tell him I've bought him a beer. He looks disorientated, but I shove a can of lager into his hand he that seems to placate him.

We cheers, crunch the cans together and have a swill and I offer the sweets around. Kevin declines and climbs over us to go to the bog once the stewardess has moved the cart out of the way. He shuts the door behind him and spends a good ten minutes in there. When he eventually comes out, he looks like Rudolph the Reindeer. Oh I wonder why. Tight bastard doesn't even offer me and Giles any. He gets up twice more during the flight, and I'm itching to say something, but I know that he'd love me to ask him for a line, just so he could feel the intoxication of power and say "no". I say nothing.

Kevin slides the shutter up as we come into land and I lean over and see the old part of Ibiza Town beneath us. The sea is brilliant blue and the island is positively glowing in the sunlight. It looks fucking beautiful. My spirits soar and the last of the hangover is swept away in a torrent of excitement and anticipation. I'm gonna enjoy myself today.

The Resort Manager Part 1 : San An In The Morning

A muffled thud wakes me from my slumber. It takes a moment for the white noise in my head to tune back into reality and I work out where I am. San An. Shit. I'm still only in San An. Every time I think I'm going to wake up back in England. When I was home after my first season, all I could think about was being back here. But these days, when I'm here, I want to be back there. I'm getting tired of this. It's nowhere near as much fun as it used to be. *I'm* nowhere near as much fun as I used to be. I used to love it here. Now, it's just a never ending stream of bullshit and stress, with fun very thin on the ground.

I'm supposed to be flying over to Mallorca for a jolly with the other managers tonight, but a problem has presented itself that I have to deal with first. One of my reps has "gone native", as one of his colleagues put it last night. And now I've got to reel him in and clean up the mess. Great.

I roll over and look at my alarm clock. Fuck. It's only 6am. Practically the middle of the night. I think it was the front door of the block slamming that woke me. I live in the flat above the reps, opposite the hotel we work in, so I dare say they just got in from last night. As if to confirm this, I hear the balcony door being slid open and shut downstairs, and the muffled sound of an afterparty kicking in. I fold my pillow in half and try and squeeze some more sleep out of it.

A few hours pass before my alarm clock beeps into action. My bed has become so comfortable it seems to have developed magnetic powers that make it nigh on impossible to peel myself off the sheets. But I manage to do it, and stumble into the en-suite bathroom. I plonk myself on the seat, and let myself lean sideways until I hit the wall. I rest my face against the relatively cold tiles while fighting the urge to fall asleep on the throne. God, it's so knackering out here sometimes. I was really looking forward to having a day off today. I was going to have a lie-in, then get the midday flight over to Palma to go for a slap-up dinner with the top-brass. I still haven't written off my chances of getting over there, but I'm more than fucked-off about having to postpone my departure because of Sean's antics. What should have been a nice easy day now has "pain in the arse" written all over it. I don't want to have to sack Sean, but the bosses have been quite clear about how pissed off they are, and I want to show them I'm one of them now, not an ex-rep who happens to be at a manager's level. And if that means Sean has to go, well, so be it. I have to put my job before my friendships now. It doesn't sit particularly easy with me though. But then he shouldn't be doing shit on his own with company money.

 I strip off and climb gingerly into the shower. I turn the taps on and a jet of cold water rushes out and jolts me further into consciousness, rinsing the night's sweat from my body. It slowly warms up and I coat myself with shower gel and give my hair a good going over. Feeling considerably fresher, I turn off the taps and step out onto the floor. It's soaking wet, and my foot slips out from under me and I skid across the room. I manage to grab the sink and stop myself going over, but the pang of panic I feel for a second makes my heart pound like a jack-hammer and a burst of adrenaline screeches through me. *Not* the most pleasant sensation at this time of the morning. I wrap myself in a towel and slouch back to my room. My phone beeps to let me know a text has arrived, and I stretch over to the bedside table and grab the handset. It's from my boss.

"Make sure you deal with Sean before you get the plane. We're going for drinks at Abaco then dinner at Chopin in Palma at 10. Don't be late!"

I text back in the affirmative, and chuck my phone onto the pile of clothes next to the bed. I momentarily think I might be making a mountain out of a molehill with the Sean thing. I emailed my boss about it yesterday when I was stressed, but now, I feel that might have been a mistake. Going running to them with any little mishap or potential disaster will mark me out as weak. I should've dealt with this, asserted myself, and then told them about it once it was a problem solved, not a problem pending. Lesson learnt.

I get up and shuffle into the kitchen to put a pan of water on. I swear there used to be a kettle in this flat. It's a proper arse-pain making coffee like this, but there's no way I can function or even leave the flat without being dosed up on caffeine. As the water begins to bubble, I take a sachet of cappuccino from my cupboard, rip the end off and tip the fine brown and white speckled powder into a mug.

I can't fucking wait until I'm back home and can go to Starbucks for a bucket-sized latte. I pour the boiling water in and whip the frothy liquid until it has the consistency of weak porridge and head out to the balcony. I scrape one of the chairs along the floor in the living room and plonk it outside, and grab my cigarettes from on top of the telly.

It's just gone 11, and it's quiet and peaceful outside. San An can be a lovely place at certain times of the day, and of the year too, come to think of it. Last season, I stayed until mid-October, and witnessed the town transform from a noisy, garish and puke-stained hellhole to sleepy Spanish seaside town. All the bars festooned with flags and blaring out way too loud Euro-dance slowly shut down, and a host of hidden Spanish bars suddenly appeared – places I didn't notice during the summer, either because they were closed, or because they were just drowned out by the seasonal bars surrounding them. It became so much nicer. This time in the morning reminds me of the off-season a little bit. It's beautiful.

I draw a cigarette slowly out of the pack, and attempt to light it with the shitty disposable lighter I have. The wheel doesn't turn properly and makes a crunching noise before a twang announces the departure of the flint and the death of the lighter. Bollocks. I set my coffee down on the floor next to my chair and go into the kitchen to light it off the toaster. I push the lever down and poke the cigarette inside until it catches. I whip it up to my mouth and hyperventilate the fag into life, taking a nice long lug before leaving the kitchen. I'm looking forward to the next ten minutes of calm before I get started today. Hopefully, it won't be the stress I think it is.

Hopefully.

I make my way back outside to enjoy the peace, quiet, fag and coffee. Unfortunately, as I step back onto the balcony, a sharp pain in my toe and a clattering noise tells me that I'm not going to be drinking my coffee. I look down and see the remnants of the shattered mug lying against the metal pole that forms the balcony railing, the dark brown liquid slowly bleeding into an ever growing pool around it. It trickles to the edge of the balcony and starts dribbling off the edge like some pathetic waterfall. Fucking hell. It's going to be one of those days, is it? In a fit of pique, I kick the fragments of the mug off the balcony, and immediately regret it. Some pissed tourist will probably fall over and cut themselves on the shards. Probably one of our guests. Fuck it. I'll pick them up on my way into the hotel. I flick what's left of the fag down into the street and go and get dressed. I'm out of the door two minutes later.

The alleyway our apartment block opens onto is littered with fall-out from the night before. Broken bottles, take-away cartons and spent johnnies all jockey for position on the pavement, with only the frequent lake of vomit breaking up this disgusting mosaic of debauchery. Luckily the broken mug hasn't landed in anything sticky. I collect the biggest pieces together and chuck them in the big green recycling bin on the corner before heading into the hotel.

I enter the lobby, and get my phone out and bring up Sean's number. I press call and listen to it ring. I know he won't be up yet, but I know if he wakes up to a few missed calls from me, it will underscore the severity of the situation. Which is this: last week at the programming meeting, he suggested putting on a 'secret party' and taking a load of the guests out to a secret location with a soundsystem and a bar, which we'll have stocked ourselves, and charging them 30 Euros a pop. I actually thought it was a good idea, but the powers that be would never go for it, so I chucked a wet blanket on the idea straight away. But a wet blanket is never going to stop Sean from doing anything, and it would appear he's gone ahead and organised it anyway. A bundle of receipts I found in the office yesterday and an email that came into the group inbox leads me to believe he's up to something. The thing that worries me is these aren't invoices that are asking for payment. They are receipts for things that have already been paid for. And I know that Sean hasn't liquidated his ticket sales yet, so he's got thousands of Euros of company money at his disposal. Great.

I get into the hotel office and have a poke around to see if I can find any more evidence on Sean's desk. I also give him a couple more missed calls. I gather up the receipts and photocopy them, and also print out the email about the dancers. My phone goes. It's Mike, my superior. His thick Scouse twang squeaks into my ear.

"Alright, you around for a meeting in the office at 3.30? Just a few things to go over, and we can discuss what Sean is up to as well. Have you seen him yet?"

"No, I heard him come in at about 6 this morning though. I'm just in the office at the hotel now, finding out a bit more about what he's doing."

"OK, cool – don't act on this until after the meeting. I've got something that sheds a bit of light on it. Anyway, I need a favour – can you get over to the hotel in Playa D'en Bossa and pick up some posters and banners?" He doesn't wait for me to say yes. "Cheers for that. I'll see you at HQ at half three."

"Cheers Mike."

"See you later, Amy."

I finish up in the office, being careful to leave Sean's chaotic desk as it was when I got here. I don't want to forewarn him that I've got wind of his plan, although he's not stupid, so I'm sure he's got an idea I'm on to him. I head back through the lobby and see two of the reps, Ash and Kirstie, coming through the main doors to start their shift. Kirstie still looks fucked from last night, and Ash looks less than impressed with her. I don't really want to see them, let alone talk to them right now, so I take the long way round and exit the hotel from the side entrance, straight into the car park. I get into my little Golf convertible and stick Ibiza Global Radio on and head out of San An. I check the time – it's 11.30 now, so I reckon I can get over the other side of the island, grab the stuff for Mike and have time to treat myself to breakfast at JD's before I come back for the meeting. Wicked.

The Bouncer Part 1 : A New Toy

I sit up like a jack-in-a-box. I'm picking up my new super fly iPhone this morning and I can't wait. It arrived a couple of days ago at my sister's house in London and she's Fed-Ex'ed it over to my mate Stefan's office in Ibiza Town. I'm well excited – I've been using this plastic 20 euro handset since I got out here! I go through my morning routine – stretching and massaging this, un-kinking that – before I have a shower and throw on some clothes. One cup of hot water and lemon later and I'm out of the door.

I bound out of the dark, dank hallway of my apartment block and into a brilliantly bright morning. For a moment, everything appears iridescent and blindingly white, but then my eyes adjust and I remember to put my aviators on. I yomp over to the spaceship-like bus station and hop on the bus to Ibiza Town, enjoying the ride and scenery on the 20 minute journey. There are so many contrasting sides to this island, and the road between San Antonio and Ibiza Town gives you a glimpse of how beautiful this island can be, with the lush green hills that roll away to each side of the motorway. I've remembered my camera this time, so I snap off a couple of shots of the passing 'campo', as the locals call it.

The bus pulls into Ibiza Town and deposits me on one of the main thoroughfares that run through the town. I walk back towards the centre and duck into one of the gated doorways right on the street. The coolness of the hallway is lovely, and I float up the stairs to the second floor. In the cool twilight of the landing, I feel around on the door for the bell. I press it and a shrill, old school ring echoes around the stairwell. I love the lack of carpets in this country – really does wonders for the acoustics. I hear the bolts being slid across on the other side of the door and it creaks open, revealing a clearly hung-over Stefan. I step through into the hallway and give him a hug.

"Morning brother. You look like you had fun last night. Where'd you go?"

"Ugh. Pacha for Subliminal, then at about four we went to Grial. Ended up getting wankered with this group of workers from San An. Funny little fuckers. One of them is doing an all-night party up north tonight if you're game?" He croaks. "I feel rough as badger's arse this morning though. What did you get up to?"

"Working, innit. Stopping kids from killing each other down the West End."

"Why on Earth would you want to stop them from killing each other? Surely, the fewer of them about, the easier your job?"

"Hmm. Interesting way at looking at it. I prefer to think of my role as the facilitator of a good and safe night out for the little oiks."

"Man, you've really changed. I can remember when you would've been the worst one of the lot. You've certainly mellowed with age."

We go through to his kitchen and he sticks the kettle on. He sparks up a joint and sets about making us two cups of PG Tips. He motions to a brown jiffy bag on the table.

"I believe that's your new toy in there."

I pick up the package and rip the end off. I tilt it down and a box slides out on to the table. I prise it open and take the phone out. Wicked. My sister, as per my instructions, has already charged the battery for me and stuck a load of tunes on it – I left her my CD collection before I came out. It's now full of the finest in northern soul, Stax, Motown and Trojan reggae. Excellent. I've been without a personal stereo since our flat got robbed a couple of weeks back. Whoever ended up with my iPod has one of the finest collections of music on the island. Oh well, not to worry. I crack open my old handset, and switch the sim card over to the iPhone.

I start fiddling around with it while Stefan tells me more details about his antics last night at Pacha. They got chucked out of the VIP at Subliminal for openly snorting lines off the table.

"I would have chucked you out for that, silly boy."

"Yeah, but they didn't get our gear, so then we just went next door to Grial and got roaring drunk on hierbas with these young 'uns. I think I may have thrown up on the dancefloor in there. Oops."

"Doesn't sound too Balearic to me."

We finish the cups of tea, and I bid Stefan farewell. He's off down the beach to get stoned and look at women. I'm invited along, but as I'm working later it's probably best I give it a miss. I head back into the street from the relative cool of the building and enjoy the slow cooking sensation on the back of my neck as I head towards the old town. I cut across Placa Del Parq, and take the road that skirts along the base of the wall that surrounds Dalt Villa. I weigh up whether or not to head up into the old town – the view from the top is breath-taking – but decide I'll stay down here today.

The Stags Part 1 : London

The T-shirts are ready. Fucking tidy they are as well. I was beginning to think the cunts wouldn't have them done in time – we've got to be at Stansted in four hours – but thank fuck they came through this morning. Wouldn't be much of a stag do if we didn't have a team strip, would it? There are six of us, including the stag, and yours truly, the best man, and I've got us all identical t-shirts with "Johns Stag Rampage" printed on the front. On the back, each of us has been assigned a nickname and a squad number. Our names have been taken from the nastiest serial killers and monsters history has to offer. It's all a bit of fun, innit? Better brace yourself, Ibiza, because the boys from Peckham are on their way! Oi oi!

I jump in my XR3i. It's got a wicked spoiler on the back, and rims that cost more than the car itself. It's an older model, but I've been flexing this motor since I passed my driving test in 1989, and over the years I've added to it, tinkered with it and basically turned it into the finest set of wheels this side of the Thames. This motor is legendary on the mean streets of SE15. You can hear it coming a mile off, and it goes like shit off a shovel. I screech through the backstreets of Peckham Rye, and skid to a halt in the car park behind Burger King. I notice the group of girls hanging around outside eyeing me up and giving me fuck-me looks. This car's a fanny magnet and no mistake. Stick me behind the wheel with my driving skills, and it turns from magnet to black-hole, drawing in skirt from miles around. There's no resistance any tart can put up against this.

I lock up and run over the road to the T-shirt printing place next to the pie and mash shop. The printer geezer hands over a massive white plastic bag with all the clobber in. I take one out and hold it up against the window. It looks fucking wicked. White with red lettering. The number 4 is just the right size, and the name "Huntley" forms a nice crescent over the top of it. Wicked. I stuff it back in the bag, chuck the money across the counter at the man, missing him and sending a shower of notes all over the shop. Ha.

"Bet you wish it rained money like that all the time in here, don't ya mate?" I say as I take in the dilapidated shop, with its filthy counter, grubby machines and tacky photos on the walls. It's disgusting. What a dump.

"You should spend that on tarting this shithole up, you cunt," I advise him as I strut out the door. I get honked by some twat driving too fast as I cross back over the road, and hold my arms up at his rear view mirror. I'm game if they are. But they disappear off down the road, the shiteing bastards. I get to the car, and pop the boot open to put the bag of shirts in, taking another one out to examine the handiwork. This one bears the name of Peter Sutcliffe, and the number nine. It's mine. Maybe I should've grown a beard like Mr Sutcliffe's for this little trip. Always did think he was the most stylish of the mass murderers.

The group of girls over by Burger King are still giving me the eye, so I decide to road test the clobber and take off my Millwall top and stick my stag uniform on. I peel the footy strip off to expose my impressive torso. Some people would describe me as stocky – if they wanted a slap – but underneath the extra padding I'm as hard as a rock. My biceps look like Popeye's, and the lion tats on my arm and the dragon on my back just add to my appeal. I make eye contact with one of the girls and wink at her.

"Who you fucking winking at you fucking nonce? Cover yourself up, you fat bastard!", the little bitch says as her mates double up in laughter. I slam the boot shut and march over to her, covering the ground between us in no time. I'm right in her face, craning my head down to her until our noses are nearly touching in some sick Eskimo kiss.

"You want to say that again, you fucking cunt?" I hiss under my breath as my eyes burrow into hers. I hold her gaze, pouring every ounce of malice I can muster into my stare. I can see her eyes begin to water, and her lip begins to tremble as she keeps schtum. Stupid little bitch. I've completely taken the wind out of her and her little cunt mates' sails, so I take a step back, before jumping quickly into a fighting stance. They crap themselves and are chased away by the sound of my laughter. Ah, kids. I was just the same, but not always as stupid or lucky as this lot. If they'd pulled that with some of the lads that are going to be on this stag, it would've got fucking nasty fucking fast. I head back to the car, realising that the little ding-dong has given me a semi. Better head home and do something about that. I don't want to start this trip with a loaded gun in my pocket, do I?

The Resort Manager Part 2 : Breakfast By The Beach

It takes me 20 minutes to get to the hotel in PDB, and a further ten to locate all the promo gear I need to take back to Mike. One of the reps helps me load the car, and two minutes later I'm parking up in the plot of derelict land behind JD's that passes as a car park. I walk round to the sea front and along to the café, taking my favourite table right on the front as Jo comes over and says hello. I love this place. It's right on the beach, they have proper English bacon and English bread. I used to practically live here when I was based in PDB a couple of seasons ago. I order a bacon and sausage sandwich and a cup of tea, and sit back and enjoy the view for a few minutes. Darren comes out from the kitchen and delivers my sarnie personally, asking how I'm getting on.

"Yeah, not too bad, Darren. I'll be a lot better once I've got this down me though."

"How's it going this season? We hardly ever see you anymore! You got your big promotion and now you're forgetting all your old mates, eh?"

"Yeah, I know. I'm sorry. I'm stuck over in San An – I've got to stay close to all my misbehaving reps so I can keep them in check."

He laughs and heads back into the kitchen. I squirt some brown sauce into my sarnie and mull over the state of affairs with Sean, and what the possible outcomes are going to be. If he loses our money, which there's a very good chance he will, he has to go. There's no two ways about it. If he makes money, then he's still gone against what he was told to do, but there's a reason not to sack him. Either way, he's made me look like an idiot by ignoring and defying me, and there has to be some sort of price to pay for that or I'll appear completely impotent to everyone in the company – the bosses, the other reps and the other managers. I've got to be seen to be hard on errant reps.

I take a large bite out of the sandwich and look out over the sea and try to push all stressful thoughts out of my mind so I can enjoy my breakfast. As I chew, I focus on how delicious the mush of bacon, sausage, sauce and bread in my mouth is, and how my tea is now at the perfect temperature to sip.

The waitress takes away my spent plate, and I go back to gazing out over the sea. I order another cup of tea and think back to last summer and the problems the reps caused then. Including me. I broke my arm halfway through the season after going arse over tit in Upmarket, and that pissed my boss off no-end, especially as I was his most reliable (and profitable) rep and having me out of the front line was a proper arse pain for him. Perversely, I have that to thank for my promotion. They made me help out in the office while I was recuperating and I turned out to be too good to let back into the wild this season. But some of the others last summer…..fuck me, we really did pick them. One ended up getting nicked for serving up to the guests – he's still in prison on Mallorca – and another did a runner with his liquidation and was found in hospital a week later with a record-breaking amount of mandy and ket in his system. He spunked upwards of eight grand on that week long bender. That's why there's this hoohaa about Sean's antics – there *cannot* be a repeat of that. This is why I've got to be so on it with this one. I can't show weakness or leniency. Not after last year.

Generally, though, we've been luckier this season – I've only had to properly discipline our reps at the San An hotel a couple of times, and that was for high jinks, nothing too serious. One of the reps, Jake, on his first weekend, ended up coming home in an ambulance because he got so ketted up at the Zoo Project. They charged 185 euros for it. Fucking idiot. And guess who ended up paying for it? And then I caught Charlotte, our team-leader no less, leaning over the balcony of the flat pouring vodka down into a guest's mouth. But all that needed was a quick bollocking and it was done and dusted. I wish that was all that would be called for today.

The Reps Part 2 : Perfect Party Planning and Preparation

It takes us less than ten minutes to get there. I had the generator delivered yesterday, along with the lights and some bamboo torches, and in no time we've got the soundsystem up and running. We give it a little tester and bang out a couple of tunes full blast on each of the decks. Because of the steep incline of the walls of the cove, the acoustics sound wicked. I get a little tingle in my balls. If this party works, this is going to be fucking immense. We spend the next half an hour running cables through the trees and putting floodlights in strategic places, as well as encircling most of the clearing with fairy lights. When it gets dark and these are the only sources of light aside from the moon and the stars, this is going to look like something out of a fantasy film. We then follow the route out of the clearing, through the tunnel and down to the small jetty on the other side, placing the large bamboo torches at three metre intervals.

We head back up to the shack and put up the finishing touches – a massive banner goes on the roof of the shack, and four more at quarter-intervals all round the clearing. They're done in a sort-of Keith Haring/hippie style, and I reckon it will give off a Goa/Thailand-type full moon party vibe. I've never been that far east, but if I did, I'd want it to look like this. Jody and I walk into the centre of the bowl and look around us, and we both nod at each other in satisfaction. It looks smart. This should be one wicked fucking party.

We head through the trees back to the car and drive to the big Eroski just outside of San An. We'll need to make two trips in the next couple of hours. The first to get us somewhere in the region of 50 cases of lager, a couple of cases of vodka and a load of Red Bull. After that, we'll come back and buy as much ice as we can. Because we've not got any fridges up there, we'll be putting all the beer into 15 massive dustbins I took up there yesterday and packing them with ice. Proper old school festival style.

We get back on the road to San An, and I take in the dimensions of the car and work out how much booze we can fit in. There's no way we're going to get everything we need in two trips. I lift my bum off the seat and rummage around in my pockets for my phone and call my mate Joe the sound engineer, who also happens to be a sound guy as well. He has the skills of a modern day MacGuyver. Give him a ball of string, an empty Pringles packet and some cable ties, and he'll make you a fully working satellite TV antenna. With all the sports channels. The man's a fucking genius. And he also has a transit van. He answers my plea for help and says he'll meet us at the supermarket in ten minutes. Wicked. That's one potential headache removed.

We swerve into the car park and nab a space next to the mess of shopping trolleys that have been slung into the corner. We liberate a trolley each from the mangle and enter the shop, thrusting our way through the bevy of Saturday afternoon shoppers to where the pallets of San Miguel reside. We load them up and I duck out and grab us a couple more trolleys while Jody begins queuing with the first mountain of cases. Luckily, as I'm struggling across the car park with them, Joe shows up in the van and gives me a hand. We pile more slabs of beer onto them and sidle up next to Jody in the queue, tactically ignoring the tuts and clucks of the people waiting behind him.

There are still quite a few people in front of us, and it would be expedient to take advantage of Joe and his van, so I go and get the ice. It looks like some fucked-up version of Titanic as I steer it towards the queue. When it comes to our turn, the check-out girl looks startled at the amount of grog we've got, before she rolls her eyes and mouths the word "Ingles" and cracks a wry smile. Yeah baby, you know no-one boozes like the English. Something to be proud of, really, isn't it? Once we ruled the world, teaching cricket to far-off exotic types, spreading civilisation and the written word to the darkest corners of the globe. Now we just go to those corners and piss or throw up in them. We used to rule the waves, now we just use them for booze cruises. Oh well, never mind. Greatness is fleeting, and we had a good innings. The manager comes over to see if we need a hand getting it out the door, and kindly dispatches a couple of lackeys to help us get our boozy booty out to the motors. They begin wheeling it all out of the shop and I settle up the bill, which is just shy of a grand, what with the vodka and mixers Jody usefully remembered to get at the last second. Fucking hell. That's a lot of booze and ice.

We pack it into the van and the car with a little space to spare, and head back to the shack to set up our stall, as it were. It takes the three of us no time to pack the beer and ice into the bins and leave them in the shade. I whip out my phone and check the time. All good, plenty of time. I chuck my phone on the trestle table that will later on constitute the bar and help Jody drag the last couple of bins out of the sun.

Joe, God bless him, gives the soundsystem a quick once-over, and fiddles with a couple of things, moving a couple of the speakers around before bidding us farewell and wishing us luck with the party. He disappears off down the dirt track, and Jody and I do a quick run around checking everything's cool before we go back to San An. The rig is good, the path from the cove is sorted, and the bar is built and stocked. The only thing missing are the plastic glasses, which we'll pick up from the hotel. Everything seems to be in place, so we walk briskly through the brush to the car and begin driving back to San Antonio.

The Bouncer Part 2 : Croissant Show

Just next to the old city gates, there is this amazing little bakery called Croissant Show. The proprietor possesses the rudest handle bar moustache this side of a WW1 German officer. I go in and get a still-warm pain au chocolat and jamon y queso croissant and a can of coke and stick them in my bag. I duck off into the warren of alleyways that comprise the old part of Ibiza Town, emerging a few minutes later right by the wall that divides the harbour from the open sea. I jump up onto it and climb down onto the rocks that face out to the Mediterranean. Finding a nice, relatively flat spot, I sit down and take my top off. The view out to sea is beautiful, and the different shades of blue meld at the horizon, making it impossible to tell where the sea stops and the sky starts.

I sit there in silence and eat my breakfast. There is a gentle breeze wafting the sea air over me and it feels fanfuckingtastic. I finish off the pain au chocolat and half the coke, before setting it down next to me and letting out a satisfying belch. I stretch out on the rock, and feel my muscles twinge as they reach their limit. I cross my legs and take up the lotus position. I straighten my back and pinch my thumb and forefingers together. Thank fuck no-one I know can see me. Where I'm from, meditation isn't exactly something that would be understood. Especially if practiced by a former bad boy like me.

I rest my hands on my legs and rock back and forth very gently, breathing as deep and as slow as I can. I close my eyes and zone out.

Beginning with my toes, I flex each part of my body, from the tiniest bones in my foot to my calves and thighs, through to my diaphragm and up to my neck. I feel the tension being squeezed out of my body as if I am a tube of toothpaste and someone is slowly pressing the gunk out of me from the bottom up. My body relaxes and I become aware of all my senses. I notice how the rock feels underneath me, and how the fabric of my shorts drapes across my legs. I taste remnants of the chocolate and the coke in my mouth. I take a deep breath through my nose, and smell of the sea fills my nostrils.

My eyes remain closed, but I focus on an imaginary point just in front of my face. A ball of purple and green light materialises on the back of my eyelids and I hold my closed-eye stare for a few moments. Then, I listen as intently as I can, zeroing in on the tiniest noises; those out at sea – a distant bird, the waves lapping against the rocks; and those behind me – the hum of the town, the sounds of the cars and the hubbub of the port.

I feel a wave of calm and nothingness engulf me, and become totally relaxed. I clear my mind, and allow any outside thoughts and influences to pass through my consciousness and go on their merry little way, paying them no attention and refusing to claim ownership of any external distractions. I stay in this tranced out state for around 30 minutes before I come back down to Earth. I open my eyes, and everything seems sharper, brighter; the colours are more vivid, and the background noise more clear. Nice.

Remembering my can of coke, I drain the rest of it, and put my t-shirt back on. I pick up the paper bag containing my remaining croissant and head back to the wall and climb over. I chuck the coke can in the bin, and take the croissant out of the bag and munch on it as I walk along the quayside. I'm feeling so fine and relaxed, in a way that I never felt on the most down of downers that I was once so fond of.

There are some awesome ships in port at the moment, so I fish my camera out and take some snaps of the posher ones. Some of these ships must cost as much as a small African country's GDP, and it's hard not to think of them as vulgar, especially in an economic climate where so many people are screwed for cash. But I brush that thought aside and appreciate them for what they are on the surface – beautifully crafted pieces of art, and a triumph of man's mastery of both engineering and the sea. I check the clock on my new phone, and see that it's nearly time for my bus back to San An. I make my way back through town, taking a detour to go to the paper shop and get a copy of The Sun. Some habits from home die harder than others.

The Stags Part 2 : Stansted

The train from Liverpool Street is fucking packed with suits. Half of them have their phones glued to their ears and the other half are texting. The birds are all slagging people off and bitching and moaning, and most of the geezers are making battle plans for a night out on the sauce in whatever provincial shithole they live. About five minutes before we pull into each new stop, more people get on their blowers and bleat, whine and grovel for someone at the other end to pick them up from the station. My heart bleeds. It must be knackering sitting on your arse at a computer all day, stalking your ex on Facebook. Finally, we approach Stansted, and I leave the half-dead worker ants behind me. I bounce across the platform using my Head bag as a shield/battering ram, slicing through the crowd like a Stanley through a Chelsea cunt's cheek.

The escalator takes me up to the main building, and I head over to the pub to meet the lads. I get there and John is already sat at a table with a couple of youngish, scruffy, straw-haired blokes who look identical. There are already nine empty pint glasses and six upturned shot glasses on the table. John gets up as he sees me approach and grabs me in a headlock as soon as I'm close enough. A swift elbow to his chest sorts the wanker out and he coughs out the word "cunt" and sits down, making a bad job of hiding the fact I've just winded him.

"Alright John-o. See you've got a head start on me there." I reach down and grab his pint and flush half of it down my gullet in one gulp. He croaks something about getting a round in and I tell him I'll get them. I drop my bags on a spare chair and John does the introductions. His voice is straining to sound normal after me winding him.

"Terry, this is Ashley and Frank. They're from Manchester, but not too bad for northern scum."

I shake their hands firmly, trying to crush the bones. It's important to have a vice-like handshake, otherwise people won't know from the off that you are not a person to be fucked with. I see them wince, and know they've got the message. I ask them what they want to drink. Predictably, being northern, they ask for some pissy bitter shit. I duck off to the bar and get two pints of John Smiths and two Carling. I carry them all back to the table, and dish them out. We raise our glasses and take a big swill.

"Where are Jimmy and Graham then? We should be checking in now." I ask, as my phone goes at the same time. It's them. "Speak of the devil. Where you at Jimbo?"

He starts to reply before the phone cuts out.

"I'm right fucking here you bastard!" Jimmy bellows in my ear, makes me jump out of my seat and spill half my pint on the floor. My cheeks flush and my hairs stand up a bit. I can hear the air rushing in my ears. Cunt. John, Graham and the two northerners are having a right old laugh. I feel like I'm in a goldfish bowl, with everyone in the pub staring at me. It makes me feel small and I struggle to suppress my rage. Luckily it passes quickly – I don't want to ruin the trip before we've even left the country by starting something here, so I let it go. I'm sure an opportunity to get the cunt back will arise over the weekend. I'll panel him later when he's shitfaced, maybe even put a glass through his face. Cunt.

Jimmy does the right thing to avoid any lingering unpleasantness and gets a round in, with a shot of Aftershock for everyone as well. As he sits back down, I fish out the T-shirts and dish them out. John is number 4, Huntley; Graham is 11 and Hitler; Jimmy is 7 and Fritzl; Ashley is 3 and Shipman; Frank is 5 and Bin Laden; and I'm number 9, the one and only Yorkshire Ripper, Peter Sutcliffe. They go down well with the lads and everyone changes into them. They look good, right size, snug around the arms, but not homo-snug.

I look around the table at the motley crew and a jolt of excitement jumps through me. Jimmy and Graham I've known for years – us three and John all grew up on the same estate and have been tighter than a nun's twat since we were kids. We've been through everything together. Fucking hell, even my first time inside I was with John, after we bollocksed up knocking off a jewellers down Nunhead. Only fucking stalled the motorbike as a copper drove past. How unlucky is that? As for the two northern monkeys, these twins, John met them when he did a stretch for GBH a few years back in Belmarsh. Apparently they're soldiers for some big nasty gangster up north, but so fucking what? They better not try anything with me. I'm not fucking scared of some dirty Mancs. Come any of that with me and they'll get a spanking.

We drain our pints and head over to the check in. The queue is miles long and seems to be full of kids, some dressed in multicoloured day-glo get up, and others a bit more classy. A lot of the boys look like they're queers with too much hair gel on, and the girls look like wags-in-waiting. I swear we never used to take our appearances so seriously when we were that age. I mean, I'm only 38, but when I was a kid, a bit of Studio Line on the Barnet was as far as anyone went. Maybe some lippy and eye shit for the girls. But this lot, judging from what they're loading into their plastic see-through bags, are bringing half of Boots with them. It's softening them up, all this pampering. And it's churning out a generation of fucking poofters. Makes me fucking sick. My granddad didn't kill fucking Nazis so cunts like that could wear make up. The girl in front of us is rummaging around with her bag, crouched down in front of us, the top of her g-string forming a "T" at the top of her perfectly rounded arse. Now that's a modern fashion trend that I can go with.

"Nice builder's arse love!" Jimmy says loudly, always the womaniser, prompting the rest of the lads to laugh. The girl gets a bit self-conscious and pulls her cardigan down, and the lad with her gives us a dirty look.

"Oh yeah, mate? Got something you want to say?" Jimmy asks him. The boy has the good sense to shake his head and turn away from us, as six pairs of eyes will him to start something we'll be happy to finish.

This is gonna be my first time in Ibiza. I ain't really into the whole fucking bleepy bleep shit arse dance music, but doing Ibiza is something you really can't do after you hit forty, so I reckon it's a good choice for John's stag. I've planned our three night stay pretty well: West End; Cream; Bora Bora; Pete Tong's night; Boat party; and even a posh fucking restaurant. Then flying home on Sunday morning, back home in time for EastEnders. Should be a right fucking laugh. Drugs and dancing and fucking and fighting. What a great way to send John off before he becomes a boring married twat.

The queue has gone down loads and the bird with the nice arse and pussy boyfriend check in and clear off, taking great pains to not make eye contact with any of us. We get to the counter and hand our passports to the ugly slapper behind the desk. She's older than us, and has more make-up on than all of these kids put together. It looks disgusting. She checks us in, quicker than most because we've only got hand luggage, and issues us with our boarding cards and asks stupid and annoying questions about our bags, who packed them and what we've got in them. Luckily she seems to have taken a shine to Jimmy, and he's laying on the charm almost as thick as her make up, so she doesn't notice my growing impatience with her babbling. We fuck off and head through the security check, behaving ourselves impeccably. We've all seen too many away trips in Europe spoiled by some twat acting up in customs. We know better than that. We waltz through the baggage check and head to the pub to stake our place while we do the duty free shop in shifts. After a couple of rounds we're all back from the shops, fully stocked with fags and booze and giant Toblerones. I'm starting to feel a little bit lagging, so I get up to go and grab a burger, but as I do, our flight changes from "wait in lounge" to "boarding" on the video screen. Bollocks.

"That's us then chaps." Jimmy says in a fake posh accent. He's a funny cunt is old Jimmy, and he's a fanny merchant of the highest order. He's pretty tasty in a scrap as well, but not as tasty as some – as he'll find out if he makes any more jokes at my expense this weekend.

We march down to the gate, strutting with the kind of confidence and swagger that only a group of fucking hard lads have. We must look like a right tidy firm – four well built skinheads, and two young casuals with typical shaggy Manc haircuts in tow. Kinda like a hard-nut Benetton advert. The music from Reservoir Dogs plays in my head as we walk up to the gate, and we give the girl our boarding passes. It must be said she is considerably better looking than the troglodyte that checked us in. Why not have the fit girls on the counters where they can be seen more? I'll have to email that in as a suggestion to that bubble that owns the airline.

The plane is rammed, packed to the gills with excited young kids. I feel like I've walked into an episode of that show on the telly, Skins. I find myself resenting them their youth for a moment, before getting over it sharpish. I can remember what a ball ache it was being

20. You think you know the lot, but you know fuck all and can sometimes be reminded of that in the most brutal way.

We colonise a couple of rows near the back, asking a couple of day-glo cheesy quavers to move so we can sit together. They bugger off, not looking too happy about the situation, but what are they going to do? Exactly. I stash my bag in the overhead, and sit down, putting a bottle of duty free vodka down the side of my seat and covering it with my hoody. The trolley dollies get funny about you drinking your own booze on planes these days. No smoking as well – no wonder you get that air rage bollocks.

I'm settling in and doing up my seatbelt when I become aware of a doings a-brewing in the seat behind me. I hear some snotty voice saying "your top is really offensive." I turn round to see one of the twins, I can't tell which, has grabbed some geezer in glasses by his lapels and looks like he's trying to pull him over the seat. Not the wisest move. You need to behave when the plane is still on the floor.

"What was that you said about my shirt, pal?"

The bloke splutters and stutters, and the other twin wrenches his brother's grip from the boy, shoving him back in his seat at the same time. He rises up out of his chair and turns menacingly to the four-eyed mouthpiece.

"You better watch your fucking mouth, mate." He then turns to his brother and warns him: "Don't be fuckin soft and get us chucked off the plane before we've even left."

Everyone pulls their necks in a bit, and we watch the air hostesses go through their "what do to if the plane crashes" bullshit. We taxi away from the terminal, and soon we're hurtling down the runway. My seat feels like it's trying to push through me and then we bounce up into the air and Essex drops out of sight through the window on my right. The plane tilts almost all the way on its side and shudders like an alky's hand as it levels out. I twist the top off the vodka bottle and take a nice long slug before passing it to John on my left. My ears begin to go, so I yawn and the left one pops. Then I pinch my nose and force air into it, making my right ear crackle and re-pressurise with a high pitched whine. I stretch my legs out as far as they can go and bundle my hoody up into a makeshift pillow and close my eyes.

The Journalist Part 2 : Pikes

We're already out of our seats and ready to steam off the plane when the stewardess pops the door open. I sling my bag over my shoulder and slide on my aviators as we clatter down the stairs and speed-walk the short way to the terminal building. We go straight through passport control and through the arrivals lounge. Our lack of hold baggage means we beat the crowds, and within 10 minutes of touching down we're in an air conditioned cab speeding down the motorway towards Pikes.

We go past Amnesia and Privilege and fly through the tunnel that sits roughly in the middle of the island. We leave the main road and head through some dusty back roads, past fields of watermelon and citrus fruits before the driver deposits us in front of the hotel. We get out of the cab, and I'm struck first by the brightness, second by the heat, and third by the lack of noise save for the rhythmic call of the crickets. The difference between this and the hubbub of San An, only a couple of miles down the road, is immense. I love Pikes. I've stayed here a couple of times before. It's easily the best hotel on the island, at least in terms of character and rock'n'roll pedigree – Freddie Mercury used to hang out here, and it's where they shot the video for Club Tropicana. Fucking priceless. Unfortunately I'm with Kevin and Giles though, not Pepsi and Shirley.

We check in and head to our rooms to dump our stuff before we hit the beach. I empty my bag onto the bed, and repack it with my netbook, notepad, a towel and my Dictaphone. I lock up and bounce down to the bar where Giles is already waiting. My mobile goes off. It's Kevin.

"Jack, I'm staying here for the afternoon. I'll call you later." His nasal tone snuffles down the phone. Well, isn't that a surprise? Kevin's sitting in his room snorting coke by himself. Never done that before. I'm relieved though, I don't really want him getting in the way. We call a cab and head back across the island to Bora Bora. We need to come back with shots of bikini clad girls dancing on beaches, and Playa D'en Bossa is where we can get them. And it's also where we can get drugs – within seconds of arriving on the beach we are offered some MDMA by an old crusty. I give him 50 Euros for a gram. I stick it in my pocket for later. It's going to be a long day and I don't want to peak too soon.

Bora Bora is rammed, with the stretch of beach in front of it knee-deep in bikinis, board shorts and speedos, all bobbing away to the music. On the outskirts of the crowd, we find an unoccupied parasol and drag a pair of nearby sun-beds into its shadow and make ourselves comfortable. Giles starts fiddling with his camera equipment and doing his technical gubbins.

I shuffle my lounger round a bit so I'm facing the crowd. I stretch back, enjoying the warming glow of sun on my skin, and lay there people watching. There are a group of Italians at the waters edge, all perfectly chiselled, with speedos clenching their tackle into a tight bulge. They're prancing around and posing, seemingly oblivious to the fact that most people are openly mocking them. Well, at least the English are. Further up from them are a group of teenage boys, clearly on their first holiday without their parents. They're swaggering and staggering around, clutching 40s of San Miguel, wearing their t-shirts on their heads. I think back to myself at their age and feel envious that they've got it all to come. The next ten years of their life will be the best, at least in terms of carefree shenanigans, drug taking and casual sex. I point them out to Giles as potential targets for his camera. They're our readership, and they'll be happy to ham it up for the camera. I've brought a couple of back issues as props, so we'll get some shots of them holding it aloft like a trophy in front of Bora Bora.

My view of the boys is obscured by a group of women wearing matching pink t-shirts. They're the hens that I saw at the airport. They'll be bang up for some pics I reckon – coming back with shots of them in their bikinis, frolicking around with me and a copy of the mag will be the money shot for the picture editor. Predictable, but that's the nature of the beast I've sold my soul to. The Hen party take a plot on the beach not far from us and start passing around the booze. Three of them peel off their pink t-shirts and start dancing around to the thumping house music that is bleeding out of the speakers and rolling across the beach. One of them doesn't. The cute one from the shop.

I nudge Giles and tell him we need shots of the group of lads and then the Hen party. We heap our stuff on the sun loungers and jog over to the boys. I mention to them the name of the mag and they immediately get even more excited and tell me how much they love it.

"Brilliant. Can we take some pictures of you fucking around then? You guys wanna be famous?" I joke with them. They're only too happy to piss around in the water for us and ham it up for Giles' camera. I get them waving copies of the mag around and we get the required shots of them enjoying themselves with Bora Bora in the background, reading the mag and one with me in the middle, looking like the cheerleader for this motley crew. I go to the bar and buy them a round of drinks. One of the less shitfaced of them starts asking me about how I got the job.

"By being able to bullshit very well, make excellent tea and luck. I was in the right place at the right time. It's all a blag mate!" I tell him.

He tells me I'm the luckiest bloke in the world. I feel bad when he does, because while I know deep down that even though I've had a right result doing this for a living, and for so long, I'd be happy to walk away from it tomorrow. I don't tell him this and instead I just raise my pint to him and tell him meeting the readers like him is the best bit of it. He's pilled up to the nines and gives me a big hug, the sweaty bastard. Still, him and his mates are immensely likeable. We all shake hands and I take one of their email addresses so I can send them some swag from the office.

Now we have the part I don't really like. Where we walk up to a group of girls and ask them if we can objectify them. Well, we don't put it so succinctly, and it's not really we who does it – this is Giles' realm. And it's where his patter comes in very useful.

"Hello ladies, I wonder if you can help me. My camera has just had to suffer taking pictures of a load of ugly boys. If I was to die right now, I wouldn't want the last thing I shot to be a bunch of spotty lads, so can I take some pictures of you for our magazine?"

His waffle, combined with the crazy Vietnam-era photojournalist style he's wearing today (sleeveless khaki flak-jacket and cut off combat shorts), and the mention of the name of the magazine has the girls like putty in his hands. Well, nearly all them. The cute one looks uncomfortable and has moved slightly away from the gaggle, as if she's trying to blend into the background. No chance, as her mates keep shouting at her to get her top off and get into the shot. She shakes her head and sits down on a lounger, rummaging in a bag for something. Giles turns around to try and get her involved, but I step up to his side and subtly tell him to leave her be and concentrate on the girls in front of him who are well game. So game in fact one of them has already whipped her top off and is giving us an eyeful of her pendulous boobs. Giles needs no encouragement and is giving it the full porno-snapper routine. I know these are the shots that will go down well in the office when we get back, but it sits uneasily with me. I go over to where the cute girl is sat and plop down opposite her.

"Hi, I'm Jack."

"Hi. I'm not getting my kit off for your camera."

"I wasn't going to ask you to. Your friends seem more than happy to hog the limelight," I say, smiling. She looks back at me, seeming rather unimpressed. I feel compelled to explain myself to her. "Please don't judge me for this. There's more to me than running around asking girls to flash their boobs."

"I wasn't judging you. The exploitation runs both ways as far as I'm concerned."

She doesn't seem like she wants to talk to me, so I shut up and turn back to watch Giles and her mates whooping and cheering. She seems on the verge of tears.

"Tell me to fuck off if I'm being nosy, but are you ok? You look like you're about to cry."

"I'm fine."

"Can I get you anything? Do you wanna go somewhere less lively and have a coffee. I can leave Giles here for a bit. And to be honest, I could do with some peace and quiet for a bit."

She goes to say something, but then stops herself. She gives me an evaluating stare and takes a deep breath.

"Yeah, alright then."

We get up, and she wraps a towel around her legs. I shout over to Giles that I'll be back in a bit, but he's having too much fun to acknowledge me beyond a dismissive swipe of the hand in my general direction. I ask her name. She says it's Vicky. We walk down the beach a bit and then cut down the side of one of the hotels and go to a little bar sandwiched between the beach and the main road. It's a

German place I know that does amazing schnitzel sandwiches. I dump my bag at one of the tables and ask her what she wants to drink. She says coffee is fine. I order two coffees and two schnitzel sarnies, and then go back and sit down opposite her.

I'm struggling to think of something to say that doesn't sound trite and cretinous. I fail.

"So, er, how long are you on the island?" I wince on the inside. It's become second nature for me to act the braggadocio when chatting to people when I'm on a story. But the last thing I want to be in front of this girl is some Charlie Big Potatoes twat. I don't want to impress her with the "Hey look at me I get paid to fuck around" line, and she looks like the last thing she needs is someone giving it the big 'un.

"Only until tomorrow."

"Then where are you going? Where's home for you?"

"Liverpool." She says. She looks like she wants to say more, like a torrent of words is bubbling away at the top of her throat, but something's holding her back.

"Look, I know I'm a complete stranger, but if there's anything you want to talk about, I'm a very good listener. And I won't repeat a word of it to anyone."

"Do you know where the lav is in here?" She says without looking at me. I point towards the back of the bar and offer an apologetic smile. As she moves off I think I should just leave it. I don't know this girl at all, there's clearly some kind of shit going on with her and I don't need to involve myself. But something in me wants to help. Yeah, I fancy her, but there's something else. This side of me has got me in trouble before, this compulsion I have to try and get involved in other people's problems.

The coffees and the sandwiches arrive, followed shortly after by Vicky. She looks like she's been crying. She sits down and it all comes out. How she's been with this guy for seven years, how he was lovely at the start, how he beats the shit out of her now, how she can't take off the pink T-shirt and frolic around on the beach in her bikini because her back is black and blue from the kicking he gave her a couple of nights ago, how she wants to be chatted up like all her mates are, but she feels scared and worthless and ugly. I'm shocked. Christ. I can feel anger brewing in my stomach. How fucking dare anyone treat another person like that, let alone a bloke subjecting a woman to it? It fucking disgusts me. But I keep a lid on it. The last thing she needs is another male exhibiting aggression.

"Shit. I'm so sorry. That sounds fucking dreadful. I don't know what to say." I bleat. I wish I could think of something that would make it better for her. I don't think it's really appropriate to tell her I think she's gorgeous and I think there's something special about her.

"There's not really much you can say. But you did ask. Bet you wish you hadn't now."

"Not at all. You looked like to needed to vent. That's a shitty situation for you to be in. Why do you bother staying with him?"

"Because I'm scared. He's taken so much from me. Believe it or not, I used to be the life and soul of the party. I had loads of friends, I was popular, I was out all the time. But he alienated them, he stopped me from seeing them, he guilt-tripped me out of a life of my own. He isolated me. He became the only thing in my life. And he took my self-esteem and self-confidence. He took everything. It's only recently I've had the guts to come to my senses. I'm doing something about it now."

"What are you doing about it?"

She goes quiet again. The shutters have come down. She draws her towel around her and looks furtive.

"Enough about me. What about you? What's your story then? Is it fun running around trying to get girls to strip for the camera?"

"Not as much fun as you think. I used to love it loads, and I'm sure it beats the shit out of working in McDonalds, but I'm getting a bit tired of it to be honest, strange as it sounds. I guess I'm growing up. I need more of a challenge."

Another silence descends between us, but it's not an uncomfortable one. The way Vicky is looking at me it's as if she's trying to figure me out, before her features relax and she appears to come to a conclusion. She swivels round in her seat towards the bar and summons the waitress.

"Do you want a proper drink?"

"Er, yeah. Jack and Coke for me."

She orders two of them, and takes the final bite of her sandwich, giving the empty plate to the waitress. She doesn't say anything while we wait for the drinks. They arrive and she picks the lemon out and holds the JD aloft to cheers me.

"To challenging ourselves."

We chink glasses. She looks at me in the eyes when the glasses touch.

"So where are you going tonight?"

"Ah, we've got to go to some club in San An. Some idiots from Big Brother are doing a PA in one of the clubs, and I have to go and interview them. I'm very tempted to actually say and write what I really think about them and stir up something of a shitstorm."

"And what do you really think about them?"

"That they're holding back evolution, and providing kids with shit role models. You should be famous for a talent, not getting your knockers out in some tatty magazine."

"Like the one you work for."

"Exactly. And yes, I'm fully aware I'm a total hypocrite. But if I write anything negative, they won't publish it. Maybe I'll write what I really think and stick it on my blog."

"You'll have to let me know the address."

I tear a page out of my notepad and scribble it down for her.

"So, where are you girls going tonight?"

"We're going to Cream. I can't wait. I've not been clubbing for years. He didn't like me getting dressed up and going out. He wouldn't let me do pills, and he didn't like me drinking – he said it wasn't me he didn't trust, it was other men. Our nights out would always end with him twatting some poor sod who'd made the mistake of looking in my direction, or heaven forbid, talking to me. So tonight, I've got a lot of dancing to get out of my system."

"Wicked. I'll try and make it down to Amnesia after I've committed career suicide over in San An."

"That'd be nice."

I suggest a shot of hierbas, and she agrees. She's lightened up considerably since her little revelation, and it's certainly put things in perspective for me. Any grievances I had with my job are exposed as the petty quibbles that they are. This girl's got real problems. I've got none at all. We go up to the bar and do the shots, before going back to where we last saw Giles. The sun isn't as high as it was, but the beach is still fucking hot. We find them all sat in a rough circle in the sand, Giles holding court. A barrage of laughter erupts from the hens as we approach, before Giles notices us and waves.

"Thought we'd lost you there, soldier. Where'd you go?"

"I needed to line my stomach, so I treated Vicky here to a schnitzel sandwich from the Kraut place."

I sit down and Giles throws a lit joint in my direction. I take a long toke and pass it on to one of the girls. They all seem well up for it – you can tell a night out with them would be a fucking riot. We should definitely come back and find them after we've done San An.

As if reading my mind – and he does that a lot – Giles pipes up and asks what the plan of attack is.

"Back to the hotel, freshen up, pick up the twat, dinner, West End, club. The PA's at 12.30, so we can be out of there by 2.00. I'll interview them as soon as they've done their turn. And then I think we should go to Amnesia for some rich Creamy goodness with our new friends here."

"Capital idea."

The girls murmur their approval, and me and Giles, knowing to always leave before we've outstayed our welcome, bid the ladies farewell and go looking for a cab outside Space.

The Hens Part 2 : Bora Boring

The queue at the cab rank is long, and it takes us about 20 mins to get to the front. It's sweltering outside, so the air-conditioned cab comes as a massive and refreshing relief. It only takes us ten minutes to get to our destination, some flash hotel called Es Vive in Figuretas, halfway between Ibiza Town and Bora Bora. It's all done out in pastel colours and is a bit art deco, and wouldn't look out of place in Miami. The check-in is swift, and we're soon disappearing into the hotel's bowels to our rooms, but not before Sharon has dished out some horrendous black t-shirts with "Keeleys Hen Do" emblazoned across the chest in pink. Ugh. Don't even get me started on the grammar.

    I get to my room – I'm not sharing with anyone – and put my suitcase on the bed. I unzip it and remove the contents, rather more carefully than someone else did last night. I take the Sainsbury's bag out and carefully unfold the dress I have in it. I got this gorgeous skimpy Michael Kors number from TK Maxx during the week especially to wear at Cream tonight. I look hot in it. It has a plunging neckline and makes me look and feel like a million dollars. I hang it up on the front of the wardrobe and take it in. The thought of wearing it out tonight makes my stomach tingle, and I think how great it will be to be able to get all glammed up without the ever-present fear that the night will turn into a maelstrom of threats, accusations and violent retribution.

I take my bikini and my one piece out and chuck them on the bed. I'm going to have to check out what the visible damage is to my torso before I decide what to wear on the beach. I strip in front of the mirror. When I bend down to take off my tights, the pain makes me grimace. I look at my naked self in the mirror and tentatively twist one way and the other to see how much of me is black and blue. Luckily, it's not too bad – nothing a superficial slap of foundation won't cover. But I still go for the one-piece. Just to be on the safe side. Safe from what though? That wanker is still informing my decisions as to what to wear from over a thousand miles away. Argh. I almost throw the one piece down, and plump for the bikini, but it'll raise eyebrows and questions I just can't be arsed to deal with right now.

I plonk myself on the edge of the bed and take in my reflection again. I look haggard. I'm only 26, but I look like I'm well into my 30s. I used to sparkle. Now I'm lucky if there's a flicker every now and then. I used to take such pride in my appearance when I was going out, even if it was just to the shops for a pint of milk. But now, getting dressed for an excursion seems like a preventative exercise in damage limitation and pre-emptive fire-fighting. Such is his control over me.

The only area of my life I've maintained any semblance of control over is in my career, and he's still managed to leave his mark on that. I actually have a half-decent job, much better than his, but I've not progressed as far as I should've. A promotion was offered about three or four years ago, but it meant relocating to the south, and he wasn't having it at all. He literally ordered me not to go. That was around the time he started getting more and more controlling and abusive. And since then, the only promotions I've been offered are pissy little baby-steps, mostly sideways ones, on the career ladder. So that's something else he's taken from me. There's been a lot of give and take in this relationship. I gave him my self-esteem, my confidence and my life-force, and he took my happiness and my soul.

    I get up and climb into my swimming costume, before wrapping a towel around myself. I chuck my phone and a magazine in my beach bag, and go down to meet the others. We ask reception to call us a cab, and within a few minutes we are getting out of it and walking towards an arched doorway bearing the name Bora Bora Beach Club. The thump of house music and murmur of laughter gives me goose-bumps, bringing back distant memories of being young and being able to enjoy myself free of fear. It makes me think about tonight and how much I'm going to enjoy letting my hair down. We go in and order a round of vodka limons and shots of Zambucca, and then head down to the beach to sit on the recliners.

    A group of hard looking lads are bobbing around at the water's edge. They're clearly pilled up and obviously are struggling with working out what to do other than pick fights and stare people down. They look like *him*. Beyond them, there is a group of young lads frolicking by the surf. They are hamming it up for a dude with a camera. He's getting them to hold up one of those dreadful lads' magazines and pose with it. The bloke next to him I recognise from somewhere. I think I saw him at the airport this morning. He looks bored.

My phone beeps and tells me I've got a text message. It's lunchtime now, so he'll be getting tanked up with a liquid lunch. I know his team are playing away tonight in some pre-season tournament, so he will be gearing up for a night sat in front of the TV getting drunk. I hope they win. When they lose, so do I.

Actually, you know what, fuck it, I hope they fucking lose and all their players get sent off.

I open the message. It reads:

"How is it? What are you up to?"

I send one back, saying where I am, what I'm doing and who I'm with. His lunch break will be over in about 15 minutes I think, so if I can keep him cool until then, he'll give me some peace and quiet for a couple of hours. The phone goes again. Another text from him. It says:

"Remember – I'll know if you misbehave. ;-)"

With a winking smiley face? Is this his attempt at stealth in his mission to intimidate me? Subtle. I'm feeling a little cheeky, buoyed by the shot and the half pint of vodka limon I've glugged, so I give him some back.

"Don't you trust me? :-p"

Ooh, a tongue sticking out smiley. This is almost verging on cute, this little exchange. He replies with:

"It's not you that I don't trust, Vicky. It's other people."

Aw, he's so *sweet*, isn't he? Where's the smiley gone though?

I don't reply, and by now the game is on so I have some respite.

The bloke who was pissing around by the sea with the camera has come over to us and is chatting up Sharon. I try to make myself invisible, and sink into my lounger, pulling the towel around me. He wants to take some photos of us for his mucky magazine, and Sharon, Kelly and Keeley are loving the attention, so they agree straight away. They whip off their t-shirts and Sharon even gets her tits out without prompting. She always was a classy girl. Kelly and Keeley start shouting over to me to get up and join them, but there's no way in hell that's going to happen. Luckily their desire to be the centre of attention overrides their desire for me to get my kit off and join them, and they leave me alone as I start rooting through my bag as an excuse to break eye contact with them and become invisible. The bloke with the camera tries to get me involved, but his mate clocks my discomfort and says something in his ear that turns his attention back to the others. He's actually being quite funny with them, acting like the clichéd glamour photographer. He reminds me of Austin Powers. I suppress a grin, not wanting to be dragged into it. They're all having a laugh, and part of me wants to get involved and frolic with them, but the fear occupies a bigger part of me, so I keep schtum and try not to draw attention to myself. It doesn't work though as the photographer's mate, who I assume to be a journalist, if you can call writing about boobs journalism, comes over and sits down on the sunbed next to me.

"Hi. I'm Jack."

I tell him I'm not interested in having my picture taken.

"I wasn't going to ask you to. Your friends seem more than happy to hog the limelight. Please don't judge me for this. There's more to me than running around asking girls to flash their boobs."

Oh, give it a rest. But I decide to be magnanimous. He seems unthreatening and a bit nerdy, to be honest.

"I wasn't judging you. The exploitation runs both ways as far as I'm concerned."

He turns back and looks at the scene with Sharon, Kelly and Keeley. We sit there in silence and I find myself welling up. I want to be having fun in front a camera, pissing around and having the confidence to show off my body. I feel robbed. I blink back a tear behind my sunglasses. Jack turns back to me and looks at me for a moment.

"Tell me to fuck off if I'm being nosy, but are you OK?" He says. "You look like you're about to cry."

I tell him I'm fine, and consider telling him I think he's nosy anyway because he's a journalist. Then he asks me if I want to go and have a coffee somewhere more peaceful and quiet. I'm about to tell him to "Fuck off", but when I look at him, he seems calm and quite gentle. He seems nice enough, and he doesn't come across like the kind of bloke who would take advantage of a damsel in distress, although my judgment when it comes to men has proved to be a little off before. I decide to take him up on his offer.

"Yeah, alright then." I find myself saying.

I get up and wrap the towel around me, covering myself. He shouts over at his mate Giles that we'll be back in a bit, but he and Sharon, Kelly and Keeley are all so engrossed in each other they don't even notice us leave. He asks me my name and we start walking towards the back of the beach and one of the little roads that lead off it. He doesn't persist in a lame line of questioning, instead letting things fall quiet. But it's not uncomfortable. I feel OK with this guy. After a minute or two we arrive at this German pub and he goes to the bar and orders us a couple of coffees and some sandwiches.

He comes back and slides into the seat opposite me.

"So, er, how long are you on the island?"

"Only until tomorrow."

He asks me a couple more inane questions. I can't help but feel a little irritated, thinking maybe this is a clumsy attempt at pulling me after all. I want to talk to him though. I want to get it all off my chest. I want to blurt out everything that's going on for me right now, and how this is one of the most important crossroads of my life. But I just keep quiet. Should I say anything to this total stranger? It would be a bit crazy, even if I do have a good feeling about him. The next thing he says momentarily makes me think he can read my thoughts.

"Look, I know I'm a complete stranger, but if there's anything you want to talk about, I'm a very good listener. And I won't repeat a word of it to anyone."

His directness throws me a bit. Nosey bastard. But then again, that's probably a good thing in his line of work. I need to take a minute, so I ask him where the bathroom is. I head off to the loo and lock myself in one of the stalls. I have a little cry, nothing major, but just enough to release the pressure, as it were. I decide to tell him when I get back out there. I sit there for a minute or two, compose myself and go back to our table, where our coffees and a couple of chicken sandwiches are waiting.

I start to tell him everything. Well, nearly everything.

His face looks shocked, and I can see anger dancing around in his eyes, but he then fixes his jaw and put his poker face on. I finish up and he sits there staring.

"Shit. I'm so sorry. That sounds fucking dreadful. I don't know what to say."

I'm impressed he hasn't come out with some macho bullshit about how he wants to kill Paul. He gets points for not playing the knight in shining armour card.

I tell him there's not much he can say. He asks me why I've stayed with him. I tell him the truth. How I was scared. How my self-esteem and confidence have been leeched out of me. How the person I was before, who wouldn't have stood for this shit was crushed and ground underfoot over the course of seven insidious years with *him*. I tell him I've only got wise recently. But then I stop. I don't want to shoot my mouth off more than I have already. The alcohol has loosened my tongue too much.

I retreat into my shell a bit and ask him what his story is. He tells me he's not happy in his job because he feels unchallenged. There, there – I wish I had problems like that! Haha. But he seems harmless enough, and I actually find him a little cute. Bless.

I order a couple of JD and Cokes, and finish off my sandwich. We toast and chink our glasses and I catch his eye. I ask him where he's going tonight. He says something about having to cover a club appearance by some Big Brother contestants. How vacuous. But to his credit, he has a little rant about them being the idiots that they are and how they are holding back society. I'm inclined to agree with him. He says he dislikes it and wants to write what he really thinks, but it'll never be published. He writes down a website where he says he'll post it.

"So, where are you girls going tonight?"

"We're going to Cream. I can't wait. I've not been clubbing for years. He didn't like me getting dressed up and going out. He wouldn't let me do pills, and he didn't like me drinking – he said it wasn't me he didn't trust, it was other men. Our nights out would always end with him twatting some poor sod who'd made the mistake of looking in my direction, or heaven forbid, talking to me. So tonight I've got lots of dancing to get out of my system."

The thought of going out and the fun I intend to have makes my heart sing. He says he'll try to make it down, and that makes me smile on the inside. We knock back a couple of shots of the local liqueur and head off back to the beach. The photographer is still entertaining the girls, but they're now sat in a circle on the sand, not pretending they're at the Playboy Mansion.

There's a joint going round, and Jack has a toke before passing it to Keeley. She takes a puff on it and stares at me while she draws the smoke in. If looks could kill....I wonder if she texted Paul and told him I went off and my whereabouts were unknown for all of, ooh, 30 minutes. I'll find out soon enough, I'm sure.

Jack and Giles say their goodbyes, and leave the beach. I hope I see him at Cream tonight. I might give him a little snog. That'll send a message back to Paul. Haha. This booze is making me feel mischievous. I look round to see a combination of inquisitive and accusatory faces looking at me.

"What's going on there then?" Keeley says, in a voice that drips in false sweetness. Like a knuckle duster on an iron fist in a velvet glove. So like her brother. As I answer her, I get a text.

"Nothing, Keeley. We went for a coffee and a sandwich. Is that alright with you?" I say with enough attitude to fend her off.

I look at the message on my phone. This one is enquiring as to who I am with. I go through my sent messages folder and resend the one I sent earlier. He responds with accusations of there being other people there, and that I'm not telling him. He says his sister told him I went off with some bloke. Un-fucking-believable. What a fucking shit-stirring bitch.

Over the next hour or so, the messages, which I am now mostly ignoring, get progressively worse and more offensive as he gets more livid he gets. Kelly has noticed I've got another text and makes an unintentionally disturbing cooing noise.

"Is that from Paul again? Aw, I think it's really sweet how you two keep texting, you must be so happy together." She clucks moronically as I finish tapping out the most subordinate apology I can muster to Paul.

"Oh yes. He's ever so sweet. And passionate. Isn't he Keeley? My Paul? Very passionate." I chirp, completely deadpan. Keeley shoots me an evil stare that cuts right through me. She looks *just* like him. Only for a second though. That family, God.

"I think it's lovely he cares so much," Sharon spouts. "Gary probably hasn't even noticed I've gone. It must be great to have a boyfriend who pays you so much attention."

Ugh, God, yeah it's great, I think.

"Oh God, yeah. It's great!" I say.

By now the sun is pretty low in the sky behind us, well on its way to setting on the other side of the island. Keeley says we should get back to the hotel and get ready for tonight. We're going to a restaurant before we go to the club, and our booking is at ten. It's only six now, so I might have a little siesta and try and sleep off this afternoon's indulgences.

We get in a cab back to the hotel and I flop onto my bed, setting the alarm on my phone for 8.30.

The Dealer Part 2 : Delegation

I get the gear back to mine and call up my number two, Niko, and tell him to come round and help me step on the gear. I've been working with him a couple of weeks now, since my previous colleague, a nice Romanian chap called Nagi, fucked off. Or disappeared. Whatever you think happened. I'm not stupid enough to ask, but I know he was stepping on the gear again before he sent it out, and I think he was starting to hold money back. Working for the firm we do, you've got to be a complete fucking idiot to do that. Nuff said.

So bye Nagi, and hello Niko. Niko seems a bit more clued up than his predecessor. I wonder about the turn of events that has led to him working for Charles and Eddie. Again, sometimes it doesn't pay to ask. My own route to "employment" with this altruistic pair was the result of something going disastrously wrong back home. To cut a long story short, I ended up owing their other brother 20 grand. And not having any means to pay it, no family and few possessions, they offered me the chance to work off the debt by ferrying gear back and forth and serving up and helping run things in Playa D'en Bossa and at their club in San An. Some people would call it enslavement, especially as they confiscate my passport whenever I return, but fuck it. At least this way I get to live. And it's way better than the life of signing-on and petty crime that I had back home. And the work is not without its perks. I'd rather be enslaved in a place with sunshine, fit birds and wicked music than be a prisoner of Camberwell Green dole office.

Niko arrives with a few bags of cut, and we empty it all in a big bowl with the gak and mix it all up. When I'm satisfied with the blend, I get two huge sandwich bags from under the sink and fill them with the gear. It just about fits. I give it back to Niko and he leaves. From here he'll take it round to another apartment we use, where it'll be split into .7 gram bindles and divvied up between our street team, who will then go and shift it for 50 euros a pop in the bars and clubs and on the beaches of the island.

I go through to my room and begin to get ready for the evening. I lay out my smart clothes on the bed. Beige chinos, pristine trainers and a white shirt. I have a shave and jump in the shower and scrub myself vigorously, making sure to give my arse a proper going over after my not 100% hygienic dump at Eddie and Charlie's earlier. I towel off, put on my clothes and go and sit on the balcony with a beer, looking out over the beach. The sky is getting darker, and the moon is now visible. The sea is very calm, with the distant throb of a house beat the only noise. I think about how things are going here. By the end of the season, I'll have cleared my debt and will hopefully have accumulated enough cash to fuck off and start all over somewhere else. The line of work I'm in is a high-risk and dangerous one, but if I can hold on just a couple more months, I can leave it all behind. I'm thinking of going to Thailand and doing a diving course and getting qualified as an underwater guide. My old man used to take me along with his dive club before he popped his clogs. I used to love the feeling underwater. It was the closest to what I imagine flying would be like, floating over all the flooded landscape. It was the only time I've ever felt totally free.

I spark the joint that's been left in the ashtray, and float away on my thoughts, thinking about a paradise with clear, turquoise water, reefs festooned with coral and shoals of multicoloured fish. I drift off into a doze, my daydream sliding into a real dream. I'm cruising along just beneath the surface, when, all of a sudden, nothing comes out of my aqualung. I gasp for breath and feel myself sinking to the sea bed. My feet are sucked into the sand, and I sink further until it covers my head. I feel smothered, drowning, but it feels warm and comfortable at the same time. Panic battles with resignation to my fate and I struggle before realising there no point and serenity takes over. My feet suddenly feel free, and I feel myself fall through the sand into a pocket of air. My lungs fill up and I can breathe again. I look around, and see nothing in the blackness except for a luminous, phosphorous conical shell. It starts ringing.

The Resort Manager Part 3 : Meeting

It takes me about 15 mins to get back over to San Antonio. When I park up in the car park of the hotel I notice Sean's car is there, so he can't be far. I enter the lobby and go and check some of the new arrivals' info behind reception. We've got a few in today, most of whom are dispersing from a welcome meeting that Ash has just wound up. I trot over to the reps desk.

"Good morning Amy. And how are you today?" Ash says bombastically. He's a good rep, but there's something about him that I don't like. He's smarmy.

"Have you seen Sean or Jody?"

"You just missed them. Sean's up to something though. You want to keep an eye on him." Ash says. He really is a sneaky fucker this one. I can't understand someone who gets such obvious glee from shit-stirring and dropping people in it.

"And you want to stop telling me how to do my job, Ashley." Nobody likes a snitch, especially when they don't venture any useful information.

Kirstie sits there with a rictus smile on her face, but I can tell she's suffering.

"How are you feeling this morning, Kirstie? You're a bit quiet. Did you overdo it at Pacha last night?"

"No, no, I'm fine, Amy. Takes more than a night out disco-dancing to fell this mighty tree," she says with an admirable amount of conviction. She then erupts into a guttural sounding coughing fit. Bless her. I'm not going to give her shit about it, not when I've got the Sean situation to deal with as well.

"OK, well, why don't you go and get something to eat. I'm sure Ash can hold the fort here."

Kirstie smiles, this time it seems a bit more genuine, and slides off her stool.

"Yeah, I think that might help. Cheers."

She walks off towards the restaurant, her spaceman-like gait giving away the fact that she's probably got a fair amount of ket, mkat or whatever it is still flying round her system. I feel a little pang of jealousy. I have a lot of fond memories from last year of me and Kirstie sitting at the reps desk enduring comedowns together. It was always painful, but the banter was always good, and the shared adversity of a comedown at work always engenders some serious bonding. I miss that. Now I feel like they see me as the disapproving adult that they are all nice to because they have to be, not because we're mates. And that saddens me. But fuck that, I've no time for melancholia today. I say bye to Ash, who sleazily gives me a kiss on both cheeks, and holds me in a sweaty clasp that is a second too long for it to be affectionate, and I get the fuck out of there and head down to the office.

It's still fucking baking outside, and the glare from the lowering sun flash-blinds me for a second when I emerge from the hotel. I slide my sunnies down off the top of my head and strut down the hill towards the office, stopping off at the Tabac for 20 Lambert and Butler, and at Eroski for some milk. There's hardly ever any in the office, and when there is, it's usually been left out and is halfway between yoghurt and cheese. I skirt the West End, which already has a few squads of lads gorging on shit fry-ups and shit lager. Most of them are shirtless, shitfaced and scarlet. They look like pigs snuffling at a trough full of fizzy beer and fatty bacon. I go up past the Ship and on into the back end of San An, arriving at the office just before half three.

Mike is already there with Lucas and Toby, my two co-managers from the Bay and Playa D'en Bossa. They're all watching something on Toby's laptop. From their reactions, it's more than likely scat or something else disgusting. The fact that they don't turn it off or even try to hide what they are watching when I come in speaks volumes about the maturity of my other managers.

"Alright Amy. You seen this – Two Girls, One Cup? Fucking hilarious."

"I'm sure it is, but I'll give it a miss, ta."

Mike and Lucas say hello, and then spy the milk.

"Oh, you fucking legend. I'm gasping for a cuppa but some twat left the milk out. Do us one as well, will you? Cheers Amy." Lucas says. "Two sugars."

Please? Not likely. Rude bastard.

"Do you two want one as well?" I say to Mike and Toby. They both do, and have the manners to say thanks. They all go back to gawping at their scat and I stick the kettle on. The hunt for some clean mugs takes a while, but eventually I round four up that don't have any life forms evolving in them and give them a quick rinse in the bathroom sink. I finish up making the brews and pull up a chair with the others. Thankfully, their film is over. Mike motions to a couple of bulging plastic bags on the table.

"I went to Croissant Show this morning – help yourself to a Danish or a chocolate croissant."

Wicked. I love Croissant Show. I fish out a sticky almond pastry and dip the end in my tea. Mike closes his laptop and starts talking.

"OK. The guys at head office wanted me to talk to you all, as managers and team leaders, about how you guys need to be making more club tickets sales and bringing in more revenue from any extras we can. We were down the last month compared to last year, by quite a bit. I know you guys are working flat out, but I got my balls squeezed by them this week, so I have to squeeze yours. Shit rolls downhill and all that. Do whatever you can to bring in more cash. Incentivise if you have to, offer the best rep something, whatever you need to do, just get them to rake in as much as they can."

"Yeah, we'll try, you know that. But it's fucking difficult – there's a recession on, and these kids are a lot more savvy these days than they used to be. It's hard to get them to spend on anything if they can do it by themselves on the cheap." Lucas says.

"Yeah, yeah I know. But as I said, I'm just passing on a message. I know what it's like out there. Anyway, I want to get off down the beach, so Amy, what's happening with Sean? Is he trying to do that stupid fucking party? If he thinks he can just present a fait accompli and put it on anyway, he can fucking think again. I want that shut down."

"Well, it looks like it. The Animador at the hotel mentioned something yesterday, and I found a load of receipts for boat hire and some dancers from the lap dance club. And it looks like it'll be tonight."

I consider telling them how much cash I think he's into it for. I decide not to, opting to keep this problem as small as I can until it's necessary to blow the lid off it. Mike sets down his cup of tea with a little more force than I think he intended, spilling a little on the table.

"Sean's a cheeky little cunt," Mike says. "I take it this is his liquidation he's dipping into? Why hasn't he given it in yet? It's Thursday. I thought collections were done on Tuesday?"

"They're supposed to be, but we generally do it at the end of the week," I reply, a little too meekly. "You know that, Mike, we've always let that slide until the end of the week." It's true. Timetables are very movable out here, always have been.

"Stupid fucking Sean," Mike says. "If he's lost a load of money, he's fucking finished, and head office may even want to prosecute him."

"I'm on it," I say with forced confidence. "I'll deal with it this afternoon."

"You better," Mike says. "Oh yeah, and sorry, but there's no Mallorca for you this week. They want you to stay here to keep an eye on your reps. And if you need a hand dealing with Sean, call Lucas or Toby."

Fucking great. I was looking forward to Palma. Wankers. And what's this 'If I need a hand' shit? Implying I can't deal with it myself? Cheers for the vote of confidence.

"It'll be fine. I can handle it."

"Right, that's that then. I'm off down Salinas for a bit. I'll ding you later on."

And with that, he's out the door quicker than a schoolboy on the last day of term, taking one of the Croissant Show bags with him. No sooner is he out the door than Lucas, Toby and I pounce on the remaining bag. A tug of war ensues, with me as the ultimate victor. I can be pretty feisty when I want to, and while being on the whole childish imbeciles, neither of them are the type to physically overpower a woman, even if it's for food.

"What ever happened to ladies first, eh boys?" I chide.

I look in the bag and see one almond Danish and two chocolate croissants. I take one of the pain au chocolate and toss the bag back on the table. Before it's even touched the surface the two of them are tearing it to shreds to get at the grub. Hehe. The tussle is soon over and we sit there, enjoying a rare moment of mirth. Toby is grumbling about getting the almond one and lunges at Lucas to take his instead. Lucas swerves in his seat, leaning backwards and stuffs the whole croissant in his mouth in one go, giving himself the look of a gerbil with mumps. Toby sits back down and we all start giggling as Lucas sprays bits of flaky pastry over the table. I polish off the last of my croissant and get up to go.

"Give us a shout if you need a hand controlling your staff, darling." Lucas sings in a patronising tone as I go out the door. I head back to the hotel through the back streets, taking a route that leads through the square at the top of the West End. I need to come up with a plan. And I need to find out more info about the party. I'll have another poke around in the office, and see what I can glean from the other reps. Kirstie won't be much use, nor will Jody, but Ash is enough of a treacherous bastard for me to be able to hopefully trawl some information from him.

When I get there, the reps are busy chatting to some guests. I slink past and get into the office without them seeing me and lock the door behind me. I want to maintain a low profile for now, and maybe lull Sean into a false sense of security. I'm fairly certain the others will be keeping him updated on my whereabouts.

Wheeling a chair over from by the water cooler, I sit down at the desk that Sean has colonised. It looks like someone has upended the contents of a paper recycling bin all over it. Whenever I've pulled him up about this in the past, he says there's a system, and he knows where everything is, naturally. It's a fucking mess though, system or not. I begin to sift through the papers again, feeling a little twinge of excitement as I do. It's not often you get to partake in some espionage in this job. I fire up the desktop computer, and make a cuppa while it boots up. It takes ages, so I open the fire exit door and have a quiet fag. In the distance, the din from the pool party echoes off the surrounding buildings. I can hear the increased traffic in the lobby as the guests come down from their afternoon naps to recharge themselves with sun and booze. I finish my cig and go over to Sean's computer and click on the Outlook icon. The window opens up and I'm pleased to see that this machine is plumbed into both the general inbox and the reps' individual ones.

    I have a quick look through the group one, and notice the emails regarding the dancers have been deleted. I check Sean's inbox and sent folders, but there's nothing in there that sheds any light on today's proceedings. A light bulb pings in my mind, and I move the mouse to the start menu and hover over the recent documents tab. There's a photoshop document there called "party flyer" which looks hopeful. I click on it, only to be told windows is searching for it. Ha, seems someone's had a right old clear-out this morning.

    I check Facebook. It's possible he could have posted details on there of where and when and so on. Unfortunately there's nothing on his profile or in his events. On the right side of the page, there's a link to a photo album from last year. I click on it and am greeted with a picture of me, Sean, Jody and Kirstie at DC10's closing party. That was such a wicked night. I get a little misty eyed and nostalgic. We used to be such a tight little unit, and it's mainly because that has been missing that this summer has been so shit. I thought I'd be able to combine the role of boss and friend, but despite my efforts, it just hasn't panned out like that. Yeah perhaps I've been a bit heavy handed, but they could've cut me some slack. They've not made it easy. Although my ostracism makes it easier to be the one who has to piss on Sean's chips today. That night at DC10 was the last time I really felt part of the gang, anyway. I look through some more pictures of this season, group shots of them all at Space opening, one of the gigs at Ibiza Rocks, and some on the rock where we all used to go to watch the sunset. I'm in none of them.

I log out of Facebook and shut the computer down.

Sean's still not answering his phone when I try him again, so I leave the office and go into the lobby and head over to the reps' desk. Ash and Kirstie have been joined by Wine-Eyes. As I get closer, they notice me and a sneering grin spreads over Ash's face.

"Oi Amy, I think you might want to see this." He says, waving a piece of paper in the air.

Kirstie jabs him in the ribs.

"Oh my god, you are such a fucking grass," she says as she tries to snatch whatever it is from him. Ash is tall and spindly, and with no effort he holds it beyond her reach and let's go. The paper floats down to the ground and lands in front on me. It looks like half a sheet of A4 that has been photocopied and guillotined, given the roughness of one side and the shite printing. Having seen Sean's attempts at mastering Photoshop when designing promotion fliers for events we did last summer at the hotel, I recognise his own inimitable and shonky style a mile off. I crouch down and peel it off the floor.

A cartoon picture of a boom box on a beach surrounded by palm trees is the image, with graf-style lettering spelling out "Secret Party at a Secret Location. Meet at Club Tropicana Hotel at 10, or on the good ship *Erebus,* right next to the Egg by the dock at 10.15pm. EUROS30"

Bingo. Nailed him.

I can feel Kirstie and Wine-Eyes studying my face for a reaction, so I keep my features set. Ash is squirming in his chair, barely containing his joy at dropping Sean in it, Schadenfreude dripping from every single one of his odious pores. What a shit he is. I've never understood why some people feel the need to undermine and sabotage their friends in the name of 'banter'. It strikes me as the actions of someone cruel and very insecure, which is pretty much what Ash is. But in this instance, his treachery serves a purpose. Mine.

I fold the flyer and don't pay it a second glance, being careful to act like I don't give a shit. I tell the reps I'm going out for a fag, in a tone of voice that leaves an unspoken invitation for someone to join me hanging like an unwanted fart in the air. But none of them want to smoke with me. I leave the lobby and head out to the front of the hotel by myself. I think I hear hushed tones and stifled giggles recede behind me, but I could be paranoid.

Lighting up outside, I look down at the flier in my hand and scrunch it up. Little cunt. I'm going to have him. This is a direct slap in the face, not only to me, but to my authority, the company's authority, and it's tantamount to theft. He's spunked money that isn't his. End of. I finish my fag and light another one straight away. I don't really want to go back to the lobby and hang out with Kirstie, Ash and Wine-Eyes any longer than I have to, such is the unpleasantness that hangs in the air. I head back over to the flat and flop onto the bed. I set my alarm for 9.00 and fall asleep within minutes.

The Thief Part 1 : Commuting

This is my last week out here. I've had a good run, but I've been here for a month, and only an idiot would press her luck. I can get out of here with a nice bankroll and my nose clean if I go now and don't get greedy. There's still enough of the season left for me to go and put in a good shift in Malia and still make it back here for closing. So tonight will probably be my last night working in Ibiza for a bit. I'd better make it count.

    This evening's job involves relieving a group of workers of their laptops, cameras and anything else that will fit in my trusty record bag. Everyone works nights here, I have the advantage of always working in the dark. I wander around with my bag and a pair of headphones on, completing my inconspicuousness. Nobody gives a DJ a second glance out here. They're ten a penny. As are thieves. But not good ones like me.

    I've tried rationalising what I do in order to make myself think I'm not as much of a cunt as my main occupation would suggest, but I must admit, I come up short. But then again, I'm not alone in being one, especially here. So I try to redress the karmic balance wherever I can. In every other aspect of my life, my real life, I'm a good person. I'm a stand-up gal. I never bully people, I never treat anyone like shit. I give generously to those who are genuinely unfortunate. Unlike most of the snotty-nosed trustafarians and gap year students that I rob.

They're insured up to the gills anyway, so apart from a minor inconvenience caused by the loss of their gadgets, the only real victims here are the insurance companies. Fuck 'em. My heart bleeds. Anyway, by removing all these creature comforts from these kids, I'm returning to them the joys that belong to the pre-digital age. I'm helping them develop their social skills more by forcing them out of the virtual world. They'll converse more in person. Hell, they might even read a book or write a letter. Ha. Yeah right.

I set off just before eight. I'm staying at my ex-boyfriend's flat just outside Ibiza Town. It's in the middle of the Can Bufi industrial area, next to all manner of dusty and noisy workshops and factories. My ex, Dennis, lives here with another dude, Ian, in a three bedroom apartment, and they rent their spare room out over the season to mates who are visiting. They both work in a bar down by the port, not far from Pacha. I love this side of the island. It's so much classier than the wretched hive of scum and villainy that is San Antonio. But however horrific San An is, it's the best place for me to work while I'm here.

I leave our apartment block next to the noisy recycling depot and stroll down the road past our local bar. It's a bit Spartan, but we're so far off the beaten track here that the only people that drink here are the local bin men. You find them there at five in the morning knocking back shots of hierbas before their shift. We sometimes stagger in here on our way home from the clubs, and get funny looks from them.

Outside the bar I walk past a cat. It got run over just after I got here. Over the last four weeks I have watched in fascination as a) no one has bothered to clear it up, and b) its decomposing corpse has slowly been steam-rollered into a black, oily, cat-shaped silhouette on the tarmac. It's rank, but compelling.

I reach the end of the road, where it feeds onto the dual carriageway that serves as the main artery between Ibiza Town and San Antonio. I wait for the oncoming traffic to clear, and jog over to the central reservation and pause, again waiting for my chance to get across to the other side. The roads here are fucking treacherous. The Spanish drive like maniacs with feet made of lead, and the tourists drive like maniacs full of booze and drugs. I saw more crashes here in my first season than I had in England in the rest of my life. I make it to the other side in one piece and take a pew at the bus stop next to Maison D'Elephant, which has to be the best named furniture shop in the world. I feel a little leap of joy in my stomach when I remember a recently pilfered iPod is in my bag. The previous owner had fantastic taste in music, with 80 gigs of funk, soul, rare groove, proper old school house, every Essential Mix since 1993 and the entire back catalogues of The Stones, The Beatles, The Clash and the Mondays. I felt like leaving him a thank you note.

The headphones are fished out and stuck in, and I circle my thumb around the jog-wheel until I get to Oakie's Goa Mix. I look over to the west, at the azure expanse of sky that sits over the hills like a massive blue sombrero. I feel the sinking sun still warming my face, and let the wave of contentment wash over me. I press play on the iPod and let the wishy-washy synth intro breeze into my ears, before the beat drops and my mojo flickers into life. A lovely way to start the evening.

The bus flies over the roundabout and pulls up at the bus stop. I give the driver my fare and take a seat at the back of the bus as it rattles out of the bus stop and heads down the motorway. Soon after we pass Amnesia, I see Privilege rising out of the side of an escarpment on our right. With its bulbous dome and huge hanger, it looks like a spaceship has landed in the countryside, even more so late at night, when the hum and thump of the music rolls over the fields, accompanied by the attendant lightshow. We go through San Raf and I think how sad it is that most tourists will never venture north or south of this road, and see what the island is really like. But on the other hand, as a result of this non-straying, there are still parts of this island that are completely unspoilt. As we climb over the crest of the hill and emerge from the canopy of trees, the sky opens up and I see the expanse of the San An Bay spread out in orange glow in front of me. The sun hangs low over the horizon at just the right altitude to give me time to get to my favourite spot to watch the sunset. The bus deposits me at the terminus, and I trot off into the back streets of San Antonio.

The Shop Girl Part 1 : Daytime Dullness

Late afternoon in the shop always drags like a school-kid on a Benson out here. The place doesn't get busy until everyone comes out on the piss, so from four until around nine, I have fuck all to do. When I get there, it will take me all of half an hour to tidy the shop, rearrange and rebuild the displays, and take care of any other lingering business left over from the day shift. Which leaves a huge swathe of time in the early evening for me to think, be bored and get antsy. I'm not even allowed to read a book. God knows why. And as there are so few punters, the chances of any conversation are not high. They don't even have wi-fi. I spend most of my afternoons wishing my life away and waiting for it to be time to go out with my mates. But still, saying that, it beats the shit out of a rainy afternoon back home.

    I set off for the shop at about half three. I only live five minutes away, but I know that Natalie is doing the shift before me, and she's probably the messiest person I've ever known, so it's in my interests to arrive ahead of time and try to limit the disruption her end-of-shift tidy-up will cause. She's scatter-brained, forgetful, unreliable and, quite literally, all over the shop. She's also one of the funniest girls you could ever hope to meet. And she's been a very good friend to me on more than one occasion. So I'm getting there early so I can sort out the shop for my shift, and so we can have a bit of a gossip and a natter. We've both got boy trouble at the moment, as in trouble finding any.

I leave my apartment block and head up towards Ibiza Rocks, taking the alleyway opposite which will take me in the direction of the West End. I nod to the workers I see as I pass the Ship – this world is exceptionally small, and you can't travel more than five metres in any direction without bumping into someone you know. I feel a surge of joy as I see my friend Matt walking across from the direction of the Egg. He's carrying a watermelon.

"Hello beautiful, how are you this fine day? We must stop meeting like this." He shouts over at me. "You know, this is the exact same spot where we first met last season. It must have some kind of cosmic significance."

I crack a smile. I love Matt. He's the best friend I've got out here. We worked together last year and kept in touch over winter. This season we've hardly left each other's side. He's like a gay best mate, except he's straight. I can't fathom why he hasn't got a girlfriend. He's the loveliest dude in the world, and is pretty cute too. We're going out tonight to our friend's party in the countryside, and I cannot fucking wait. He's the best partner in crime you could ask for. He's sharp-witted and funny, can handle his drugs, never takes too much and becomes a liability, and is a wicked dancer. I've never had a shit time when we've gone out together.

"Alright my love. How are you? That's a nice looking watermelon you've got there."

"Yeah baby, I'm going to take it home and try to eat it all in one go. You still up for tonight?"

"Of course. What time are you finishing?"

"I'll try and get off about 3. We meeting at the OK?"

"Yup."

"OK sugar-pie, I'll see you then. I've got to get home and make a dent in this."

He holds his watermelon aloft like it's a trophy, pecks me on the cheek and struts off down the road. He turns and starts walking backwards, shouting to me as he departs.

"I'll try and pop into the shop before work to alleviate your boredom if I get the chance. Love ya."

I hope he does, I really do. Come and see me at work, I mean. I wave at him as he spins round and carries on his bounce down the road.

I head down the West End and turn down the quiet-ish side street where the shop is. I go in, and surprise, surprise, the place is a tip. Nat is trying to gather the strewn garments into tidy little piles, but is in reality mucking up the displays even more.

"Hello Hannah, how are you doing, my dear?"

"I'm good. Let me do that. Why don't you stick the kettle on?" I suggest, hoping to draw her away from making more of a mess. That's the one thing I really love about the shop – the owners are English, and there's always a full box of PG Tips in the storeroom and proper milk in the fridge.

I scurry around the shop, chucking the right clothes in the right places and generally undoing all of Nat's work. She comes back from the back of the shop with a couple of steaming mugs and plonks herself down on the sofa with a sigh. Given the state of the shop, she must be knackered – it can't be easy creating this much carnage out of a load of pre-ripped t-shirts and hot pants.

"So how's your day been so far?" She enquires.

"Pretty non-descript. A couple of hours down at Kanya beach this morning, then I had some lunch, and then came to work. I bumped into Matt on the way here. And that's about as exciting as it's been. How's it gone in here?"

"Yeah, pretty busy for a couple of hours about lunchtime, but that's it. So how's Matt then, eh? I'm surprised he didn't walk you all the way to work," she says, mischievously.

"Oh, he had a date with a watermelon. I wouldn't have wanted to come between the two of them. It looked like love." I reply flippantly, trying to work out what she meant.

"Tell me about it."

Whatever she's alluding to, I let it go. She starts telling me about her boy woes. Or lack of. She's not shy of male attention, but as is so common out here, it's more the quality than the quantity that's the problem. So we start making a list of all the single guys we know, and methodically go through it, trying to identify a suitable beau for her. And for me. This kills about 15 minutes, and by the end of our little virtual-cruise through the eligible bachelors of San An, we're probably feeling more disheartened than before. Not the most fertile of breeding grounds, if you'll excuse the pun.

"But then again," she says sagely, "if you're looking for a high calibre man, like your Matt, I don't think San Antonio is the best place to shop."

"My Matt? He's not mine! We're just mates." Jesus – can't anyone be friends without someone thinking anything of it?

"Yeah, right. You're always with him. You look good together. He's a catch, and he's obviously devoted to you, so I reckon you two should pair off."

"Yeah, whatever." Her bluntness is a little unwelcome, drawing attention to something that I'd rather was left alone. A couple of customers come in and start asking about the clothes, and I welcome the distraction. I start pulling out various garments for them, and Nat starts packing up her stuff. They buy a couple of t-shirts and dresses, and then scoot off. Nat asks me what I'm doing tonight.

"Off to Sean's party with the gang. I think we're heading down about 3.00 if you want to come?"

"Who's going then?"

"Me, Ryan, Jordan, Lucy, Starkey. It should be fun."

"And Matt?"

"Yeah, of course."

She says nothing, but her raised eyebrow and silence speaks volumes.

"Nat, seriously, fuck off. You're barking up the wrong tree with that one."

"Yeah, whatever. Well, if it looks like a couple, smells like a couple and sounds like a couple….."

"You're starting to annoy me now, Nat!" I say, only half-joking.

She apologises, and then goes straight on to say that because me and Matt look like we're together, it might be scaring off potential suitors. She then says that me and Matt should just stop fucking around and get together. She doesn't pull any punches, this one. I'd be lying if I said the thought hadn't ever occurred to me, but we're just mates. He's never expressed any interest in me – surely if he fancied me, he would've made a move. And he never has. So any crush I may or may not have on him is totally irrelevant, and has been denied the oxygen of any attention.

Anyway, she finally shuts up and picks up her bag. She gives me a wink, and flounces out of the shop.

"I'll ding you later, my sweet," she says over her shoulder. And off she goes down the road.

I turn my attention to what needs to be done to get the shop ship-shape. As I fold and replace the errant clothes, my mind keeps drifting towards Matt. He's such a dude. But he doesn't really seem to believe it himself. He can be really self-deprecating, to the point where it's unattractive. Not many girls will fancy someone who doesn't even fancy themselves a little bit. I really wish he wasn't so down on himself. He's a fucking catch. He needs to start loving himself a bit more, because his personality is brilliant. And that's what happens to matter most. At least I think so. And between me and the four walls of the shop, I actually do think he's pretty cute. But I push those feelings down into myself – they more than likely are the result of some form of cabin fever, down to the amount of time we've been spending with each other. A holiday romance type thing. And there are things that seem real on this island, but when you rotate them back to the real world, they aren't. But then again, our friendship remained real back home over the winter. Anyway, it's a moot point. There's nothing that's going to happen there. He's my mate. I'm his mate. And that's just great.

The Holidaymakers Part 1 : Arrival

It seems like we've been driving round in circles for hours. Trying to find a parking space in Ibiza Town is like trying to find a virgin in San Antonio. It's proving to be a challenge. What a drag. I'm still not over the drive down here, and I could well do with getting out of the car. We left yesterday morning and two days of being folded up in a Capri has probably given me deep vein thrombosis.

It was a fucking wicked road trip though. Me and Kenny shared the driving. We drove through the Eurotunnel and across France quicker than a Panzer division, stopping off in Toulouse for the night, before burning down to Barcelona to get the ferry. I fucking love road trips. We had a lump of hash the size of a golf ball, and a couple of grams of Charlie to keep us going, and it rocked. Just like Johnny Depp and Benicio Del Torro in that film about Las Vegas. The only bit of bad luck was we left our draw in the Novotel in Toulouse – but hey, our misfortune is someone else's score, so good luck to the cleaner who finds our wad of Afghan. I'm sure we won't have any problems picking up again now we're in Ibiza.

Eventually we find a space big enough for the Capri, and we slide it in backwards between a couple of land-cruisers. There are fucking millions of those things over here – the environmentalists must love it. We've not checked into a hotel tonight, due to lack of funds. There's a tent in the boot, so the plan is to hang around Ibiza Town for the rest of the day, have some fun, score, then find a secluded beach to pitch our tent on. We'll probably check into a hostel tomorrow, but I'm happy to slum it tonight so we can save some pennies.

We wind up the windows and get out of the car. I lunge one way, and then the other, giving my legs a much needed stretch. The joints in my knees and groin both show their gratitude with a series of satisfying pops and clicks. I take a look around and drink it all in. Even though it's just gone midnight, the streets are rammed. And not only with tourists. All manner of locals are out and about, from young Spanish groups of mates to middle and old age couples strolling around. One thing that stands out is how classy and well dressed everyone is. It really makes you think that we're the scruffy bastards of Europe. I love the way the elder Spanish men walk around really slowly with their hands clasped behind their backs. It makes them look so distinguished. It's also very calming. Their quiet dignity is a stark contrast to what lies in wait for us over the other side of the island. But for now, we're lucky enough to be in Ibiza Town, not San Antonio, and for that, I am grateful.

I look over at my companion, and see him stifling a yawn as he stretches his back out.

"I don't know about you, Lee, but I could murder a fucking pint. Let's go to that place Simon told us about. The Rock Bar."

"Spiffing idea, Kenneth."

I kneel on the front seat of the car and rummage around in the back for my bag. I pull out my passport and wallet – if the car gets nicked, I don't want to lose all this shit as well. I lock the motor and we cross the road, heading in the direction of the harbour. We wander into a pedestrianised area of the old town. It's brightly lit, the dazzle amplified by all the white painted buildings and it glistens like a wonderland in front of us. Down this particular alley, there are a load of stalls selling all manner of holiday tat from stupid hats to porno cards. The side streets are dotted with poncey boutiques displaying ludicrously expensive handbags and some lovely directional knitwear. Not really my thing, but probably very becoming on your elegant middle-aged Ibicencan senorita.

We spill out of the alley into a bustling square, with hawkers hustling even more tat. Hippie chicks are selling shit jewellery and African dudes are selling fake Ray-Bans. I remember these sorts of markets from holidays to Spain as a kid. I'd forever be hunting for some kind of butterfly knife or switchblade that I could show off to my mates at school. We'd always try to recreate that scene in Aliens where Bishop does the knife trick in the canteen. And we'd always stab ourselves pretty much immediately. I have a nice scar on my index finger to prove it.

In order to avoid the crowds, we walk out into the road that runs along the harbour and down to the Rock Bar. We pull up a couple of stools at the high tables outside and the waitress comes over immediately. We order two vodka limons and a couple of shots of hierbas. The drinks arrive and we neck the shots, before dousing the resulting fire in our throats with a big glug of our long drinks. We then settle back and start people watching. The parades of freaks, trannies, musclemen, queens, midgets, dwarfs, hobbits and ewoks that trickle past with clockwork regularity is fascinating. They've always got the most freakish at the front, holding the banner for whichever club it is they are promoting, like some skewed standard bearer for a marauding army of the extravagant and extrovert. It looks fucking immense. And the fact that there are a lot of super-fit girls on stilts with nothing but glitter covering their nips is just the icing on this crazy visual cake. Ah, Ibiza.

The Bouncer Part 3 : Sunset

The alarm wakes me at 6.30. I don't have to be at Mambo's until 8.00, so I whip myself a huge plate of scrambled eggs, grilled mushrooms and tomatoes and wolf it down while watching the Simpsons on my flatmate's laptop. I let my dinner go down a bit, then do some stretches and sit ups. I grab a shower and put on my black trackie bottoms and my black t-shirt before heading out the door just after seven thirty.

    I only live about five minutes walk from the Egg, and by the time I get to the main drag, it's already teeming with tourists and lobster-red kids out to line their stomach with some cheap egg and chips before they fill themselves up with vodka and Red Bull. I can remember the first time I was out here as a teenager, and a large mix of empathy and nostalgia brings a cheesy grin to my face. I hope I'll be able to hang on to this benevolent feeling later on, when these same people will be staggering around the West End trying to fuck or fight each other. Bless 'em.

    I get onto the posh new path that skirts along the coastline to the sunset strip, and head round to where all the sunset bars are. Café Del Mar and Savannah are already heaving, as is Mambo's. I check in with Cliff, the guv'nor, and assume my usual position in front of the DJ booth. There's a little step there I can stand on, which given my already sizable form, makes me seem like a giant protector of the decks. With my aviators on, I imagine I cut quite the clichéd image of a man in black.

Taking in the view and the atmosphere, I sense the buzz in the air that all the positive vibes are creating – the beautiful scenery, the anticipation of a storming night out, the possibility of a fuck – it's all there, playing its part. The gentle tribal rhythms of the music seem to tease the sun down out of the sky, and as it comes to rest for the briefest of moments on the horizon, a rumble of applause and cheers lifts out of the crowd. I love this part of the evening. I don't even consider myself at work right now – I've got the best seat in the house and I'm getting paid for it. Nice. Doing evening at Mambo's is a cushy number. No fighting, ever, and one of the best sunsets in the world is the view from my workspace.

Sometimes I think about my occupation in terms of my cod-Zen leanings, and how it's a job that sometimes has to utilise violence, or at least the threat of violence to achieve its goals. I've been doing security work since I got out. I'm a big lad, and luckily that has proved to be deterrent enough for me to have not had to twat anyone. I can block and restrain someone in the blink of an eye without any need to hurt them. Unlike a lot of security guys I know, I don't believe you're doing your job properly by hitting a punter – in fact, when you do so, you're failing. Our job is to provide a safe and non-violent environment for these kids to have their wild night of debauchery. We're the grown ups at the party. We stay sober and keep things cool so that the kids can go bananas. If it gets to the point where your only recourse is to twat someone, you've fucked up. You've not seen it coming, and you've let people down by allowing a situation requiring violence to develop. I tell this to the other security guards, but they just laugh at me and call me an old hippie. But they never call me anything stronger and put my pacifist principles to the test. It's just a shame that so many of them are haters and just look upon the job as a licence to hit drunk people. I would even go so far as to say I hate they way some of them are, but hate is something I try not to feel these days.

But there's none of that down by Mambo's. It's purely a chilled vibe down here. The second part of my shift is in the West End, where there's always a ruck waiting to be found.

The Thief Part 2 : Sunset Vibes

I scurry through the warren of backstreets and make my way towards the sunset strip. I move fast, passing by the Ship, and carve a route down the mostly deserted West End, past garish joints like Highlander, Capones, Ground Zero and Koppas. The proprietors and PRs are steeling themselves for another night of drunken pukiness – it's quiet, but there's a feeling of anticipation. This bit is the calm before the shit storm.

    I cut up a side street and drop into the supermarket to pick up a couple of cans of cider, before padding the hoof up towards Cafes Mambo and Del Mar, both now ruined by expensive drinks and cheap clientele. I go round the back of Mambo's and cross the derelict plot of land next to it. There is an outcropping of rock there, next to a spot that the workers call Ket Cove. Perched on this rock you can see as good a sunset as you can at the over-priced Mambo or Savannahs (no-one goes to Del Mar anymore, except Germans). I plop myself down on a smooth rock and crack open a cider. I have a swig and stretch my legs out in front of me as I feel the day's captured sunshine radiate out of the rock and warm my arse. The music on the iPod gets changed to something suitably chilled (React Records' Real Ibiza 3 comp – God, I really do owe the previous owner a pint) and I let the hypnogogic sounds of Bliss's 'Song For Olabi' massage my mojo. The sun floats down and kisses the horizon in a truly beautiful spectacle. The only thing wrong with it is the distant sound of a clichéd round of applause from the sunset bars. But I choose to ignore this blemish on an otherwise perfect moment and turn up the tunes a notch.

I stretch out and lose myself in the music and the view as the sun finally dips beneath the horizon. The sky fades into a palette of intense reds, oranges, purples and blues that layer themselves over the horizon. For all the trappings of 21st century life, there's nothing that compares to the beauty of a sunset as viewed from the western side of Ibiza.

I finish off the cider and head back towards (un)civilisation to grab some food before I go to work. I stroll back along the sunset strip, past the now thronging bars and head back up towards the West End. I duck into Pennsylvania Burger, a tiny '50s style diner round the back of Koppas.

I order an egg, bacon and cheese burger from the cute guy serving, and take a pew at the counter, swivelling round to watch the kids trickle down from their hotels and head towards a debauched night of fighting, fucking and frowing up. My burger arrives – it's so gargantuan it can only be eaten with a knife and a fork to start with, but I won't need to eat again for a couple of days after I tuck away this baby. I reach the halfway stage of the burger, and scoop the more manageable sized meal up into a napkin and head out the door. I want to be done with work by midnight. I have tentative arrangements to go to Space with Dennis and Ian once they've finished work, and don't want to get waylaid over here. I slip round the corner to Koppas, cramming the rest of my dinner down on the way, and greet my old mate Fish with a quick squeeze on the bum. He slips a drink token into my hand and tells me to get one down me. I take the stairs into the bar two at a time and am hit with a wall of hi-energy house and air conditioning as I go through the door. It's exhilarating for all of two seconds, before my ears seem to scream at me for subjecting them to this cacophony that passes as music. Christ, house isn't supposed to be this violently offensive. I mean, where's the love? I stop these thoughts, realising I'm beginning to sound like someone's dad, and I go over to the bar and order a shot of Hierbas. While this place isn't really my cup of tea, it serves a purpose for me tonight. The shot gives me a tiny bit of Dutch courage, and the music shakes off the last of the comfortably complacent chilled feeling I have after watching the sunset.

Pulling out a 20 Euro note, I motion to Conan the barman for another shot, and offer him one as well. One thing I've learned over the years is to take care of the people who serve you booze. They invariably have the inside track on everything, know what is going on, where to get the best drugs, which to avoid, and where some of the best secret parties are. And having worked a bar in my time, I know how much easier a shift can be if your punters treat you like human beings, and not some subservient twat who is there to cater to your every whim. Conan and I snap the shots back, and I feel my eyes wobble a little as I crash the glass back onto the bar.

"Eeeurgh! That tastes rank! You're a fucking barbarian!" I shout at Conan, and he looks round furtively before pouring us both another.

"Get that down you, sweetheart. You off anywhere good tonight?"

I hold the glass to my lips and take a sip, letting the sickly sweet liquid coat my tongue, before knocking it back.

"Dunno babe, just gonna have a poke around and see what mischief I can find."

I give him a wink and push my way back out of the bar, stopping to pilfer a pint glass from a table by the door, which I slip into my bag. I'm happy to leave behind the throbbing kick drum behind, and pat Fish on the arse again as I go past, and thank him for the drink. The West End is getting rowdy now, but it's not too busy for me to be able to walk up it unhindered, save for being nearly knocked off my feet by some roughneck bouncer getting punchy with a punter. I navigate my way through a crowd at speed, and before long I've made it to the top and I'm walking across the square past the Ship, heading towards where my target apartment block is this evening.

It's a relatively new block, opposite one of the many 18-30 hotels, and is populated by a some workers I followed home after eavesdropping on them the other day. From overhearing their bragging in a couple of bars, I've ascertained that they are reps from the hotel over the road, and they live in one of three occupied flats in the block. They were speaking with plumy voices that sound like they are from the home counties, but in reality they are from somewhere up north, but their lack of a broad regional accent gives away the fact they are from an affluent background – all good for my conscience.

The Reps Part 3 : Boat Trip

The temperature inside the car is stifling, and even with the windows open and the fan on full, its stuffiness threatens to overwhelm us. The low sun burns through the windscreen, and before long sweat is streaming off us. We get onto the concrete road that snakes through the hills back towards San An, and thankfully are able to pick up enough speed to generate a slightly chilling breeze. As we go past Sa Cappella, we take a right and head into the arse end of San Antonio and back to the hotel. Unfortunately we get stuck behind some fuckwit in a Land Cruiser, who for some reason thinks their motor can fit through spaces where a Smart Car would struggle. It would appear he's taken the wing-mirror off another Land Cruiser, the owner of which is a local, and is gesticulating wildly. They're now having a stand-up row in the street, and surprise, surprise, another car pulls up behind us and boxes us in. But we've made good time so we can afford to enjoy this little sideshow for a couple of minutes. I use the time to run through the plan with Jody again for the final time.

"OK. So we'll meet at the hotel around 10.00. I'll lead whatever straggling guests there are down to the boat. I've told everyone to meet there at 10.15 for a 10.30 departure. So while I'm doing that, you're going to drive over there with the security guards and a couple of bar staff and await our arrival. Get all the lights on and torches lit, and have the soundsystem on and ready. We should disembark by 11.00, I reckon."

"Sweet. Who have we got doing the security then?"

"Harry, Brown and Sweeney are. And Sam, Nat and Nicola are doing the bar. Sam, Brown, the DJs, dancers, fire eaters and stilt-walkers are coming on the boat with me. Grainger and Nicola Bear from Ibiza Rocks are DJing. And another guy – that fat one that does the back room at Es Paradis."

"Wicked. Grainger's been smashing it down the bar this season. The fat one ain't too shabby either. I can never remember his name though. I've been calling him variations of mate, matey and chum all season."

"Haha. I'm not going to tell you his name then."

"Fuck you. Anyway Sean, me old mucker, you know there's a good chance of running into Amy tonight at the hotel. How are you going to deal with that? If she sees you, she'll probably try and shut it down."

"Well, she was supposed to be going to Mallorca this afternoon, so hopefully it won't be a problem. But if she's still here tonight, I'm going to ring reception and tell them that someone from head office is in the office waiting for her. That should distract her. She's enough of a suck-ass jobsworth now to go running whenever one of the brass click their fingers. I only need five minutes to round everyone up to follow me down to the dock."

"Yeah man, you don't want to run into her while she's on the warpath. Remember that time last season outside Trops when that bloke grabbed her arse? She's got a punch on her like a drunken sailor. Mate, I'd be worried. You're going to get slapped by a girl! Hahaha."

"Fuck off." I remember that happening. It actually made me fancy her a little. Some thug groped her, and she punched him, then grabbed his head as if she was going to snog him and stuck the nut on him. I love a fiery chick, but fucking hell, I hope I don't end up on the receiving end of her ire. Although I doubt she'd do the same in this situation, what with her being all 'professional' now.

The altercation between the Land Cruiser owners is far from resolved, so Jody gets out and gestures at the dude in the car behind us to reverse. He backs up 20 metres and is able to peel off down a side road. We follow him and pull into the hotel car park just before 7.00. Perfect timing – we've got a couple of hours to kill, so we go back to the flat and make a few pre-rolls to go and watch the sunset with. I try to go and sit on the rocks and watch the sun go down every day. It's free and it's fucking beautiful and has an invigorating effect on me.

We pick up my iPod dock and head down to the rocks outside Kanya, clambering over them until we're at the furthest point out, right next to the sea. There's only a few others here. Some girl with headphones is smoking a joint on her own. I put on some reggae and blaze up one of the reefers, handing it over to Jody after a couple of pulls. I then light the other one. Gotta have a spliff each for sunset. Standard.

The sun is only a few degrees above the horizon, and by the time we've smoked the jays it's buggered off and we are treated to the wicked pastel painting that the sky and clouds become soon after the sun goes down. We head back to the flat and get showered and changed and ready. Just before 10.00, we bound down the stairs and erupt into the alleyway and almost skip across the road to the hotel.

The security, bar staff and dancers are waiting in the car park next to a pile of boxes of plastic cups. I bring the car around and jump out while Jody, Harry, Sweeney, Nat and Nicola get in. I load the boot with the cups. I tell the others to wait outside the main gate for me, and fondle my pockets for my phone. Shit. Fuck it. I've lost it. Again. Bollocks. I jog over to the car and ask Jody for his. He belms at me and pats his chin with his palm.

"Why do you always lose shit Sean? You lost our fucking draw in the cab on the way back from Pacha last night, and now you've lost your phone. I would say you'd lose your head if it wasn't screwed on, but it's clearly held on with chewing gum and gaffer tape, you big spastic."

He gives me his iPhone. I punch in the number for reception and put on a thick Scouse accent.

"Hi, la, is Amy there please? It's Mike from head office. La."

"Yes, hang on a moment. She's just over with the reps."

Shite. Never made it over to Mallorca then.

"Actually, la, could you ask her to come and meet me in the office? It's urgent. La."

And I hang up. I give the phone back to Jody and he drives off. I squat behind another car and moments later watch Amy stride purposely out of the hotel and down the hill in the direction of the office. It's about five minutes away, so I've got at least double that to get in and get out of the hotel.

As soon as she's round the corner, I jump up and jog into the hotel. Shit. The place is deserted. There are only about fifteen people in the lobby. And it appears that the only people who are there to come to the party are the lads who bought the Cream tickets, a group of girls and a pair of spotty kids. Shitting hell. I fucking hope there's a better turnout down by the jetty or I'm well and truly fucked. I go over to Kirtsie and Ash who are at the reps desk.

"Where the fuck is everyone?" I say, probably a bit more curtly than I intended.

"I have no idea. Amy was just bitching about the same thing. And she's very interested in your whereabouts. I think you've been busted, matey." Ash says with a generous dollop of schadenfreude. Wanker. I bet he grassed me up as well. My arse clenches involuntarily. In my excitement, I hadn't genuinely considered the prospect of failure. This could be really bad, especially if I don't make back the money I've already spunked on this shindig. I look to Kirstie for some moral support. She's draped a towel over her shoulders and tied it in a knot at the front.

"What else did Amy say?"

"She was whinging about how the hotel are giving her shit about the guests going out and not spending money at the bar here," Ash chimes in. "And how she's going to make your bollocks into tapas when she finds you."

"Fuck it." I turn and head over to the guests. I put on my happy face and round them up, telling them that most people are meeting us at the boat. The pair of spotty teenagers confer and then fuck off. Arseholes. The rest seem up for it though, and I lead them out of the hotel to the main gates. We pick up Brown and the dancers, whose presence swells our numbers enough so we now seem less of a motley crew than before, and more of a party in waiting. And the fact that the dancers are wearing next to nothing is guaranteed to maintain the high spirits of the group of lads. We walk up to the Ship, and head down the main drag. I give the dancers wads of flyers and get them to hit people up on the way, and we gain a few more bodies, pushing the count to over thirty which alleviates my anxiety. Well, only a bit, but enough to restore a little faith.

We pass Koppas, and cross over the plaza past the big puddles of piss, amusingly touted as fountains, and onto the boardwalk where the boats are moored. About 100 meters in the distance I think I can make out a crowd. I squint, and my stomach twitches a little. Fucking hell. As we get closer, I think of Roy Scheider in Jaws, backing into the cabin on the Orca when he first sees the shark. I turn to Brown and smile.

"We're going to need a bigger boat."

As we approach the dock, I see Grainger, Nicola Bear and the other DJ and march over to them.

"Dude. Fucking hell. There must be over 150 people here!" Grainger exclaims as I near him.

"I know! Fuck me, I thought we were fucked when there was hardly anyone at the hotel."

He laughs and they, Bear and the other guy follow the dancers up the gang plank and start setting up their laptops. I stand on a bench and look over the crowd. The city suits from last night are there, and give us a wave. There are quite a few workers there as well. Wicked. I think I could be onto something here! I shout a loud "Oi" to get everyone's attention.

"Right, ladies and gentlemen, if you'd all like to board now, that would be great. Just have your 30 Euros ready for me as you get to the top of the gang-plank."

I run over and onto the boat and take up position with Brown and the cashbox at a little wooden podium by the entrance to the main cabin. It's quite a big tub, with a couple of decks and a large outside area through the back. We get everyone on board in under ten minutes. In total, there are 172 people. I take just over five grand. I'm already in profit to the tune of a couple of thousand. I almost piss myself with joy. I bundle the cash up and go into the toilet and put it into the money belt I'm wearing under my t-shirt. The wad of notes makes it considerably heavier. Fucking brilliant.

I come out and see the deck hand climbing around the front of the ship like a sea-monkey as he casts off. The engines splutter into life and the captain starts backing out and executes a three point turn before we start cutting through the waves on our way out of the harbour.

As we zip past the harbour walls, the captain rings a little bell to let us know we can start playing music and I hear the opening synths of Inner City's 'Good Life' reverberate around the cabin. Nice. Our passengers need little encouragement, and within seconds nearly all are jumping around like Mexican jumping beans or standing on the benches punching the air around them as if they're being attacked by invisible bats.

The Resort Manager Part 4 : Super-sleuthing

The beeping on my phone gets progressively louder, and I roll over and smash the buttons to stop it. I feel groggy, so I have another shower and feel a bit more alert. I make a cup of tea, and being careful not to smash it or spill any, I head onto the balcony for a fag, before getting dressed and going to the hotel to wait for Sean. The flier says to meet in the lobby at 10, or down by the boat at 10.15. It's 9.55 now. And there's nobody here. Oh dear. Sean's fucked this right up. He's going to be completely thrashed for this. He's fired for sure, especially as he's blown thousands on this ill-advised shindig. I go over to the reps desk where Ash, Wine-Eyes and Kirstie are.

"No sign of Sean then?" I ask, trying to sound as nonchalant as I can.

"So, tell us Amy, how much trouble is Sean in, on a scale of one to ten?" Ash snickers.

"Ooh, are you going to thump him? I like it when you get punchy, Amy." Wine-Eyes says, deadpan and all innocent. She's such a wind up merchant. She knows I'm embarrassed about that. I can't work out if it's banter or bitchyness. I turn my back to them and scope the lobby. It's deserted, which momentarily makes me feel bad. Sean's obviously tried hard to make this work, but apparently to no avail. So a tiny pang of pity shoots through me, but it's soon chased away by that far more powerful emotion, anger, of which I have plenty right now.

One of the reception staff comes over.

"Erm, that was Mike on the phone for you. He said to go and meet him in the office immediately. He says it's urgent."

I check for my phone, but realise I've left it in the car. Arseholes. Bollocks. The fucking timing of this. I'm slightly relieved that the confrontation has been delayed, if I'm honest. Oh well, I'll get Sean down by the boat. The office is kind of on the way there, and I'll have time unless Mike keeps me there more than ten minutes.

I get out of the hotel, stopping to retrieve my phone, and hot foot it down to the office. If Mike has asked me down there, it's probably something important. Upon arriving there, the only person I find is Toby. He's listening to some extremely loud house music. He turns it down a fraction when he sees me, but it's still deafening.

"Hello Amy. Found Sean yet?" He bellows.

"Where's Mike?" I shout.

"Haven't seen him since this afternoon." He hollers.

Fucking hell. I go and turn the speakers down.

"Oh. I got a message up at the hotel just now saying to meet him here immediately."

"Here? Nah, someone's having you on. There's no way he'd be in the office at this time of night."

Bollocks. I work out what's gone on in a nanosecond. The crafty little bastard. It was Sean who placed the call. One of the things we all used to do last year was impersonate Mike's absurdly broad Scouse accent. And Sean was very good at it, so much so you couldn't tell the difference over the phone, as he used to call me from the office and mock bollock me, pretending to be Mike. I feel my face flush, and my stomach starts pretending it's a tumble dryer. The rage is swelling up from deep inside me, and I'm either going to explode violently or tearfully, so I head towards the toilet to calm myself down and collect my thoughts in peace. I reach the door of the bathroom, and turn to face Toby with exasperation.

"I really don't need this shit."

"Then why are you going in the toilet then?"

The door closes behind me to the sound of Toby giggling at his lame joke. Cock. I lock the door and turn on the taps. I splash some water on my face and feel my anger recede a little as the cool liquid lowers my temperature a notch. My mind clears enough for me to realise I've still got a job to do, and I need to get down the harbour to intercept Sean. I must keep a cool head though. I want nothing more than to tear him a new arsehole after his little stunt on the phone, but I have got to remain professional. Twatting the little shit isn't going to do me any good. In fact it'll just show me up as being totally incapable and incompetent. Which is exactly what I will be if I hit a misbehaving member of staff. But Christ, I really want to.

I check the time. It's now ten past ten. Shit. I'm going to have to run if I want to intercept Sean at the dock. I begin to jog down the road that leads past David's and towards the promenade. It's hot and humid and sweat is soon seeping out of my brow and nearly blinding me as I hit the seafront. It's taken me a few minutes to get here, and

I've still got the most of the dock to get around before I get to the Egg. I pause to fill my lungs with air and carry on jogging past the rows upon rows of glass bottomed boats, catamarans and speedboats that line the side of the harbour.

My feet feel like they have been replaced with bowling balls, and my canter has become more of a stumble. Halfway to the Egg, I realise I'm not going to get there in time, and even if I do, I'm going to be out of breath, sweaty, and not in any fit shape to deal with Sean. I stop running, sit down on the nearest bench and double up, gasping and concentrating hard not to have a violent coughing fit. It doesn't work, and I hack up half a lung anyway. Christ, I really need to give up smoking. I look up and out at the bay and see the Erebus chugging past in the distance, I think. I can't really tell from here, but whatever boat it is doesn't look or sound very lively.

The out of breath, lightheaded sensation is swiftly shoved aside by a much more energetic frustrated and angry feeling. Bastard. I'm not letting this one go. I reckon the other reps are going to go and join him at the party when they finish work at midnight. And I'm going to fucking follow them. I am *not* going to lose today: Sean is not going to win this one. I'll head back, loiter around and then follow them in my car. This isn't over by a long shot. I turn back towards the hotel.

When I get back to the hotel, Wine-Eyes and Kirstie are at the desk pissing around. Kirstie has wrapped a towel around her shoulders, and is draping another over Wine-Eyes. I decide to go over and try to be a bit matey with them. They're not having any of it.

"Did you find Sean then, Amy?" Kirstie says, her happy demeanour evaporating as she sees me approach.

Wine-Eyes takes the towel from her shoulders and looks a little like a school-kid who's just been caught doing something naughty. Have I become that much of a kill-joy? My presence amongst them has rapidly given rise to an atmosphere thicker than a bowl of porridge, replacing the carefree, happy vibe I could sense when I entered the lobby.

"No, I didn't find him. I'll leave it until Monday I think. This is supposed to be my day off anyway." I say with a forced lack of urgency.

Normally, well, at least last year, the conversation would have flowed easily, as would have the banter, but they just clam up. I try again.

"Still loving the capes, eh, Kirstie?"

"Uh, yeah, sorry – I know they aren't part of our official uniform." She says defensively.

"I wasn't having a go. I like your cape-fixation."

She says nothing in reply. Neither of them even make eye-contact with me. I feel like I am the most hated person in the world. Fuck this. I turn to go, and walk straight into the manager of the hotel.

"Ah, Amy. I was hoping to see you," he says. He produces one of Sean's fliers. Oh for fucks sake. "Sean said this party was for people outside of the hotel – why did I find this has been delivered to all the rooms? I would never have let him use our security and soundsystem if I knew he was going to be taking our guests away. Maybe if he'd offered us a cut of the tickets, but he hasn't."

"Don't worry Paco, we'll give you a share – I'm sure it's just an oversight on Sean's part to not offer you one."

"Yes, I hope so."

I can't believe I'm defending Sean to this twat, but much as I have beef with Sean, one thing I will never do is side with the hotel over one of our own. We can fight as much as we like behind closed doors, but you should always maintain a united front when dealing with outsiders.

Paco seems placated, and he waddles off to bollock the reception staff for whatever it is he deems they're not doing right tonight. Prick. I exit the lobby and take a seat just outside, lighting up a cigarette while I try and think of my next move. Which, if I'm honest, I'm not sure of. I've failed to stop Sean's party from happening, but to be honest, that makes no odds now – Sean's already spent what he's spent. There's not much point in closing the stable door now the horse has bolted. But what I can do is find that horse and wrestle him to the ground. Then tie a fucking lasso round its neck and string him up from the sign outside Koppas at the bottom of the West End for all to see. Well, some sort of public bollocking at least.

I flick my fag butt in the general direction of the bins, and get up to go back into the hotel office. I see a van pull into the car park and Joe gets out. He sees me and waves. I like Joe – he's one of the few people from last year who is still cool with me. He's not a rep, he's a sound engineer, so he's not involved in any of the politicking, and as a result has absolutely no bullshittery around him.

"Hello Amy, how are you?" He says cheerfully.

"Been better, to be honest." I reply.

"Oh yeah, what's up?"

"Everything." I croak. I feel like I'm about to cry. I swallow hard and squeeze the lump in my throat back down inside me, compressing my sadness into a little pellet of hate, to be expelled later on. Preferably in the direction of someone who deserves it.

"Wanna talk about it?" Joe says.

Do I? I feel like getting it off my chest might help, but I resolve not to mention the party, not while that game is still being played out.

"Oh Joe, it's really getting to me, being public enemy number one as far as the reps are concerned," I sigh. "These are people I called my friends last year, and this year, they absolutely fucking hate my guts. If I'd known that taking the new job would lead to this, I would never have said yes. I've tried to be as cool as possible about it, but they're just total dicks to me the whole time. I know I'm not the best manager in the world, but it's my first year doing it, and you would've thought with our history together, they would have cut me some slack."

"I'm sure they don't hate you, Amy. From where I'm standing, I think you're just struggling with the new dynamic. You don't know how to be a boss and friend, and they don't know how to treat you as a boss and friend. The thing is, you're always going to have to sacrifice something if you step up a level. It won't always be like this, you just need to clear the air with the reps I reckon. You're still the same person underneath, it's just your priorities are very different this year, innit. They don't genuinely hate you, it's just I think they're as crap as you at handling this new situation. Talk to them. Explain it to them. Get fucked with them one night and clear it all up with some E. Hahaha."

He has a point, and I feel a little better. I give him a massive hug and ruffle his Flash Gordon hairdo, and duck back into the hotel, feeling buoyed by our conversation. I'm nearly skipping as I pass the reps desk, and I mischievously mutter "I still love you" as I go past Wine-Eyes and Kirstie and on into the office.

I pop the kettle on and make a cup of tea, and turn on my laptop to check through my emails. There's nothing doing, so I flick through a copy of DJ magazine and enjoy my cup of tea. I reckon Kirstie and Wine-Eyes are going to go straight from here to the party, so I ready myself to go after them. They're finishing their shift soon, so I wander out into the lobby to check the situation out. Joe's talking to them, so I hold back and eavesdrop from the little mezzanine balcony just above their desk.

"…..well, Sean's just got in touch, asking me to bring more booze down, so if you want you can jump in the van with me." I hear him say. Wicked. If they need more booze, that means they're selling it, which means Sean's little do might be turning a profit. Also, Joe's big white transit van isn't going to be the hardest thing in the world to follow. I go back to the office, grab my stuff and lock up. I'll wait for them in my car.

I've barely had time to wind the windows down in the Golf before they come bounding out of the hotel. Ten minutes before the end of their shift, I note. They jump into the van and pull out of the car park and start heading towards the main road out of town. I try and keep some distance, but I end up right up their arse for most of the snaking journey out of San Antonio. We get to the first of a series of roundabouts before the motorway proper starts and I let a few cars in between us to not look too hot.

The road gets a little busier as we leave the outskirts of San An and I get stuck behind some tourists in a hire car, who are clearly uncomfortably with the steering wheel and their car both being on the wrong side for them. I can see the driver faffing and getting flustered, feelings that transfer to me as I see Joe's van shoot off down the road towards the motorway. Finally I get past the tourists and screech off in the direction Joe went. I get to the junction where the routes to San Raf, San An and Ibiza Town fan out from a roundabout, and scope the different roads. Shit. Fuck. I can't see the van. I punch the steering wheel in frustration and shout a series of random swearwords at no-one in particular. Brilliant. Great. Some spy I'd make.

A wave of defeat washes over me, drenching me in the energy-sapping feeling of failure. Fucking hell.

A cacophony of horns brings me out of my funk momentarily to let me know a queue has built up behind me, so I pull onto the roundabout and take the exit that will lead me back to San An. Fuck it. I go past the Egg and get held up as a group of hooligans being all drunk and lairy dance into the street outside Wips. There's a cabbie up front who's remonstrating with them – he's got out and is gesticulating wildly, in the inimitable Mediterranean style. I use the opportunity to fire off a text to Sean, threatening him with the sack, and immediately regret it. I take a look out at the bay, and I see a familiar boat chugging towards its moorings. No fucking way. It's the *Erebus*. A flash of inspiration ignites my mind, and I back up and pull a U-turn, parking up in the plot of derelict land opposite the Ibiza Rocks Bar.

The Stags Part 3 : Hotel Playa Sol

The plane thumps down in Ibiza and I wake up with a start. Most of the plane is shouting and cheering at our arrival, but for a split second I think the plane is crashing and their screams of joy are actually those of panic. After a moment's disorientation, I come into the present. I feel like shit. I feel like crying. I dig my nails into my palm on one hand and rub at my eyes with the other, camouflaging any watering by clawing at any eye snot that's accumulated while I was asleep. I breathe deeply and try to pull me head together. This doesn't need to become a thing. I look around at all the boys and everyone's got a cheesy grin splattered across their mush. I copy them, but on the inside I just want to smash their fucking faces in.

    The plane decelerates and comes to a stop. The doors open up and we spill out onto some rickety stairs and pile into a couple of bendy buses which drop us off at the terminal. We march right off the bus and breeze through passport control, going straight past baggage reclaim and out of the exit.

    It's fucking stifling outside. It hits us like a wall as we pass through the sliding doors. It's 10 o'clock dago time, and the sky is dark with an orange tint to it. We walk past the groups of holiday reps waiting to pounce on their guests, and go straight to the front of the taxi queue. We take the first two taxis, and I end up with the twins, which I'm not over the moon about. They're well full of themselves, like every other fucking Manc jailbird scally I've met has been.

Our driver, some Arab terrorist looking bloke starts blabbering away at us in Spanish.

"Mate, speak-o the English?" I speak loudly over him. I've found when speaking to foreigners, if you want to be understood, you just need to speak slower and louder.

"Eeenglish, eeenglish. David Beckham, David Beckham. Where you go boss?" he parrots at me. Me and the Mancs look at each other and start pissing ourselves, before we treat the driver to a chorus of "Chris Waddle", like that sketch off the Fast Show. He looks confused for a bit, and I tell him to take us to San An Bay and the Hotel Playa Sol.

We're soon on a motorway, flying past some sort of industrial area, with billboards at the side advertising all the big clubs on the island. The cabbie has some god awful wailing music on, so I reach down and turn it off and talk to the cunt.

"Where you from mate?"

"I from Morocco my friend."

The one that might be Frank lights up a fag in the back seat. The driver clocks this straight away and starts flapping around and getting the arsehole.

"No smoke. No smoke. Please stop."

Frank takes a long drag and then breathes it all out over the back of the cabbies head.

"Why don't you fucking make me you fucking Taliban cunt? Just shut up and drive the cab."

The other twin butts in apologising on his brother's behalf, and being over friendly to the cabbie. I've seen this shit a million times before. Fucking with someone's head using the good cunt, bad cunt system. I've done it myself loads. The good cunt starts blathering away to the cabbie, asking him about his family, faking enthusiasm about the man's kids. He then starts asking him if he knows any good swearwords. I like where this is heading. Frank finishes his fag and stubs it out on the back of the head rest behind the cabbie. He then flicks the butt out of the window.

"So, what swearwords do you know then, mate?" Frank sneers.

"Um, yo no hablo mucho Ingles," the cabbie spouts.

"Do you know what a wanker is mate?" Frank says back to him.

"Yeah, yeah, do you know what a wanker is?" Ashley echoes again.

The cabbie has a confused look on his boat. He turns to us and says something that sounds like "I no understand."

"Don't worry about it, mate. You're a wanker. A fucking massive wanker. But that's a cool thing. Call all the English people you have in here wankers. They'll give you big tip, you huge wanker."

I tell you something, I aint't too keen on these gobby Manc twats, but they are fucking funny and I'm in stitches for the rest of the journey. He drops us off in front of our hotel, and we shout our goodbyes at him as we get out the car.

"See you later, wanker!"

"Adios you fucking wanker!"

"Ta-ta, wanker!"

We walk the short distance to the hotel, which is right on the beach. The other cab pulls up across the road and Jimmy, Graham and John get out. We all go into the hotel, which is a dump with a minging swimming pool, a minging bar and some minging girls propping it up. Hotel? Fucking hovel more like. The receptionist takes our passports and money and gives us our room keys, saying we can pick up our passports in a few minutes when she's photocopied them. She says one of the reps will come and say hello, and we go to the lifts and head up. We've got two rooms. I'm the best man, so I'm staying with John-o and Jimmy in one, and Graham gets to share with the two savages from the wild lands of oop north in the other.

The room's pretty basic, with a sofa that splits into two single beds and a tiny double by the window that leads to a balcony. There's a fridge and a shit hob, but there's also a kettle. Nice. There's a knock at the door and Graham and the northerners come in.

Graham, who has been mostly quiet for the whole time, makes his first meaningful contribution to the stag do and pulls a glasses case out of his trousers. He pops it open and pulls out a large bag rammed to the hilt with gear. He dishes a baggie and wrap out to everyone.

"Right. The baggie is an eighth of Charlie, and the wraps are an eighth of ket. I haven't got any pills, but there's not going to be any trouble scoring them out here. And the gear's on me as a present to

John-o, but I don't want to have to buy a fucking drink this weekend boys. You get me?"

We all nod in agreement and within a matter of seconds we've each commandeered a surface and are chopping out some gargantuan lines of chang. We all sniff them back in unison and roar a battle cry. There's a banging at the door and Graham opens it up to find a pretty young girl in a holiday company t-shirt. She comes into the room and starts telling us about cheap tickets she can get us for the clubs, and waffling about packages and excursions. There's some banter, but I can tell she feels a little bit intimidated, so I put my arm round her shoulder to let her know she's alright in a subtle way. I can see she fancies me a bit, because she gets all nervous and bashful. Ah, still got it. We get some tickets off her for Cream tonight, and she wishes us a good night and turns to go to the door. As she goes past one of those fucking twins, he reaches his hand out to grab her arse. I quickly move over and grab him by the upper arm, moving his hand away from her. She doesn't notice a thing, and leaves the room. I eyeball him a little and release my grip. Things are fucking tense for a moment.

"Mate, we don't want to shit on our own doorstep here." I say, by way of an explanation. Not that I need to explain myself to this twat.

"Too right," chimes in John. "There'll be plenty of time for birds after dinner. Which I suggest we do right after another line."

We dip into our baggies again and hoof another one down. We all jump up, and jostle our way out of the room, chanting and wolf-whistling. Ibiza won't know what's hit it.

The Dealer Part 3 : Collection

My eyes snap open as I'm woken by my phone. It's Perry. I answer it.

"Chop chop, Rocky. I'm outside."

"Right you are. I'll be down in a minute." I go to the bathroom and splash some water on my face. I grip the sides of the sink and stare at myself in the mirror. I go to the kitchen and pour a few shots of hierbas into a mug and sling it back. The taste takes my breath away, and I gasp and feel a little nauseous. It works though, and takes the edge off.

Slamming the door shut behind me, I take the stairs down three or four at a time, and run over to the 4x4. I see Pez is driving Eddie's motor tonight. Not as good as Charlie's, but still, it's got a bad-ass soundsystem, and it's exceptionally comfortable. I bump fists with Perry as I get in. He's another junior manager in the firm, about my age (late 20s) and a right geezer. He's not the sharpest tool in the box, but his imposing frame and 'direct' manner of sorting out problems mean he's respected and, even better, efficient. I wouldn't want to get on the wrong side of him, having seen him in action. But saying that, seeing others get on the wrong side of him is like having front row seats to Steven Segal film. He's like one of those Shaolin Kung-fu monks that you see in those shows. Except with Perry, I think the philosophical teachings behind all that are a little beyond him. He's just exceptionally good at battering people.

He tells me we've got two stops to make. The first one in Figueretas, the second in Ibiza Town, then we'll head over to Mammon, Eddie and Charles' club in San An. We drive the short distance to the first pick-up, and park up outside a lap-dancing club called the Pink Oyster. Subtle.

We go in and there's a tidy looking girl on the runway prancing around in her pants. I see her gravitate towards a group of lads at one of the tables closest to her. She leans off the stage and puts her hands on the shoulders of one of the boys, perching on him, giving him a face full of boob and rocking back and forth. Without warning, the chair gives way, and she tumbles off the stage and onto him. Poor girl. She looks mortified as all his mates erupt in baying mob laughter. She gets up and legs it out the back. Jesus, as if this job wasn't demeaning enough. Still, it looked fucking hilarious.

The owner is sat at the bar and clocks us. He jumps up and comes over, being super-friendly because he knows who we work for. We're given a drink each, and he leads us into the office out the back. He gets on his knees behind his desk and opens a safe built into the floor. I sneak a peek inside over his shoulder and see a load of cash, a shooter and probably half a key of ya-yo. He takes the bundles of cash and puts them in a duffel bag. There's fucking loads in there. I don't know what part this geezer plays in Charlie and Eddie's operation, but it's got to be at least a hundred grand he's handing over. Thank fuck Perry is with me.

We go back through the club with the bag, watching another future X Factor reject going through the motions on the stage. I don't understand blokes who spunk hundreds of Euros in a place like this. Who wants to pay to be teased and frustrated? They can go down any beach on the island if they want an eyeful, and it doesn't cost 20 quid a pop. Still, it's the pack mentality thing innit. A big group of lads egging each other on to get seriously aroused. It's a bit suspect and soggy biscuit if you ask me. I like to do all that kind of thing in private. Still, their money invariably ends up in our pockets, so who am I to complain?

The PR Part 1 : Fishing

Another day, another dollar. Well, another night, another Euro, to be more accurate. I've just got to the bar, which occupies a prime corner spot halfway down the West End. It's my job to get the punters in. I entice them with some banter, the promise of ludicrously cheap drinks and by being so persistent it's just easier for my victims to acquiesce and give in than put up any real resistance. It's a dirty job, but someone's got to do it.

It's been a hard week. It's got to that time of the season when everyone's a bit strung out on too much work, too many drugs and too little sleep. But to everyone's credit, we're all in the same boat and we're all looking out for each other. The feeling of family and camaraderie that permeates through the workers out here is a strong one. It needs to be, because it can be fucking tough working out here, seven days a week, seemingly for 25 hours a day, for very little pay. That sense of community helps make it bearable.

I walk into the bar and say hello to the guvnor. He's berating one of the bar staff, Steve, who got properly wankered during his shift the other day. It was well funny. He swears blind that he got spiked by one of the punters, but yeah, right, whatever mate. He was falling all over the place – still managed to do his job, mind, but he may or may not have spilled a few drinks. Bless him. The boss finishes his bollocking, then sees me and points outside.

"Get out there, Matt, you're fuck all use in here!"

"Right you are, Don."

I head back outside. He's right, I have no business inside the bar, but I just wanted him to see I was here on time. I've been a bit late now and then recently, and I don't want him to think I'm taking the piss too much. As badly paid as this job is, it's one I enjoy immensely.

Lots of people who come to Ibiza are very snobby about where I work. Mention the words "San An" and "West End" to some of the more seasoned Ibiza vets, and you can almost see the bile rushing up their throats. It's coarse, it's vulgar, it's offensively loud and it's encrusted in sick. But you know what? I fucking love it. To me, it's vibrant, energetic, full of life and an absolute fucking scream. It makes me feel alive.

But tonight, I can't wait to finish work. My mate Sean is throwing a secret all night party in the countryside and a bunch of us are going. It's going to be wicked. We were all out here together last season, and have become a tight little unit. I think we're probably thought a bit cliquey by some, but fuck it, we've all got a history together and we get on brilliantly. The dynamic in the group is good, and not one of them is a cunt. We all kept in touch over winter and it's great that we're all back together this season. It's like that bit at the end of Grease, but every day. And without a flying motor.

My favourite of the bunch has to be Hannah. We worked together last year, and became really close friends. We maintained that over the winter, seeing each other at least a couple of times a week, becoming close as fuck. But then, this season, my feelings for her have developed and grown much stronger. We've barely left each other's side, which is great. I always had a very minor, manageable crush on her – she's gorgeous, both inside and out – but lately, it's become more. If I wanted to go and ruin it all, I'd probably say something stupid like I love her.

It's becoming a bit of a distraction, this feeling. At first, I could easily ignore it, but every day now, it seems to grow ever larger – at first, it was just my tummy that glowed when I saw her or thought of her; now it's my whole insides that sparkle and crackle when's she's close by. She's wiser than me, smarter than me and just better than me all over. But this is great, because it makes me want to up my game when I'm with her. She inspires me to better myself.

But I'm 99% certain these feelings aren't reciprocated, so I've resolved to keep them to myself, suffer in silence and not ruin what is a cherished friendship. I value the time we spend together immensely, and I feel like every second I'm away from her is a second wasted. Maybe it's just an infatuation, a stupid obsession. But maybe it's for real. Either way, I doubt very much it's ever going to develop beyond what it is now, and that's something I have to live with. Them's the breaks.

I take my mind off her and start barking at the groups of holiday makers worming their way down the West End. I get a couple of groups of stags and hens in without much effort. Some of the groups I completely ignore – they look like trouble, and entering into a dialogue with them would be a waste of time, and probably wind me up to the point where I'd tell them to fuck off and get a slap for my trouble. About midnight, I see my old mucker Starkey strolling down the hill towards me. She deliberately walks straight into me.

"Oh sorry mate, didn't see you there." She says as she follows up with a shoulder barge. Ha. She's good value is Starkey. Very wise, and very fucking cool with it. Her calm brain is a refreshing change to most of the wreck-heads out here. Everyone should have a mate like Starkey.

"So, are you looking forward to Sean's party then?"

"Yeah man. I can't wait. I reckon I can fuck off from here at about 3.00, so I'll come and meet you then. We've got quite the crowd coming tonight, haven't we?"

"I know. I love it when we all go out in a big gang. We don't do it enough though! You always seem to just hang around with Hannah now. I hope you two decide to talk to other people tonight." She says cheekily.

"Oh, is she going?" I say with mock innocence.

"Yeah of course she is you plum. You're going, aren't you? And are the two of you ever in a different place? Exactly. People are beginning to talk. Everyone thinks you're a couple."

"Yeah, I fucking wish."

"Really?"

"Forget I said that."

Starkey looks at me and rolls her eyes.

"Yeah, whatever!" I feel my cheeks redden a little, but I'm grateful she leaves it at that.

"We meeting at the OK then?"

"Yep. I'll be there from about 2.00."

"Wicked my dear, I'll see you there later."

We bump fists and she disappears into the crowd, and I go back to haranguing potential customers. I find the easiest groups to coerce into the bar are the ones who are clearly Ibiza virgins. The redder they are, the more perplexed they look, the easier they are to get in. I always start off chatting them up, finding out their plans, where they're from and all that shit, before I try and get them into the bar. Make friends first, then make money off your new friends. Easy peasy lemon squeezy.

The Hens Part 3 : Dinner

I wake up from my snooze feeling a bit groggy and disorientated. I drink some Evian from the mini-bar and have a cold shower. As the water washes over me, I think about him and how much I've changed since he sunk his claws into me. I wasn't always the scared and scarred shrinking violet I am now. I used to be the life and soul of the party. I used to dazzle when I walked in a room. Heads would turn, and all eyes would be on me. Nowadays, any eyes on me are likely to be blackened by an angry, jealous fist.

    It wasn't always this bad. At the start, it was amazing. Aside from his exceptional good looks and Adonis-like body, he had the power to make you feel like the most important person in the world. When he turned on the charm, he could make the rest of the universe disappear, and you'd feel like you were the only thing in existence. He could do something like that, such were his skills of manipulation. But anyone who has the power to make you feel that good also has the power to make you feel equally bad. And fuck me, he did that in spades.

    I get out of the shower and dry myself off. I'm pissed off that I've now got thoughts of him in my head, and my nervous and quite welcome excited anticipation about going out tonight seems to have subsided. I resolve not to let my mind wander down a dark path tonight and open the half-bottle of champagne in the mini-bar. I polish it off, and a miniature of vodka, while I put my face on.

The Michael Kors dress is hanging on the wardrobe. I grab it by the hanger and hold it up to myself in the mirror. It looks awesome. I lay it out on the bed and put on a g-string. One even skimpier than the one that Paul went mental over. I slide the dress over my head and wriggle into it, smoothing it out over my thighs and pulling the hem down to just above my knee. I take in my reflection in the mirror. I barely recognise myself. I see flickers of the old me staring back. I smile and feel sexy for the first time in ages. It's brilliant. I check the time and go downstairs to meet the others in the bar.

Sharon is the first one to see me. She gasps and does a double take.

"Oh my God. Is that you Vicky? You look fan-taaaastic!"

Kelly and Keeley turn round and look shocked. Keeley gives me a wolf-whistle.

"You haven't looked this good in years!" Kelly says. "I don't know why you don't dress up more often."

There's a bottle of champagne in a bucket on the bar, and four glasses. I get handed one and we all cheers the bride to be. For a moment, it feels like old times. There's a real sense of camaraderie there. And then Keeley poisons it.

"Bloody hell. I can't get over what you're wearing, Vicky. Are you on the pull tonight or something?" She sneers, sounding very familiar.

You know what? I think I am now.

"Don't be silly, Keeley!"

She lets it go, and the others haven't picked up on any malicious undercurrents between us, so we carry on enjoying the champers. We have another bottle, and ask the barman to call us a cab to the restaurant, which is over in Ibiza Town. We get dropped off at the foot of the entrance to the walled old town, and climb up the cobbled hill and through the old gates. The restaurant is right up at the top, and the view is spectacular. We get seated under a big white umbrella, and the waiter brings us all a menu.

"Would choo like anything to drink, ladies?" He says with slightly accented but perfect English. Sharon and Kelly snigger.

"I don't know. Keeley, you're the hen. What would choo like to trink?" Kelly says, displaying her deep reserves of wit by mocking someone who probably speaks better English than her.

"Vodka Red Bull I think. Yeah, can we have four of those, if choo please?" Keeley says. This so isn't the kind of place where you should be ordering vodka and red bull, but Keely lacks class. She always has. The waiter looks surprised.

"I'm eh-sorry, but we don't have any Red Bull. Is there eh-something else you would like?" He replies, his voice apologetic.

"We'll have a couple of bottles of red please. Rioja, if you have it." I butt in, nipping their opportunity for more casual racism in the bud.

"Yeah, that's good." Sharon agrees. She loves her red wine.

The waiter returns with the wine and four glasses. He gives it to me to taste, and I nod. He fills the glasses half full and leaves us. We leaf through the menus and I nearly begin drooling when I see some of the dishes they have.

"What the hell is this stuff?" Kelly says, struggling to understand what's on offer, despite there being an English translation of the dishes underneath the Spanish names.

"Do they do steak? And chips?" Keeley says, completely predictably. I'm surprised she didn't ask for us to go to McDonalds.

"Yeah, they do. It's called entrecote, and the chips are called patatas frites." I think about encouraging them to have something a bit more exciting, but then I don't bother.

The waiter returns with some olives, bread and alioli and takes our order. They ask for three steak and chips, while I go for the grilled sea-bass with salad. I can tell they think I'm being snooty and getting above myself by ordering something different, but I couldn't care less. I'm not wasting an opportunity to eat something amazing that I don't normally have at home. The waiter departs and my attention is drawn to an older couple at the table next to us. They look like they're in their early '40s. The man is giving the woman a right earful. It sounds ever so familiar.

"That's out of order." I say, after he makes a particularly nasty comment about her size and what she should and shouldn't be "stuffing her fat face" with.

"It's none of our business, that's what it is. And we don't know the full story." Says Sharon.

"So you think that there might be something that justifies being treated like that by a man? What? Did she burn his dinner? Not iron his clothes correctly?" I say with a bit more venom than necessary, almost becoming a caricature of the man we're discussing.

"Nah, but you never know." She splutters. What a clueless cow she is. "I think what happens between another couple is their own business and nobody else's. If she doesn't like it, she can always leave."

"It's not always that easy, is it? You can't just walk out of one life and start another the next day. And not to mention the fact that it's unlikely the poor cow hasn't got any confidence because of that pig. It makes me fucking sick. Look at her. She's not ugly, but she dresses ugly. He's sucked the life out her."

"You dress like that yourself half the time back home!" Keeley squawks moronically, in what can only be a feeble attempt at lightening the mood.

"Yeah, quite." I say.

An awkward silence hangs over the table like a damp towel. Luckily the waiter shows up with our food and they go back to openly ridiculing his English, which is elegant and eloquent.

Their attitude towards what we've just seen saddens me. But it doesn't surprise me. I was in the same kind of mindset when I allowed him to do that to me. It's taken me years to come up with the strength to even consider trying to do something about it. Building up the courage has been one of the hardest things I've ever had to do. But sometimes I feel I've got enough momentum to get out of it, and it makes me feel bigger than I have for ages. It doesn't last, and it vies with panic a lot of the time for control of my moods, but it's there. I want to go and tell the girl at the next table this, and I resolve to follow her into the loo when she next goes and give her a pep talk then.

I glance around the table at the three of them. My so-called best mates. We used to be such a close knit group. We'd go out and have such a good time, taking loads of drugs, going to wicked parties and having the time of our lives. But then one by one, we paired off, stayed in more, occasionally venturing out on a big night, but that was just mainly to get as wankered as possible to escape our dreary lives. What made us friends evaporated a long time ago. But I doubt if any of us could even identify what that bond was forged from in the first place. I don't even think anyone genuinely likes being part of this group anymore.

The woman from the other table gets up and trudges inside the restaurant. I make my excuses and go into the bathroom a couple of minutes after her. She's finished what she was doing and is smoothing out her shapeless and dowdy dress in the mirror. Her eyes are puffy, and she's puts a wad of tissue that is balled up in her fist into the bin. Fortified by the booze, I approach her and put my hand lightly on her forearm.

"You don't have to put up with that from him, you know. You can get out."

"Fuck off and mind your own business, you nosy cow." She spits at me through gritted teeth.

She jerks her arm away from me and looks at me with some pretty serious rage flickering in her eyes.

I say nothing more. She'll get there, hopefully if she can channel that rage in the right direction. She walks fast out of the toilet, slamming the door behind her. I feel sorry for her, but at the moment, I just don't have enough spare energy to care any more than that. I have a pee and go back to our table.

I pour myself more Rioja, and think about how hard it is to try and get out, with no support, no help from your anyone. My parents emigrated to Spain years ago, and have no idea what my relationship with Paul has become. His sister knows. She knows he beats the crap out of me. She's borne witness to the psychological beatings he's given me, the public humiliations dished out by his acid tongue. Her inaction and complicit silence over the state of our relationship makes her as bad as him. And not forgetting she set us up all those years ago. She must've been aware of what he was like. And if she wasn't, then she's incredibly stupid and unperceptive. I find myself resenting her almost as much as him. But again, I don't want to have a bad and angry night, so I let the thoughts go and think about dancing, having fun, and maybe even taking an E. I know Sharon got some down at the beach earlier on. We used to do them all the time together when we were younger. I'm definitely up for having one tonight.

By now, all the plates are clean, and none of us are going to be having dessert, seeing as we're going clubbing now, so we call for the bill. We pay up and climb back down to street level, and hail a cab to take us to Amnesia.

The Journalist Part 3 : Dinner

We get back to Pikes to freshen up and I tell Giles to meet me back in the bar at nine. I have a quick shower, throw on a clean t-shirt and pour the sand from my shoes into the bin. My phone says it's 8.30, so I give Kevin a bell. He answers after one ring, sounding agitated. What a cunt. Who goes to Ibiza and sits in their hotel room doing gak on their own? Fucking tool.

"Easy Kevin, it's Jack. I'm coming to your room, you're giving me some of that ching and then we're going out for dinner." I tell him authoritatively. He's blatantly too coked up and para to challenge me.

"Er, yeah, ok."

I hang up on him. Nob. I walk to his room and bang on the door violently. It amuses me to do things to freak out the jittery coke-fiend. He opens the door in his pants, the sick fucker, and beckons me in. It smells of booze and Charlie farts. He's been sat in here for hours on his own, probably wanking himself into oblivion as well. Sick!

He points to a pile of gear on a mirror and tells me to rack them up. I do three big ones and call Giles to tell him to come up get some. Kevin goes into the bathroom to get dressed. He comes out as Giles arrives, and we all hoof it up and go down to the bar and order a round of beers and shots. I ask the barman to call us a taxi. We sling back the drinks and have time for another shot before we jump in the cab.

We get dropped off at this amazing place in Ibiza Town called La Brasa. The maitre'd leads us to a little alcove at the back of the restaurant's cavernous courtyard. It's all rather posh, with fairy lights in amongst the foliage, and impeccably turned out clientele and staff. We ask for some steaks, by-passing the starters. They bring over a basket of bread and olives, and a dish of alioli, and we order up three beers and a bottle of posh red. Dinner is on the company so we might as well push the boat out.

The steaks arrive along with assorted roast vegetables. It's beyond fucking delicious. There are some steaks that are so good, they require absolutely no sauce, ketchup, condiment, seasoning or anything. And this is one of them. It's so fucking succulent that even Kevin, in his coked-up living hell, slavers and slobbers like a pissed dog and polishes off every last bit. We wash it all down with more Rioja, and call for the bill. They bring it, I gasp, and thank God this one's on work. I fucking love rinsing out the expenses on trips like this. They bring a bottle of Hierbas over on the house, and we sit there knocking the shots back, while we take turns to go for a toot in the bogs.

Kevin calls the waiter over, and asks him to book two cabs. I ask him why two.

"I'll meet you at the club. I'm not going to the West End. Fuck that. I'm going back to the hotel for a bit."

Fucking incredible. What a flake. I really don't know why he bothered coming. Still, I'm glad to be rid of him. Kevin pops open his phone and says he'll wait for the cab outside and bids us farewell. Yeah, shit off, you twat, I telepathically say to his receding back. As he goes through the door, he is buffeted by what looks like a group of casuals. They stick out like a sore thumb on this side of the island.

Giles pours a couple more shots for us. We've just snapped them back when an almighty ruckus erupts near the front of the restaurant. The universal declaration of war that is "what the fuck are you staring at?" is hollered, and Giles looks round in mischievous glee at the group of middle-aged skinheads facing off with a younger, rather well to do and affluent-looking group. His camera is already on and he's surreptitiously snapping away. God, he's good.

There's a couple of moments silence before a chap with slicked back hair and yellow t-shirt bleats some kind of apology. It doesn't appear to placate the hooligan in front of him, and he collapses the boy like a house of cards by nutting him on the bridge of the nose.

His mates steam in and it really kicks off. What the fuck? I thought we left San An behind? Still, this is fucking hilarious!

Some tables are upended, and for a moment it looks like it's going to turn into one of those brilliant brawls you get in westerns, with people swinging from chandeliers and some honky-tonk piano music in the background. But it's over as quick as it starts. The thuggish victors insult the restaurant and its clientele, and make a hasty exit to the feint sound of police sirens.

"Haha. What the fuck was that about?!" Giles says.

"I have no idea, but I get the feeling it's going to be one of those nights."

The waiter comes over and apologises for the disturbance, and tells us our cab is outside. We walk past a few wrecked dinners and leave the restaurant for a nice, cold cab. Twenty minutes later, we get out at the foot of the West End.

The Shop Girl Part 2 : Star Signs

It takes me about two hours to get the shop back into its pre-Natalie state, but I'm grateful for the distraction. It's not massively busy today, and I hate it when there's fuck all to do.

I go and make another cuppa, and find a relatively new glossy magazine next to the microwave in the store room. I perch behind the till, sipping my tea and leafing through the mag, glancing at the headings until I come across a piece that seems vaguely interesting. It takes a while. It's a piece promising an insight into what men really mean when they say things. After about two paragraphs I'm struggling to concentrate, so I flick through until I get to the horoscopes.

I go to mine, Libra, and scan through. Apparently, an opportunity will present itself to me and a friendship will reveal itself to have the potential to be something more. Oh for fuck's sake. I'm glad Nat wasn't reading this when I came in. I have a quick look at Matt's, Aries, and see that he's being advised to make a leap of faith, because apparently the rewards will be many. I laugh out loud and chuck the magazine under the counter as a couple of girls come in and start browsing through the racks of clothes. I sell them a belt for 60 Euros and they thank me. I feel a little bad. I know how much we pay for them!

The time-drag over the course of early evening is interminable. There's only so many cups of tea I can make, only so many times I can re-read my horoscope, and only so many times I can look at the clock before I go mad. Add this to the nervous anticipation I'm feeling about going out with everyone tonight, and it's almost unbearable. I have to laugh. After about 8.30, it begins to get busy and the minute hand on the shop clock seems to spin round a lot faster.

Thankfully, just after 11.00, Lucy and Starkey come in to keep me company until the end of my shift. We start hatching plans.

"When you're done, come round to mine to get ready," Starkey says. "We'll pre drink there until it's time to meet at the OK."

We all nod in agreement, and I give some cash to them to go and get some booze. I start packing up at 11.30 and lock the takings in the safe with the till roll. I pull the shutters down at midnight on the dot. I strut up the West End heading towards Starkey's flat, passing the heaving bars and the soon to be heaving drinkers. I flit past the Ship and down the alleyway to the apartment. I buzz the door and it clicks open almost immediately. I take the stairs two at a time up to the second floor and barge into the flat to the welcoming sound of a credit card bashing against a plate like a woodpecker. A line is thrust up towards my nose as soon as I enter the kitchen. I take the offering and use the proffered straw to hoof it up, before I switch the plate with a strong and sturdy vodka Red Bull – served in a mug, natch.

Judging from the dent already in the bottle of booze, and the noise Lucy and Starkey are making, I'd say I've got a serious game of catch-up to get involved in. I drain my drink, pour myself another and disappear into the bathroom to have a quick shower and chuck on the new dress I've borrowed from the shop. As soon as I'm done, I pull up a chair around the kitchen table and get my compact out and stick my face on.

Lucy is complaining about a boy she's been playing around with. He's been acting like a proper dick – being all super cool when it's just them two, but as soon as his mates are around, he reverts back to being a 14 year old.

"Why is it so difficult to find a decent man out here? They're all little boys, emotionally stunted. But still incredibly hot. It's a proper dilemma." Lucy sighs.

"Yeah, but the unwashed ranks of San An workers is hardly the best place to look for Mr Right, is it? Most of us are just passing through this existence on the island anyway – people would be well different back in the real world. The best you can hope for out here is a holiday romance. Don't expect anything more." I say.

"Oh I don't know about that, Hannah," Starkey says. "There are one or two decent guys out here. Matt's a catch, don't you think?"

"Yeah, of course he is, but he's also a mate," I say, hoping my cheeks aren't reddening like I feel they are. Starkey smiles thinly and raises an eyebrow. "What?!!"

"Nothing!" She says, all faux innocence. "Anyway, maybe we'll get lucky at Sean's little rave-up tonight."

"Hmm. You may be right," Lucy says. "Oh well, not to worry. I'm sure more booze will help in the grand scheme of things!"

And with that, Lucy pops out of her chair like a jack-in-the-box and goes to the counter to fix more drinks. She cackles as she measures out enough booze to floor an elephant. I chop out the rest of the gear into six lines, and we have one each before our last drinks. We decant what's left of the vodka into a bottle of Fanta Limon and get our shit together to head out. Just before we go out the door, we have the other lines. We're soon sashaying down the street giggling and swigging as we pass the bottle between us.

The Thief Part 3 : Clocking On

Next to the apartment block there runs an alley, which is dark and offers some cover from passers-by. I mosey on down there, fortified by the drink, and approach the street door. I have a Slim Jim in my bag, but it's not needed. A gentle push and the door swings open, unlocked. I ring the buzzers on the intercom, six in all – two on each floor, and wait just inside the door. When there is no response from any of them, I feel safe and satisfied and head up the stairs. Halfway up the first flight, I pull the glass from my bag, and place it strategically on a step. I want forewarning of any returning residents, and a stray glass won't raise any suspicions.

    I bound up the stairs to the third floor – I always like to work from the top down in these sort of situations, and will probably ignore the first floor tonight due to the minimised escape time should I hear the tinkle of the glass in the stairwell. I get to the third and move down the hallway. One of the apartment looks unoccupied, with nothing outside and flyers and junk mail sticking out of its letterbox. I head right past the door to the next one, and get the Slim Jim out. I slash it through the gap between the door and the frame next to the lock, and the door pops open immediately. Sometimes this is too easy. I shout "Hello" into the darkened apartment, and hear nothing in reply. I pull my torch out and do a quick sweep. Three bedrooms, a sitting room, a kitchen and a bathroom. There's a laptop on and open on the table in the front room. From the logged in Facebook account I can ascertain it is owned by someone called Tony. And from his status updates, I learn that he had a fucking awesome time at Ibiza Rocks on Tuesday – and was clearly off his tits on the VIP balcony from the accompanying pic – and at midday today, he was looking forward to spending the next couple of days on Formentera with two chaps called Martin and Steve. A quick hunt through the pile of envelopes on the table by the front door leads me to believe that Martin and Steve are the other occupants of the flat. Nice.

I breathe out and feel my heart rate slow a little.

I have a poke around the flat a bit more. The kitchen is at the back of the building, looking out over nothing but a brick wall and a small enclosed area of wasteland, so I flick the light on and have a look in the fridge. They have proper, non-long-life milk, which is something of a rarity here. I have a swig and stick the kettle on, having noticed a box of PG Tips. While the kettle boils, I get to work, liberating two more iPods and a small set of travel speakers from the living room, and about 300 Euros in cash from one of the bedrooms. The only other thing worth taking is the laptop, but I'm going to have a little fiddle around on that before I stick it in my bag. The kettle clicks off, and I pour the water into a pint glass – the only acceptable receptacle in the place. I let it stew for a bit and then add a splash of milk to turn it into a brick-red mix. Nice. You can't beat a proper cuppa – something that is in short supply on this island. I take a seat at the laptop, minimise the browser with Facebook open and have a look around. Ooh, tidy. I see the icon for Traktor on the desktop and pop it open. It would appear this Tony character fancies himself as a DJ. While the Traktor loads up, I have a look in the music folder and see that this dude's pile of tunes is nearly as good a collection as the one on my new favourite iPod. Wicked. I must play this all out one day soon. His desktop wallpaper though, I find extremely offensive – a picture of the latest Manchester United squad. I feel a rush of glee that I'm knocking off a United fan. Haha. My Dad was City through and through, and I spent many a Saturday afternoon with him at Maine Road when I was a little girl. Opening up Google, I search for a photo of City's latest squad and make that the wallpaper instead. The Traktor has opened by now and I load a tune onto each deck and start pissing around looping, phasing and flanging. I finish my cup of tea, then shut the machine down, fold it up and pop it in my record bag, making sure to take the power leads and the rest of the bird's nest of cables on the table next to it. I drain my tea, rinse my glass and make my way out of the flat to the stairwell.

My foot is just about to land on the top step when I hear a door slam and a glass smash. Fuck. I hear a brash, male voice bellow from downstairs.

"Which cunt left their fucking drink here? I could've cut my fucking foot!!!"

Oh shitting fuck fuck. For a moment, panic seizes me as I hear a stampede of people clattering up the stairs. I remember to breathe, and head up towards the roof, and thank the Lord fucking God almighty that the door to it is open. I stand just outside and lean back, straining my ears to hear the direction of the footfalls. They seem to have disappeared into the first floor flat. So I hold my position and look at the clock on my phone. I'll give them five minutes, then sneak out. I squat down in the shadows and wait.

The Holidaymakers Part 2 : A Drink At The Rock Bar

Another parade passes by, and in their wake follows a stream of less exciting but still slightly freaky normal people. Mostly lobster red moneyed Brits, though not of the chav kind, and the more seasoned Ibiza veterans who ooze cool and calm under their white linen suits as they stroll along with their incredibly glam women. Some of the men look like Peter Stringfellow and, like their female companions, seem to be fashioned from leather, such is the attention they have allowed the sun to pay to their skin. They look more handbag than human.

I wave over the waitress and order another round of shots and some beers. We sling them back and line up another couple as we enjoy the freakshow. I'm starting to feel a bit tired, and mention this to Kenny. His eyes widen a bit, and I swear I see a light bulb go off behind his eyes.

"Let's get some puff and go crash on the beach and get high then." Kenny suggests. I think it's a great idea and I nod enthusiastically. Being our first time on the island, we're not exactly sure of how to go about scoring here, but the standard method of wandering the streets looking for someone shady will probably work. We drain our beers, thank the barmaid and walk along the strip towards where it gets darker and the bars thin out. We climb up some stone steps and delve into the maze of alleyways, nooks and crannies that are built into the hill that comprises the old town.

We soon leave the last few dingy bars behind us and go deeper into the deserted warren. Tall, rickety buildings loom over us, reducing the amount of sky visible to a dark, narrow strip. As we get further away from any signs of life, a sense of foreboding grows. An opening between two dilapidated buildings leads to another winding stone staircase, and we start making our way up it. It opens out onto a small, derelict plot of land. Over the other side, there's a dude sat on a small stone wall. He looks like a druggy, so we bowl over to him, full of false confidence, and make eye contact. He stares at us with a look of contempt on his face, and I'm tempted to just turn round and run. I'm starting to feel more than a little bit anxious about this, and am not exactly comfortable with the situation we find ourselves in. We're in a town we don't know, in a dark, secluded place, trying to score drugs off someone who is clearly very fucking dodgy. Kenny takes the lead before I bottle it and turn tail and run. But I have a very bad feeling about this.

"Hola, amigo. Hablas Ingles?" Kenny says with more pluck than I know he has.

The bloke continues to look at us like we're a pair of cunts. My hand starts to go up to Kenny's shoulder to turn him and suggest we leave, but as it does, the geezer opens his mouth and speaks. My hand is hanging in the air and I feel a bit stupid, so I try and style it out by bring it up to my hair and smoothing it back. I know it doesn't work. How to give the upper hand away in one easy step, right fucking there.

"What do you want?" the dude says in a thick Spanish accent. It sounds like he's swallowed a bucket of gravel, his voice rough and intimidating. He sounds like a dago Danny Dyer.

"Um, we're looking for some, er, *chocolate*?" Kenny says plaintively. I'm impressed with his use of local drug slang. He then turns the whole thing into a clichéd game of charades by forming a circle with his thumb and forefinger, holding it to his lips and taking a strong pull on an imaginary spliff. He even coughs afterwards. It would be quite comical if the splutter was intentional, but it's just unfortunate timing – Kenny isn't that funny.

The dude looks us up and down with an evaluating stare, and his face softens a bit. He allows a little predatory grin to spread across his mouth.

"Yeah. You like hash?"

"Yeah, great. How much for how much?"

The bloke holds out his index finger, and measures to just below the middle knuckle with his other finger.

"You get this much for 50 euros."

Given the size of his fingers, he's measured out about half an ounce there. It seems like a good deal. Conflicting emotions jostle for position in my head. The sensible part of me is saying it's too good to be true, but every other part of me is saying it's a great deal, and it'll be fine; not everyone's a thieving gypsy bastard.

"Yeah OK, we'll go with that." Kenny says, echoing the predominant thought in my mind.

He gets up and beckons us. We follow him up the stairs and around the corner, before he stops abruptly.

"You have the money?"

I fish around in my pocket, surreptitiously separating a single note off the bundle of 50s I have in there, and deftly pull it out. There's no way I'm getting a fat roll of scratch out in front of this dude. I give him the yellow note and he starts up the stairs. After a couple of steps he turns to us and holds his arms out.

"You have to wait here."

"You what?"

"I have to get it from the gypsies. You wait here. They won't like if you come."

I look at Kenny, and he raises an eyebrow. The bloke notices our unease.

"Hey, man, I'm not going to rob you. I live here – you can find me, it's not a big place. My name is Alfonse."

He seems genuine enough, and he has a point. It's a small island, so probably could find him. And my drunken desire to score has given rise to some reckless wishful thinking. I nod to him and point at the floor.

"We'll be waiting right here."

He smiles and goes off up the stairs, disappearing into the warren of alleyways that burrow into the hill like the hollowed-out roots of a concrete tree.

It takes all of ten seconds for me and Kenny to come to the same conclusion. We've been knocked.

"Fuck. Shit. Fuck."

We peg it up the stairs after him. They open out into a small and filthy courtyard, with at least two other ways out that we can see. I run over to another set of steps and go up them two at a time, looking around the corner, seeing nothing but a long stretch with some clapped out houses and no sign of life. Kenny's checking out another exit on the opposite side. His body language tells me there's nothing doing that way either. We trudge back to where we left Alfonse.

"He might come back. Let's give it ten minutes." I say, realising how pathetic I sound as the words come out of my mouth. This is fucking schoolboy stuff. I mean, who fucking falls for that who is over the age of thirteen?

Well, we did.

We perch on the wall like a pair of simpletons. Christ, what's next? Are we going to try and buy some magic beans? Jesus. I pull out my fags, and hand one over to Kenny without saying anything. We smoke in silence. Regret and annoyance are gnawing at my guts, and I really don't want this unfortunate occurrence to define the night. So I flick my fag against the wall, and stamp on the glowing butt as it bounces down to the ground.

"Fuck it. Let's put this one down to experience and get out of here. Let's not allow it to ruin our evening." I say, injecting more determination into my voice that I think I can actually call on. But I mustn't let this get to me. It's my own fault anyway. I've never been able to spot when something is too good to be true.

The Bouncer Part 4 : A Fight and A Lost Phone

It's after 12 when I bid farewell to the manager at Mambo's and head back along the strip to the West End. As I turn the corner at the bottom of the hill that is the main artery, I'm confronted with a canyon of garish lights and fights, bars and PRs, which stretches up into the distance. Thousands of pissed up Brits – there's no sight quite like it. The sound they generate reminds me of a storm at sea, and it hits me like a shockwave. I take up my position outside Trops. It's right in the middle of it all, and it's as good a place for people watching as Mambo's is for sunsets. Groups of lads and gangs of girls file by. You can tell the seasoned Ibiza veterans from the virgins by the total look of bewilderment and incomprehension on the faces of the latter. It truly is a modern day Sodom and Gomorrah.

It's easy to judge these kids, acting the way they do, puking and scrapping and behaving like animals, and come to the conclusion that they are cunts. But that's not the case with most of them I reckon. For 51 weeks out of the year, they'll be doing their little job, quietly going about their lives, not hurting a fly. They could be the girl who books your mum's appointment at the dentist, or they could be the bloke that comes to fix your nan's heating. And they'll not have that much excitement going on for them, so they save up for their week away in the sun, and they'll look forward to it all year, and then when they get here…..bam! 51 weeks of mediocrity explodes out of them, producing a flurry of vomit, spunk and testosterone. And that's just the birds.

Tonight though, things have been relatively quiet so far, in terms of any problems to I've had to deal with. But it's Thursday night, so Cream and Guetta will have drawn a lot of the pillheads and ravers away, leaving us with the drinkers and the fighters.

Up the road, outside Sopranos, there's a bit of argy bargy. A group of English lads have just had a punch up. I look over at them and take them in. There's a funny dynamic in the group, like they're all very uncomfortable in each other's presence, but their macho attitude dictates that they must appear unfazed by everything. I know it well, having run with firms of nasty bastards for most of my life. At least up until I went to jail.

Seeing the group of thugs and sensing the black hole of hatred emanating from inside each and every one of them brings back memories all right. It prompts me to think about the turnaround in my life. I got out of prison two years ago after doing a stretch for GBH. Prior to my incarceration, I'd been in with a very nasty group of lads. We stole, we dealt, we bullied, battered and bashed our way through life. It was all I knew growing up. Fighting at the football, mugging the richer kids stupid enough to use our estate as a short-cut, setting fire to anything that would burn – growing up in a such a Petri-dish of hate, it wasn't that surprising I ended up in stir. But it wasn't inevitable that I ended up a wrong-un. We are all in control of our destiny. Life is just a series of choices, and you always have a choice in what you do. It might not be an easy choice, but there is always a right and a wrong path. And I always took the wrong path. Either because it was easy, or I got off on the rush of doing something bad, or I just wanted to feel power and control over others, probably because I had so little power and control over my own life. Or so I perceived.

It was while I was in jail I realised that my life didn't have to be one drenched in pain and conflict, and devoid of love and happiness. My cellmate was a lifer. He wasn't ever going to see the outside again. You couldn't blame a man in that situation for going nuts with rage, but he hadn't. He was the calmest, most zen person I'd ever met. He'd had no choice to accept he was there forever, and decided he could have a life on the inside, both literally and metaphorically. He showed me how to become impervious to the outside world, and helped me to find inner calm.

He'd been busted 15 years earlier bringing an obscene amount of cocaine into Dover. We're talking near to half a ton. As half of the Kent police force descended on him just outside the docks, he floored his car and ran one over. By accident, he says, but that didn't stop him from getting an extra-long stretch for crippling a copper with a car full of Charlie. Soon after he went down, he became a Buddhist and came to terms with what his life was. The only way it would ever have any meaning under those horrific circumstances would be for him to find inner peace and happiness. Appropriate, seeing as the rest of his life would be spent inside.

Over my time as a guest of Her Maj, I went from being a career thug to being what can best be described as a hippie. But only in terms of my ideals – I haven't quite got to the stage where I can relinquish possession of a sense of smell and thus the need for soap, and I'm not a fan of the long hair.

I smile inwardly as I look at the gang of hooligans. I hear them being obnoxious and swearing loudly at each other, the names they call each other are infused with genuine hatred disguised as banter. As they stagger past to sow havoc elsewhere, I'm relieved that I'm no longer as angry, twisted and in pain as they are.

Phil, the manager, comes to me at my spot just outside the main door, and tells me there is a punter inside that needs to be moved on. He's shitfaced and is picking fights, and has been grabbing girls' arses. Sounds like a lovely chap. I follow Phil inside and he points out this twat in a Mackenzie t-shirt with an incredibly red face and more hair gel than Peter Andre's bathroom cabinet. He's harassing a group of girls at table in the corner. I go over and apologise to everyone, before asking the boy to leave. He turns to me, puts his hand on my chest and tells me to fuck off, and attempts to push me away. I grab his arm and flip him around and drive him through the door, taking care to not rough him up. He's just had a bit too much to drink, and is acting obnoxious. No reason to hurt him if I don't have to.

I bundle the drunk away from the door, nearly knocking over a passing DJ. I frogmarch the dude down the side street, telling him in no uncertain terms it would be in his best interests for him to go home and sleep it off. I let go of him with a shove and he stumbles away from me. He staggers towards the green garden furniture we have outside, looking like he's going to do some human ten pin bowling and strike all the tables and chairs. He stops just before he hits a table and straightens up and grabs a chair, turning and raising it over his head. He lunges forward and lobs the chair at me. I step towards it, controlling its landing and palming it down to the ground.

What a nob.

He's giving it the big 'un, shouting at me, calling me every disgusting thing that bustles to the front of your mind when you're incoherently drunk and riddled with rage. And in his broad Glaswegian accent, it sounds even lovelier than it usually does. This is one of the reasons I'm very glad I never drink anymore. Anything that can turn a person into this twisted caricature of the worst humanity has to offer cannot be good in any way.

The punters have formed a semi-circle that caps the side street, arching between Trops and Capones. Groups of blokes are egging me on to batter this guy, and I can feel the adrenaline surging through my body as my face flushes, and a whooshing sensation rushes through my ears. I really don't want to thump this guy. I wish he'd just fuck off. I can feel the crowd watching every move, and I feel a momentary stab of hate towards the drunk for dragging me centre stage in this evening's street entertainment. I remember to breathe deep, and not let the anger take over and dictate my actions. I again tell the bloke to piss off, this time raising my voice and swearing. He then elects to spit at me, and that's it.

Enough is enough.

I step to him and throw a fist, missing him as he flukily sways out of the way. My air punch is greeted with a burst of laughter and wolf whistles and the hairs on my cheeks bristle and I feel about two foot tall. This is fucking horrible. He falls drunkenly into me, and we grapple for a moment before I roughly push him away. I feel my pocket lighten as my iPhone tumbles out and then clatters across the street. Shit. I swiftly move close and smack the boy twice at close range, one blow to the jaw with my left and a follow up with my right to his solar plexus. Finally, he stops acting like a nob, and wobbles off down the street, far enough away from the bar for it to not be my problem anymore. As I turn back to the crowd, a cheer goes up and the sun-burnt lobsters of the West End serenade me with an unwelcome round of applause. I look to where my iPhone is just in time to see one of the hookers that loiter round here scoop it up and start off the down the road with it.

I chase after her, and she goes round the corner towards Breezer's and disappears up the alley. I get to the mouth of the alley and see she's stopped running because she doesn't need to anymore. Even in the darkness, which is a stark contrast to the garishness of the West End and its surrounding streets, I can see the outline of a couple of geezers. They're with her. And I can sense a whole heap of malevolence and a world of shit if I go down this alley. Fuck that. Not for a phone. I turn round and trudge back towards my post outside Trops. Fucking hell. Out of frustration, I boot a bin bag and am rewarded with an eruption of bin juice which splatters all over my leg.

At least I'm wearing dark trousers, I think as I feel my black trackies absorb, then saturate with, the bin effluvia. All I need now is to tread in dog-shit or have an anvil fall on my head and I've got a full house.

I get back to the strip and am welcomed with a round of applause by the other workers and remaining witnesses to the incident. My face flushes again, and I feel like I'm under a microscope. I can hear a non-existent wind rushing in my ears, and I fight off the urge to go into shock.

"Where the fuck have you been?" is suddenly shouted in my ear. I nearly jump out of my skin. I look round to see Phil apoplectic with rage. His eyelid is twitching, his face is red and the veins around his temples look fit to burst. "You never leave your spot, you should fucking know that!" He bellows at me.

The more malevolent elements of the crowd are laughing at my public dressing down, but luckily most of them have moved on to gawping at something else.

"Some brass nicked my phone, Phil. I chased after her." I state calmly.

"I don't give a fuck. What if the Guardia come by and I've not got security out here? We'll get fucked. You gonna pay the fine? Are you bollocks. Not on what I pay you. So you fucking stay here, regardless. I don't care if some tart's chopped your nob off and is running down the street with it. You stay here at all times. Got it?"

"Clear as crystal, Phil. Clear as crystal." I say before he waddles off to further empower himself at someone else's expense in the bar.

The urge to go mental is close to overwhelming me. But that's not who I am now. So I count to ten, fix my face to stare and breathe long and deep, just as I have trained myself to in times of high stress.

One of the PRs from the bar across the road comes over and give me a hug.

"You're not having the best night, are you?" she coos. She's a sweet girl, and feeling her arms around my chest is comforting. I ruffle her hair and tell her I'm fine. She punches my shoulder and gives me a minxy grin.

"That, you most certainly are, tough guy. Don't let it piss you off. That bloke was a twat, and iPhones are shit anyway."

We both laugh at her trivialisation of it all, and I cheer up a bit. There's no use in moping. I can replace the phone, and the only real damage to that Sweaty Sock will be a sore head in the morning, and he would've had one of those without the help of my fist anyway.

I spend the next couple of hours perched on a stool that the barmaid's brought out to me as a half joke/gesture of solidarity. All the PRs that lurk around our bit have been over and said nice things to me, and I'm feeling super-cool about that. The sense of camaraderie amongst the workers is comforting, and it's always nice to know that people give enough of a fuck to try and cheer you up when you've had a mare of it. There's a lot of love here, and it's not only generated by ecstasy.

The Reps Part 4 : Best Laid Plans

I head over to the DJ booth. Grainger is lying down and looking absolutely rotten while the other DJ conducts the crowd. It always helps when the DJ gets involved and enjoys himself as much as the punters. Grainger unfortunately doesn't seem to be too happy, his face as pale as the white bits on his stripy sailor-style T-shirt.

"You alright there, mate?" I ask.

"Ooooh," he groans. "I don't have very good sea-legs."

"That's rich coming from someone who's dressed like a 1980's yacht salesman." I laugh back at him, taking in his skinny shorts and deck shoes. I fish out some seasickness pills and pop a couple out of the blister pack for him. "Get them down you and you'll be as right as rain in 15 minutes."

He scoops them into his mouth and washes them down with some water before breathing out slowly and lying back down. Bless him. The other DJ is tearing it up with an old school house and techno set, throwing in the occasional new track, and he's really getting the party going with tunes that everyone knows the words to. I head over to the bar we've installed at one end of the cabin, and get Nicola to pass me over a couple of bottles of San Miguel to give the DJs.

It doesn't take too long for us to get to our destination, and just before we arrive there, I go over to the decks and give them a CD to put on. Due to us arriving at the venue via a little-grotto like cave, I've burned some appropriate music for us to be playing as we pull into the opening – in this case, 'Nights Introlude' by Nightmares On Wax. As we drift towards the cave and its covered dock, the synths from the song wash over the boat, and start to reverberate around us as we come to a standstill. It sounds awesome, and makes the hairs on the back of my neck stand on end. It looks amazing as well – the lighting has given it an ethereal feel and it looks fucking magical. I once saw a picture of the grotto at the Playboy Mansion and, fuck me, it looked like this. Result. I look back at the faces of the punters and see that they are suitably impressed. Nice.

Grainger has positioned himself by the gangplank, to ensure he's the first off the boat and able to make it to the soundsystem before everyone gets to the clearing. He jumps off the boat before it's lashed to the jetty and disappears up into the tunnel. About 30 seconds later, I hear a kick drum start throbbing its way towards us. Game on.

I jump off the boat, followed by the dancers and stilt-walkers. I send Sam and Brown up to the top of the stairs to direct people to the clearing. It takes a few minutes for everyone to disembark and filter through the tunnel. From the "oohs", "ahs" and general cooing I overhear as they pass me, I can see the manner of our arrival at this place has had the desired impressive effect. Once the last of them has ascended the stairs, I shake the hand of the boat captain. I tell him I'll see him later when he comes to pick us up in a few hours. He's heading back to San An for whatever reason, but I like the fact we've been 'marooned', as it were – it adds to the illicit vibe of this 'secret' party.

I watch the boat drift out of the cave and turn to climb the stairs. It looks fucking rad as I follow the torches up into the bowels of the rock. It feels like I'm being birthed into a mystical wonderland, leaving the real world behind me. The tunnel becomes a magical portal, and the muffled heartbeat caused by the drums builds and builds until I clamber out of the dark and into the twinkling light of the rave. When I emerge at the top, I allow myself a moment to absorb what's going on in front of me. It's something like fucking Glastonbury, but without the fetid stench of days old human waste and hippies. The energy in the atmosphere is immense – I feel like I could reach out and touch it. You can almost hear it crackling. Whether this is down to the vibe being generated by the music and the people, or the dodgy electrics me and Jody have laid down, I don't know. But whatever it is creating it, the feeling is something pretty fucking special. The caterpillar of doom and gloom that was residing in my stomach before I got to the boat has well and truly metamorphosed into a butterfly, which is now fluttering around inside me, making my insides tingle. I love this feeling. I swear a little bit of wee just came out.

    I enter the clearing and weave my way through the mass of people up towards the bar. The place is heaving. Pumping house music blares out from the edges of the clearing – the positioning of the speakers is bang on, and it sounds absolutely fucking stunning. The music penetrates me and infuses its groove into my bones. I find Jody chatting to a couple of girls and he slaps me on the back.

"Man, I think you might have pulled it off. This is fucking sick. I'm buzzing and I haven't even taken anything. Girls, this is Sean. This is his party."

I shake hands with a couple of preppy girls. I think they say their names are Tara and Jemima, but to be honest, I can't hear a fucking word they're saying over the music. One of them Jody is clearly after, given that he's already draped his arm over her in a proprietary way. The other one talks to me, but after a couple of exchanges, I just end up nodding vacantly and saying "yeah, innit" to her. I can't hear her, and I can't really concentrate on what she's saying. My eyes are roaming around the clearing, checking out what's going on. It's not that I intend to be rude, but I need to be on my game with this shindig, not chatting up the girls. I tell her I've got to work, but say we should go for a drink later when we get back to San An. She smiles sweetly, and I inadvertently grin like a gimp. Er, be cool man. I lean over to Jody's ear and make a megaphone out of my cupped hands.

"I can't wing you on this one. I'll re-engage when we're back at base."

He nods dismissively without taking his eyes off his new friend. Fair enough. I head back and climb up the incline opposite the DJ booth and see what it looks like from there. I'm fucked off that I didn't think to hire a photographer to document this, and further fucked off that I've lost my phone so I can't even take any snaps on that. But there are plenty of people taking pics with theirs', so I'll just get on the mic on the boat back and tell them to add them to our Facebook group. It looks fucking wicked, especially looking down from the top of this little slope. As I scope the bowl full of sweaty ravers in front of me, I catch Sam waving frantically at me. I circumnavigate to the bar and she leads me round the back of the shack, to where we can nearly hear ourselves think.

"Sean, at the rate they're drinking, we're going to run out of booze in an hour. Can we get anymore?"

Shit. Running out of grog would not only probably prompt a riot, it would also be a massive waste of a captive clientele and potential earnings. I could stick another couple of grand on my bottom line here, easy. I find Jody and explain the problem.

"The hotel. We can borrow it from them. Paco will be fine as long as he makes money on it."

He whips out his phone, and rings the hotel ops manager, Laura, a mate of ours. He wanders away from the soundsystem with one finger drilled into his ear, shouting into the handset. He comes back in a minute.

"Yeah, Laura's selling us a vanload just above cost, but we have to replace it all tomorrow."

"Wicked."

I grab Jody's phone and call Joe. After he's finished laughing, he says he'll go to the hotel and bring us a re-up on the booze. What a fucking legend. That's that sorted then. I give Jody his phone back and head back to the bar to replenish the empty bins with the remaining beer. Fuck me, they've already got through 20 cases in just under an hour. God, I love the British. They fucking know how to have it larger with lager than anyone else. I finish dumping the last of the beer into the slushy water and take one for myself. I look out over the bowl. A small dust cloud is hovering around everyones' feet, so frantic is the dancing going on here. The lights are perfect and are casting trippy shadows all over the place, all brought to life by the jacking and jigging of the punters in the middle. The music is brilliant and banging – the whole scene is just totally. Fucking. Perfect.

The Stags Part 4 : The West End

We're standing outside a bar at the top of the West End when it kicks off. Our second skirmish of the night, following the shenanigans in Ibiza Town. Some posh cunts got lairy at the restaurant and we had to indulge in a bit of mayhem. Not a bad start to the weekend. Meant we had to skip the food though, so we've come straight back out to San An instead to get on the piss.

    I've been chatting up this little blonde piece, who's part of a wider group of studenty hippie types. Usually I hate these twats, but there's some fit skirt with this lot, so I'm tolerating their smarmy presence. I'm impressing the girl with stories of scraps I've had with the boys down the football, and I can tell she fancies me because she's twiddling her hair and she keeps looking at her mate. One of the lads in their gang comes over, a long streak of piss with old school NHS glasses, a stripy top and women's jeans. He introduces himself as Justin. He's a right posh arsehole, and his nose crinkles when he looks at me.

    "I must say, you're all very brave wearing T-shirts like that in public. Or are you being ironic?"

    "Do what? You're brave going out dressed like an anorexic bird. Or are you being fucking ironic?" I eyeball him long enough for him to know he's made a grave error. Unfortunately, he's given the girl the opportunity to go, and she slinks off saying she needs a piss. The lanky sap twitches uncomfortably, chewing on the inside of his mouth, before he thinks of something to say.

"So, er, what kind of music are you into then? What clubs are you going to? You should really go to Cocoon on Monday. It's fucking brilliant minimal techno. Really sophisticated and intelligent."

I stare at this bell and despise him for his pathetic attempts at arse kissing me. Fucking minimal techno? I hate all that shit.

"Fucking hate techno mate. It's fucking mindless and pointless. It goes on forever, never does nothing and there's no lyrics. You've gotta be out of your tree to like that shit. It's for cunts."

He snorts, obviously clearing some sniffle out of the back of his nose. This seems to give him some balls. Big mistake.

"What? Are you crazy? Do you need someone singing on the top of it, telling you what emotions you should be experiencing? Can't you lose yourself in the rhythm?" The student cunt goes, trying to be jokey, but again, realising by my cold stare he's not doing himself any favours.

I've had just about enough of this twat. I lean my head back and snap it forward onto his nose with a satisfying crack. His glasses erupt off his face and clatter across the alleyway as he staggers back and treads on them. His mates have shat it, and are backing away from us. I step towards the cunts and sharply raise my fist as if I'm going in for afters. Seeing them flinch as a group makes me feel formidable, yet fills me with a mixture of pity and incandescent rage. The rage wins over and I feel nothing but contempt for them. Where's their fucking balls? Where's their backbone? Where's their self respect? Fucking pussies. I tell them to fuck off out of it, and go back to my drink. As I raise my pint to my lips, John enthusiastically thumps me on the back, nearly making me glass myself in the process, and spilling half my drink over my face.

"You told that speccy twat."

"All in good fun, John-o. All in good fun." I seethe inwardly. I love a good punch up, but long after the rush has gone, I'm always left with a depressing dull anger. Usually directed at whoever it is I've slapped. I hate them for being so weak. I look at the Mancs, who I notice stayed sitting down while I was having my little run-out. No one else needed to get involved of course, but at least Jimmy, John and Graham stood up just in case they were needed.

I finish off my drink and look around. A fair bit of space has opened up around us, and you can see the other groups of people are doing their best not to make eye contact with any of us. Fuck this. We've been up the West End now for a couple of hours. We've scored some E's, and have been tanning the vodka red bulls like there's no tomorrow, but I tell the others I've had enough of it round here and we should fuck off to Cream soon. We head over to the kebab shop and get a doner each to stuff our faces into on the journey to Amnesia. As we're walking down one of the side streets, we see a bunch of geezers run out of an alleyway right in front of us. I look where they've come from and see a girl on the floor, looking roughed up. Fucking hell. What's been going on here then? Someone's been naughty. The two northern monkeys fly like shit off a shovel in the direction the girl's assailants went. The rest of us take in the view and munch on our kebabs. One of the girls from outside one of the bars has come down and is checking the girl's OK. After a couple of minutes, we get bored of watching and head in the direction of the twins, almost running into them as they jog back around the corner.

"Any joy, you chivalrous cunts?"

"Yeah, we caught up with one of them and taught him a lesson. Anyway, let's get to the club. I'm pumped and want to find a bird to fuck," one of them says.

The queue for the cabs is long enough for us to finish our kebabs and drain the bottles of beer we took away from the bar. Just before we get in the cab, we all bosh a pill. After all, to enjoy the mindless racket we're going to be hearing, you've gotta be off your tits on drugs.

The Thief Part 4 : Clocking Off

I look at my clock again. Five minutes have passed without any further noise emanating from the first floor flat. Is this a good thing? Are they in for the night or are they just changing after work and heading out? This isn't a situation I often find myself in. I've been lucky, maybe to the point that it's made me a little complacent. I shouldn't have fucked around having a cup of tea. That was stupid. It would be fucking lame to get collared for such a flimsy haul as well.

    I tentatively start padding down the stairs, walking with exaggerated movements like a astronaut, deftly moving down to the landing below. I'm just passing the second floor when I hear the muffled noise of the party on the first floor suddenly amplify, and a load of people spill out and start trotting along the hall towards the stairwell. In between the shouting and hollering, I hear the words "roof" and "party". I peg it up the stairs and down the corridor to the flat I just robbed. I let myself back in and hold the door ajar, listening to the group of people making their way to the roof. It sounds like they are mainly women, but there are a couple of blokey voices breaking through here and there. I hear them pass and the hallway and stairwell fall quiet again, as the muffled sounds of people traipsing on the roof comes through the ceiling.

    I step out of the flat, and pull the door shut gently behind me. The click the lock makes deafens me, but I know that it's just my heightened senses that make it sound so loud. Moving back down the corridor, I step onto the stairwell and cock my head up to listen in on what is going on upstairs. As I'm doing so, my peripheral vision alerts me to a couple of shapes moving up the stairs.

"Er, who the fuck are you?" One of the shapes says with a gruff voice.

Shit. Shit. Shit. Time to get proactive.

"Hi guys. Do you have any idea where I can find Tony?"

"He's gone to Formentera, I think," says the other one of them, a lanky dude with blonde hair and a cockney accent. His counterpart has short black hair and an impressive gut. He must suffer in this heat. He smiles at me creepily, so I follow up my opening gambit with more bullshit.

"Shit, do you know when they're back?"

"Tomorrow," says the tubby one. "Are you a friend of his?"

"Sort of. I met him, Steve and Martin at Ibiza Rocks the other night. We got chatting in the VIP. Well, if you call it chatting. I think we just spent most of the time dribbling and gurgling into each other's ears."

This seems to satisfy him. He apologises for being a bit brusque, before going on to explain that there has been a spate of robberies round here lately, and it pays to be a little paranoid.

"Tell me about it, babe," I concur, as I swivel and hoist my record bag up so he can see it. "I've taken to carrying my laptop around with me the whole time. It's the only way I can guarantee some sticky fingered bastard doesn't nick it!" I say with a straight face.

I tell them my name, well, *a* name, and ask if they're having a little party on the roof. They say they are and introduce themselves, before inviting me up for a drink. My initial reaction is to get the fuck out of here, but I steel myself and rationalise that it would be more suspect for me to leg it. So I give them a shit-eating grin and follow them upstairs. We step out onto the roof, and I clock about a dozen people, half girls and half mostly scrawny looking worker boys. I get involved, and introduce myself around, giving it the bollocks about meeting the guys from downstairs in the VIP at Ibiza Rocks on Tuesday. They seem like a harmless enough group of kids, not really giving much time or attention to anything other than getting off their tits and enjoying their summer in wonderland. I pay the due attention to the females present, taking on the role of the interested interloper, not paying immediate attention to the guys so as not to put their backs up. It's more important to chat the ladies up before I move onto the lads. I don't want to threaten their self-perceived alpha female status by treading on any toes. I tell them that I'm out here for a month, staying with friends and playing the occasional gig.

"Ooh, are you a DJ?" coos the black haired guy, his interest in me perking up.

"Only as a hobby, really," I tell the group, before dropping a few big names of places I've played this summer. It is only a hobby, but one I excel at. And given the people I know in the trade, a hobby that I get to indulge in some very auspicious places from time to time. They are suitably, and easily, impressed. The blonde dude from the stairwell enthusiastically suggests I play some tunes for them, and motions towards the set of mini-speakers plugged into an iPod.

"Yeah, sure, maybe later," I say, acutely aware that they might recognise the laptop belonging to Tony if I whip it out there and then. But then again, they might not – these things all look the same these days. There is a slow building commotion emanating from the door to the stairs, before a slew of fresh people erupt onto the roof.

Someone pulls out a bag of pills; others produce wraps and spliffs. Before I know it, I'm munching on one of those delightful swirls that are doing the rounds. This is pretty irresponsible and reckless, and I'm totally hanging around on the doorstep I just shat on. But, the blokes I've robbed are off the island, so that affords me some playtime. And I'm off the island myself soon enough, so fuck it, might as well get stuck in. Although it's not too clever an idea to put a human face on my criminal activities, strictly speaking I'm not by befriending these people, because I haven't robbed them. Yet! The night is young, hehe!

The pill starts to kick in, and I feel a wave of nervous anxiety break over me. The resulting nausea only lasts a moment, and soon gives way to a gentle rush. I've taken quite a few of these swirls in the month I've been here, and they're the best fucking E's I've done in years. They make you chatty, make you dance, and there's practically no comedown from then, just a general fuzziness the next day. If only pills were still like this, instead of the random mixture of speed, pips and md-prefixed chemicals most pills masquerading as ecstasy are these days. I need to watch myself on these though – I'll let my guard down, and might say something that could get me into trouble. The best way I can avoid this, I think, is to get up there and start DJing. Tony's laptop had some wicked tunes on it, and I can smash this little party to pieces.

There's a bloke loitering by the soundsystem exhibiting the proprietary stance that some males get when it comes to tunes at a party. It's not unlike when you go to a BBQ, and all the men stand around the grill, jockeying for position, wanting to be the alpha male. Me make fire. Me burn meat. Me man. How tiresome. I go over to the geezer, squeeze my boobs together to make my cleavage deeper and tell him I'm a DJ. I name drop a couple of places I've played over here, and ask him if he minds if I do a little set. He is most accommodating, no doubt due to a swirl, and he clears a space on the table next to the speakers. I fish out the laptop, plug myself in, and fire up Traktor.

Lining up the first tune – Inner City's Good Life – I crank the volume up as the drum intro bounces along, and observe the party's reaction as the tell-tale synth lick comes in. This song's 25 years old – older than most of the people on the roof – but as soon as it drops, it goes off. I follow it up with Joe Smooth's Promised Land, plugging myself into and guiding the pilled up, in-love-with-everything vibe that's drawn itself around the group like an enormous chemical blanket. I play for about an hour, keeping the music in the realms of Chicago house from back in the day and a handful of mid 90s classics, which generate quite a few cheers, especially when I mix Ultra Flava and Music Sounds Better With You. It's positively Balearic. Seeing all the people dancing and loving it, girls stood on chairs dancing in bikinis, blokes in their shorts jacking like nobody is watching, I have a bit of a moment. The E. The music. The island. The unbridled joy. I fucking love it. I breathe it all in as a rush of ecstasy makes my lungs feel like I could inhale the world. I tremble and judder as the rush peaks, and I offer my place as music maestro up to some gawky looking kid with a Mac who's been hovering around for half an hour. As I mix in my last tune, a new re-jig of 808 State's Pacific State, I hold my headphones aloft and take an exaggerated bow to let people know I've finished playing. Those not too fucked to notice make encouraging noises and raise bottles of San Miguel in my direction.

 Mac-boy starts playing electro nonsense, immediately making me look even better by the stark contrast between the happy uplifting house I was playing and his cranky trendy bleeping bollocks. I swiftly put the hot laptop back in my bag and smile as I go over to get some more beer, enjoying the numerous approving pats on the back, kudos-giving fist bumps and squishy hugs from the pilled-up partygoers. DJing is such an easy ego trip. All I've done is play music, written and produced by others, in a certain order, and I get to take all the credit. Hahaha. Fucking love it.

I grab a bottle, and take a long swig from it, taking in the scene as I do so. The new DJ hasn't completely fluffed it, and is steering it towards a wonky tech sort of noise, one that is actually very interesting and stimulating when on the correct drugs. As if reading my mind, one of the guys, this delicious looking creature with brown hair covering his face, catches my eye and comes over to offer me a bump. I accept and we take a seat and chat shit for a while. He's absolutely fucking gorgeous. I feel myself falling in love with him with the speed and intensity that only MDMA can generate. We're being very tactile, and he kisses me tenderly. He takes me by the hand and leads me downstairs to his flat on the second floor. At the door, he turns to me and we kiss again, this time with a lot more passion. It's fucking lovely. We go inside to his room and my clothes almost melt away from me as we tumble onto the bed. He is without a doubt, if I can paraphrase the great Aldous Huxley, the most pneumatic man I've ever had the pleasure of being with. And he's fucking huge and as hard as granite. The sex, coupled with the E, completely sends my brain to another plane and I ride away to heaven on wave after wave of the most ecstatic joy I've ever known. We fall asleep in each other's arms, unable to speak, just about managing to breathe, with the stupidest grins on our faces.

I wake a couple of hours later. The E has subsided, just a warm fuzzy memory. I get up, get dressed and make my way out of the apartment, almost feeling bad as I slip the boy's laptop into my bag.

The Bouncer 5 : Rough Justice

As the night cracks on, things get busier as the numbers swell and the strip becomes even more hectic, with masses of hardened boozers infesting the place. I'm just checking down the side of the bar when I see, down the end of the side-street, three guys manhandling a girl into an alleyway. I sprint down the street to them. The alleyway opens out a bit, and as I enter it I can see them pushing the girl up against a dumpster. I fly into them, grabbing two of them by the scruffs of their necks and the three of us tumble to the floor. They pin me down in order to push themselves up to their feet, and take off. I ask the girl if she's ok, and she nods breathlessly.

I give chase to the attackers.

They bomb left out of the alleyway, running into and scattering a gang of lads. I'm right behind them, gaining ground as I pound down the street. From the vocal reaction from the boys at the foot of the alleyway, they've seen the girl and are making enough of a fuss for me to know she'll be ok. At the end of the road the assailants go left down another alley, opening up a lead on me.

I turn another corner and run straight into a clenched fist. My eyes go out of focus and I feel a crunching thud between my legs before my balls seem like they've been replaced with two searing, burning spheres of pure hellfire. I drop into the foetal position and can only watch as the three would-be rapists disappear off into the night.

Bollocks.

I get to my feet and begin slowly heading back to the West End. As I turn the corner, I think I'm seeing double for a moment as I'm confronted with two identical scowling faces underneath matching blonde thatches. One of them whacks me square on the jaw.

"You should've kept running, you fucking rapist piece of shit." I hear someone say. I raise my hands to protect myself and try to explain they've got the wrong guy, but they're both pummelling me.

I feel a hot pain in my side, just under my armpit and I lose all strength. The floor rushes up to meet my face, and I feel like my lungs are collapsing. I cough violently, and feel a torrent of warm liquid pour out my mouth.

It goes dark.

Then a pinprick of light appears and I feel myself floating towards it, except now, I'm not in any pain. I feel wonderful.

I sense a benevolent presence within the light, and it draws me in, bathing me in its iridescent glory. I hear a voice permeate me, its tone soothing and familiar.

"Sorry you had to go like that. We decided to bring you home – you were way too good for that place."

The Holiday Makers Part 3 : A Bit of Good Luck

We trudge back to where we parked the car in silence. I feel fucking stupid and impotent, but the overwhelming feeling is one of disappointment – not only because we got robbed, but because I *really* wanted a spliff. And my hopes had been lifted to a lofty height before being dashed on the rocks of Alfonse's unscrupulousness. If that was his real name, the cunt. We leave the pedestrianised bit of the old town and emerge onto one of the streets that feed onto the main road. It's pretty late by now, but the place is still buzzing and there are plenty of people about. We brush past a couple of gnarly looking gangster type dudes, and I sense the larger, more psychotic-looking one snarling at us. In an effort to not walk right into one of them, I swerve and instead tread in a still moist and rather sizeable lump of dog shit. Typical. I hop down the road, not wanting to tread the shit into my shoes anymore, and look for a suitable place to scrape it off. A patch of grass, a metal grill – anything. I see a coarse looking manhole cover by the kerb next to a four by four and grind the underside of my trainer on it. It gets most of the crap off, but there's still a loads stuck into the tread. What a fucking pain in the arse. I've just finished getting rid of the majority of the poo when I glance down next to the car and see what looks like a bag. Upon closer inspection, I see that it's a green duffel bag. I do a quick 360 to check that no-one is watching me, and kneel down and scoop it into my arms, before jogging to catch Kenny up.

"Eh? Where'd that come from?" Kenny says after I finish my manoeuvre.

"It was just there, on the floor. I hope it's full of cash! Nice to have a bit of luck for a change." I joke, but I can tell from the weight, it is full of something. "Let's pick up the pace a bit."

See, now that's a nice bit of karma. If we hadn't been robbed by that cunt, we wouldn't have found the bag. Misfortune, given time, can reveal itself to be great fortune.

I want to open the bag and see what our haul is, but I don't fancy doing it while we're on the street. We hustle back to the Capri, and I get in the driver's side and rest the bag on my lap. As I pull the door shut, I think I hear a shout. Kenny pulls his door open, almost ripping it off the hinges and throws himself into the car.

"Dude, there's someone shouting at us. Get the fuck out of here!!!" He says with a nervous giggle. I look in the wing mirror and see the two hard looking cunts who diverted me into the dog shit running down the road towards us. I jam the keys in the ignition and pull out, doing a mini wheel-spin as I gun the engine and floor the accelerator. Two seconds later we're away, and the nut-jobs are nothing more than a pair of ever decreasing malevolent dots in the rear view. We turn the corner and bomb it down the wide main road. Luckily for us, the lights are green and we turn onto the slip-road that will take us to the motorway back to San Antonio. Now we're completely away, the rush subsides, and a bit of elation creeps into me. I feel like I did when I used to nick stuff from the shop at school.

I'd forgotten what a buzz being naughty can be. The bag is still sandwiched between my belly and the steering wheel. I breathe in and pull the bag out and shove it into Kenny's hands.

"Well, let's have a look at our spoils then, old chap." I say in my best Raffles The Gentleman Thief voice.

Kenny unzips the bag and gasps.

"Shit. Shit. Shit shit shit shit shit."

"What is it?"

"Dude, fucking hell. This *is* full of cash. Fucking hell." His voice cracks. "What have we done?"

"Er, how much cash?"

"Fucking thousands."

Silence grips us both. I feel sick. Anyone who carries that kind of money around in a holdall has to be involved in some kind of nasty bastard business. The kind of business that those two hard-nuts would be. Fuck. How fucking stupid are we? Why the fuck didn't I ditch the bag? They saw our car as well. And it's hardly the most conspicuous vehicle, is it? A white Capri on an island full of land-cruisers. What the fuck was I thinking? Fuck. Fuck. Fuck.

My stomach bunches up and I resist the urge to shit myself. Christ, this is going to be bad.

"Get rid of it. Chuck it." I splutter.

"Fuck off. There's must be tens of thousands of Euros in here."

"Jesus, you fucking idiot. Do you have any idea what will happen to us. We need to ditch this, and get the fuck out of here. Like, get off the island right now."

"Jesus, fucking think straight for one second. They saw us getting in the car. They don't know 100% it was us that took the bag. But they're going to be looking out for us anyway, so we might as well keep it, because they're still going to be after us even if we chuck it. And they'll be more pissed off if we've ditched it."

I take this in, and have to admit Kenny is speaking sense for a change. We've passed a few junctions on the motorway, and I can see Privilege on our left, all lit up like a Christmas tree.

"Let's get off the main road at least then," I say as we take the exit for San Rafael. The panic has subsided a bit, but I still feel fucking shook up.

We pause at the top of the slip-road and I grip the steering wheel and try to regulate my breathing. I look in the rear view and see a 4x4, exactly like the one that was next to the bag. It skids to a halt behind us, and I see the passenger door fly open. One of the thugs jumps out. Shit. I panic and slam my foot down on the accelerator, and the tyres screech as we pull away, straight over the roundabout and down the re-entry ramp. I scatter a group of clubbers walking along the hard-shoulder as we rejoin the motorway. I look in the mirror and see the 4x4 lurch onto the motorway. Fuck.

"Shit. They're right fucking behind us!"

Kenny says as swivels in his seat and looks back. He pukes, and some of it splatters on my arm.

"Oh fuck! Go faster. Lose them."

"I'm trying." The panic is almost overwhelming me now. As we approach San An, I can see the lights rising up from behind a hill. I tell Kenny to chuck the bag out the window, but he doesn't respond. He seems frozen.

"Look, if they see us launch the bag out of the window, they'll stop for it and we can get away." I shout insistently.

He refuses to acknowledge me. His mouth is open, but he's just gawping like a fish. I take one of my hands off the wheel and try and grab the bag. We struggle, and I lose control of the car. The bag goes flying out of the window just as we leave the road and flip over. We slide down the embankment on the roof and skid to a halt in the undergrowth. We lay there for a moment, hyperventilating. I pat myself down and seem mostly unscathed. I look over at Kenny and he seems ok, if a little freaked out. It's a miracle we're not dead.

I'm just about to speak when the passenger door is ripped open and set of arms drags Kenny out. I hear the sound of someone being hit very fucking hard and I fight to open my door but it jams. I feel a vice-like clamp on my legs and am hoisted out of the car the same way as Kenny. A dull thud on the back of my head dizzies me and is followed by a sharp pain in my chest as the wind is booted out of me. Then it goes dark.

The Dealer 4 : Delivery

I have the bag clenched in my lap. I don't want appear fazed or uncool in front of Perry, so I act nonchalant, even though thinking about its contents makes my heart go like a jackhammer. He starts up the motor and we head on over to Ibiza Town centre to deliver it.

Parking is practically impossible, so we go round the block a few times before we eventually find a place at the foot of the walls that surround the old town. We park up, and I wait by the motor while Perry gets a ticket from the machine. He jogs back over and asks me for some change, and I put the bag down and rummage around for some shrapnel. He gets the ticket, sticks it on the dashboard and produces a pack of fags and hands one to me.

"Right bruv, this next one is a local, so don't say anything, don't look at him the wrong way. In fact, just stare at your feet. We'll be in and out inside two minutes. But I tell you something, this geezer scares the fucking shit out of me. You ever see The Wire? This guy's like The Greek. Except he's Spanish. I call him The Spic."

Imaginative chap is our Perry, who's cracking up at his feeble wit. He goes to air-punch me, and I duck out of the way. He body-checks me and shoves me along the road, nearly bowling me into two blokes. He always seems to play fight with me, does Perry. I think sometimes he might fancy me, but I have a hunch I'll live longer if I don't investigate that one any further. Or maybe it's just his way of being friendly. We head along the street and are just about to turn the corner when I feel like my stomach has been ripped out of me.

The bag.

I've fucking left it on the floor next to the motor.

I spin round and sprint the 100 meters back to the car. It's gone. I feel sick. I climb onto a small wall next to where we parked and fight the urge to vomit. I look down the road and see the two geezers Perry nearly shoved me into disappear round the corner. One of them looks like they've got the bag. Perry arrives just as I leap off the wall and peg it towards the money, the retrieval of which is the only thing that will save my life. I go round the corner and they've disappeared. I double up and puke my guts out, before straightening up and running down the middle of the road, scanning each car I pass, and trying to control the urge to lie down on the floor and cry. Just ahead of me I hear an engine start and white Ford Capri with English plates pulls out and speeds off. I spin round and head back to our car, nearly crashing into Perry who has nearly caught up with me again.

"Get back to the fucking car, those two cunts have the fucking money."

"FUCK."

We get in the car and Perry screeches backwards out of the space. We skid through the old town, bringing ourselves round to the main road – the only place the Capri could've gone from where I last saw it. The road ahead is practically empty, and there are two directions they could've gone from the next junction. One to Playa

D'en Bossa, and the other to San An. Perry is going ballistic next to me, calling me every name under the sun. I puke again. All down my front. We head straight over at the lights, heading towards PDB. As we fly over the crossing, I look down the other road and catch a glimpse of the Capri off in the distance.

"There!!! Go back. Go back. GO BACK!!! They're taking the San An road!!"

Perry executes a hand-brake turn and the car screeches round 180 degrees. Ignoring the fact it's a one-way street, Perry guns the motor back the way we came and skids left at the lights.

"What the fucking hell happened you stupid cunt?" He bellows at me.

Fuck.

"I left the bag on the floor by the car. I forgot about it when you started playing around."

"DON'T YOU FUCKING EVEN THINK ABOUT PINNING ANY OF THIS SHIT ON ME!"

"Just fucking drive. I'll get it back. No-one ever needs to know about this," I plead. "I'm fucking sorry Pez. But we can still get out of this if we keep it together."

We approach the roundabout by the casino and cross it without braking at all. The roads are mostly clear, but the junction with the PDB motorway is coming up. It's a bit of a blind spot, but that doesn't slow Perry down. I swear we get some air as we reach the crest of the hill. We hurtle past the Maison D'Elephant, and I glimpse the white Capri off in the distance.

"There! I see them!"

"Shut up you fucking idiot. I don't want to hear another fucking peep out of you," Perry snaps. Fair enough. He'll be in as much trouble as me if we don't get it back. I doubt Charlie and Eddie will differentiate between which one of us lost the bag and which one didn't.

We fly across another roundabout, gaining on the Capri, and approach Privilege and Amnesia. The superclubs flash past us in a brightly lit blur and I see the Capri taking the road that leads up to San Raf. It stops at the top of the hill and gives us the opportunity to catch up. We screech to halt behind them and I'm already out of the door before we've stopped. I'm halfway between the cars when the Capri explodes into life and flies off down the slip road on the other side of the junction. Perry's already moving when I hurl myself back into the 4x4 and we continue the chase, rejoining the motorway on the other side of the tunnel, nearly splattering into a group of clubbers walking along the hard-shoulder.

We're keeping up with the Capri, and after a couple of minutes they begin swerving all over the road. You can tell they're panicking and must have been aware of us chasing them since at least San Raf. The Capri carves all the way across to the central reservation before they lose control and it crosses back across the lanes in front of us and disappears off the road. Shit. Perry slams his foot down onto the brakes and reverses to where they came off the road.

We jump out and fall down the embankment, rolling to our feet next to their upturned motor. Perry is absolutely raging, and nearly rips the door off the passenger side as yanks it open. He drags one of the struggling occupants out and smacks him around the head a couple of times. His arms stop flailing, and his resistance stops. The driver of the car is trying desperately to open his door. I reach into the car and grip his ankles and pull him out through the passenger side. I crack him round the back of the head before Perry boots him in the chest and he passes out. I try not to laugh. The sense of relief that we've caught up with them is intoxicating.

I get on my hands and knees and crawl into the wreck to fish out the bag. It's not resting on the roof though, so I look up into the footwells to see if it's jammed under a seat. It's not. There's no sign of it. I rip the back seat forward so I can check the boot, but again draw a blank. The relief evaporates as quickly as it arrived and I feel sick again.

"It's not fucking here."

I hear the sound of Perry booting the now comatose thieves, followed by him screaming at them to tell them where the bag is. There is no response. He's too efficient. They'll not come round for a while. We frantically search the area around the car in case the bag got thrown free as they crashed down the verge. Nothing. Shit. Shit shit shit shit shit. Not good.

After about ten minutes of scrabbling around in the undergrowth, I realise the world of shit we'll be in if the Guardia stumble across this little scene. I relay this thought to Perry and we decide to get the fuck out of there. We drag the comatose pair up the embankment and shove them in the back of the 4x4. Thank fuck it's got tinted windows. We leave the hard-shoulder and turn back at the next roundabout, heading back to Charlie and Eddie's yard. I'm shitting myself, and it takes all my effort not to spray the remaining contents of my stomach all over the interior of the car. Perry breaks the silence with some carefully chosen words.

"The first thing you do is tell them this is fucking NOTHING TO DO WITH ME!!"

He punctuates the last few words by punching the steering wheel. I'm surprised it doesn't break.

"Yes. Of course I will." If I live that long.

I get my phone out of my pocket and bring up Eddie's contact. The sense of dread and impeding doom makes me push the call button very slowly. I pray that he won't answer. After three rings, he does.

"What?"

The Hens Part 4 : Cream

The queue outside the club is buzzing, bubbling and heaving, and the atmosphere is crackling with electricity. I got Sharon to give me a pill in the cab. I think she and I are the only ones taking them tonight. Keeley was very disapproving when it was brought up. I've not taken ecstasy in years – Paul would never let me. But I wouldn't want to anyway – the thought of having to deal with him on an E comedown is the best deterrent for taking drugs in existence. By the time we get to the head of the queue and hand over the exorbitant entry fee, I'm beginning to come up. My head is tingling, and the fabric of my dress against my skin feels sensual and sexy. We pass through the doors and go straight onto the terrace. It takes my breath away. It's glittery, glamorous, sparkling, sexy and fun. Exactly like I used to be. There are massive banners and mobiles hanging from the ceiling with the Cream logo and artwork on it. And there are impossibly nubile dancers on the podiums contorting themselves into all manner of positions. It looks a vision of disco heaven.

 I lead us further into the dancefloor and let the music take control of me. I dance myself into a groove and am soon in that magical place where time has no more meaning and I become part of the music. I love it. I know the E has really kicked in when I start thinking about Paul and feeling compassion. I feel sorry for him. I think it's terribly sad the way he acts, and I understand the he does it because he is a frightened little boy stuck in the body of a 29 year old man. I can tell this particular wave of euphoria has peaked when my benevolence is quickly replaced by contempt. But fuck that. I'm not having him ruining the first pilled up club experience I've had in years. Tonight is about rebirth for me. Looking forwards, not backwards. I push all thoughts of him, and all negativity, out of my mind. My determination to dance powers me through the crowd and towards the DJ booth, and I take up residence just to the left of the decks, directly in front of a massive speaker.

The Stags Part 5 : Amnesia

It takes about 15 minutes in the cab to get to Amnesia, and another 30 minutes in the queue, so by the time we get into the club we are well and truly flying on those pills. We go into the main room where some bloke called Dick Van Dyke or something is absolutely pulverising the floor with trance. When straight, trance music can be a bit hard to handle, but with the ecstasy doing its thing in my head, tonight it sounds fucking gorgeous. I feel like I'm floating on the spot, and dancing is as necessary to me as breathing. I bend my knees and stick my arse out, while my hand hammers back and forth in a huge arc to and from the floor, like I'm thrashing an imaginary whip to make it go faster. We used to call this jacking, back when all this started. I can remember dancing like this back at Shoom and Clink Street when I was a kid. For a couple of years there, I was more interested in dancing and taking E than I was about rucking and fucking. But I soon grew out of that.

    John grabs hold of me and pulls me into a bear hug, knocking me off balance and nearly sending us both flying. Silly fucker. Some people you can trust to hold themselves together when they do pills. John you most certainly cannot. He only needs to look at a pill before his legs give way and he flops like a puppet with the strings cut. His arms slide from around my neck and brush down my side. He points to the DJ booth and leads the way.

We barge on through, elbowing and pushing our way to the middle of the dancefloor. Luckily, years of practice on the terraces have made creating space in a crowd a doddle for a tight firm like us, and we claim a plum spot right night to some lovely dolly-birds. They're all tarted up like those wags you see in the papers, tits all on show, and skirts so short they're nothing more than big belts.

One of the girls is incredible. I stare at her for what seems like forever. The way she moves, the way her hair flies round her head like a propeller, the flashes of flesh her flimsy frock reveal….fuck me, she's gorgeous. I stare at her for the time it takes to smoke a cigarette. I zone back in and realise that, from their body language and the looks on their faces, a couple of her mates are less than impressed with the presence of six burley bits of rough bopping away next to them. Fuck 'em. The beautiful one smiles meekly at me and looks away, all shy and coy. She loves me. I can tell from the smile. I know I'm on ecstasy, but there's definitely something there. I'd feel it if I was sober. All I need to know is in that smile. We're onto something here, me and her.

I take a break from dancing and run my hands through my hair. Its short crop springs back up after my fingers pass, emitting a fine spray of sweat that no-one else would notice, but in my heightened state feels like a cool shower on my face.

The girl has turned a bit away from me, and I feel like the moment has passed. The intensity and the intimacy of the look we shared has gone, and now I feel embarrassed and rejected as I notice her smiling at someone else. Fucking cow. The realisation that love, and therefore a shag, has passed me by brings me crashing down. I still feel fucked, but the happy, benevolent, warm feeling that filled me before has gone, and has been replaced by something altogether more sinister. The girl is now facing fully away from me, dancing with some other bloke. My cheeks flush, and I want to kill him. I control my breathing and make a drinky-drink motion with my hands to the others to let know I'm going to the bar. I get the thumbs up from a grinning Graham, while Jimmy points at the floor to indicate where he'll be on my return. The twins nod in unison, and one of them leans into my ear and half gobs/half shouts:

"We'll come with you, mate."

We bundle our way back through the hordes of sunburnt, sweaty kids and head to the bar at the side, passing under a massive air conditioning unit. I stand beneath it and cock my head up, checking out the balconies surrounding the dancefloor, and slowly rotate 360 degrees, taking in the spectacle. I can feel another rush coming on, and the gnawing pain that bird caused evaporates. The hairs on the back of my neck prickle and an overwhelming sense of contentment wells up from my stomach. I fucking love feeling like this.

The twins guide me towards the bar, and we start ordering drinks. I lean back against the bar and stretch, feeling an almost orgasmic ripple run through me. I am aware of someone tugging my sleeve, and turn to see one of the twins holding a drink in front of me.

I reach out to grab it, and it promptly falls through my outstretched mitt and hits the floor with a crash.

"You stupid southern cunt. That cost 14 Euros!", the twin laughs at me. I jam my hand in my pocket and give him a fistful of notes.

"Will that cover it, you northern monkey?"

He looks at me funny, like he's deciding whether or not I'm insulting him. For the record, I am a little. His face cracks into a smile and he pockets the cash. He fishes out a baggie and scoops a bump of chang out on the end of a key, and sticks it under my nose. I delicately move my face towards it and hoof it up a nostril. It has the desired effect of straightening me out a little, and my ear pops with the intensity of the snort. I tilt my head back and let the gear trickle down my throat. I bring my head down and my focus sharpens and it looks like the twins are having a bit of argy bargy with some lads. One of them, I think it's Frank, chins this massive body builder. I'm steaming in when, out of the corner of my eye, I see some rapid movement towards us. Before I realise what's happening, three bouncers have bundled me through a side door into a storeroom, with another four bringing the twins in behind me. We are shoved up against the wall, with our legs splayed uncomfortably apart. It takes two bouncers apiece to hold us there. We're all struggling and fighting against it, but they hold they have on us is like one of them fucking kung-fu grips and it's impossible to move against. One of the spare security bods roughly rummages through my pockets, helping himself to my cash. He then repeats the move on the mancs, before the smallest bouncer dispenses a couple of digs to our kidneys and then cracks one of the twins round the head with his walkie-talkie. They use me as a ram to open the fire-exit door, and I get a boot in the arse to help me on my way.

The door slams behind us. My ears adjust to the change in volume and I hear a near-silent hiss, accompanied by the dull, throbbing thud of the bass drum bleeding out of the club. "What the fuck? How come they were so fast?" The one I think is Frank says, confused.

"I think they saw me giving laughing boy here a bump at the bar," his brother replies.

I'm shocked. And more than a little gutted. The speed of our ejection from the club has made my head spin. From start to finish – from the first push from Frank to now – was less than a two minutes.

"Bastards. I was really fucking enjoying that in there." I moan. I was rushing like a bastard, and now I'm totally deflated. Anger and resentment start rampaging through my gut. First it's directed at the club itself, the massive building in front of me, the bouncers, everyone inside, everyone associated with it. I want to burn it down – I blame it for ruining my night. After a few seconds, I remember to breathe, and I feel my rage being directed towards the twin twats from Manchester. Fucking idiots. It was one of them waving around gear at the bar that alerted them, and then the other one smacking that muscle-Mary that sealed the deal.

"Fuck. They took all my fucking money." I say through gritted teeth.

"Yeah, same here. And they took my fucking blow." Whines one of them.

"Me too." Grunts the other.

Yeah, well at least they didn't get my stash. And there's no way I'm telling these pricks I've still got gear. They're the reason I'm walking home now, and they can fuck off if they think they're sharing any of my drugs.

"Yeah, mine as well. Let's go back to San An and go boozing up the West End. There'll be a cashpoint there anyway. We better start walking."

There is a nasty vibe between us. I don't like this pair, and I'm generally not very good at hiding my feelings. An air of malevolence descends over us as we start trudging up the hard shoulder back towards San An. In spite of the dark atmosphere between us, I'm still pilled up and feel compelled to chat shit. I'm stuck with this pair of cunts. So I start making conversation.

"John-o tells me you met in Belmarsh."

"John-o's got a big fucking mouth." One of them curtly replies.

"Calm down. What's your fucking problem?" I challenge.

"You ask a lot of questions. Why don't you mind your own fucking business?" the other one chips in.

What a pair of wankers. We press on in silence, hugging the side of the motorway. We get to a big tunnel, and climb the slip road next to it, passing a load of shops, which are all shut. This annoys me even more, because I've got a thirst on and I'm spitting feathers.

We carry on, re-joining the motorway after the tunnel, almost getting run over as a filthy white Ford Capri screeches past us coming down the slip road. It's followed quickly by a slick BMW 4x4 with tinted windows, causing us to scramble up the embankment through fear of getting run over.

"Wankers!"

"Cunts!"

"I hope you fucking crash you spastics."

It's probably fair to say the drivers of the cars are a convenient target for our anger at those fuckers at Amnesia. This ejaculation of swearing helps ferment the foul atmosphere between me and the twins, and fuels the dark cloud that hangs over us. The buzz of the E has run right down, a combination of our unceremonious ejection from the club, and general fatigue. I'm feeling increasingly uncomfortable in the presence of these two arseholes, and I can't wait until I can shake them off and hole up in my room at the hotel and bosh the rest of my gear on my jacks. We walk on for another 10 minutes and pass up and over a small hill, and the 4x4 that nearly killed us before speeds back the other way. One of the twins bellows more insults at its receding rear window, while the other jumps up and down like a gorilla.

The sky is getting lighter and we must be at least four or five miles from San Antonio still. What a fucking ball ache. As we descend down towards San An bay, I notice some skid marks disappearing off the road into the bushes.

Fuck. This doesn't look too good. The last thing I want to deal with or even see in my current state is some stupid cunt all mangled up in the wreckage of his holiday hire car. I point them out to Tweedlecunt and Tweedletwat and pick up the pace a bit. I stride up to the point where the undergrowth is flattened and the fence posts have been smashed into kindling. We all stand dead still as we survey the wreckage of the filthy Ford Capri. It's lying on its back, some mechanical turtle, with water and oil and all manner of fluids belching out from under the bonnet.

"Oops," laughs one of the twins. "That's no way to treat a Capri. They're classic cars, don't you know."

"Shall we call them an ambulance?" It's the only thing I can think to say.

"Nah, fuck 'em. They were driving like cunts before, so they deserve it. Let's have a look in there, though, they might have something worth taking."

I slide down the bank, the soft sand giving way and carrying me smoothly to the foot of the verge. I approach the driver side door in a half crouch, like a commando. If they're properly fucked up, I'm gonna call them an ambulance, regardless of what these twats say.

"You alright?"

Nothing. One of the twins reaches the passenger door, which is wide open, and looks in. He looks surprised. I get on my knees and peer inside the car. It's empty. Nobody's home. All I see is the gormless face of the twin looking back at me from the other side of the car.

"What the fuck?"

"Maybe they got flung out of the motor?" I say, realising as the words leave my mouth that I'm sounding like a fuckwit and an amateur.

"Ere, Frank. Come and have a look at this." Ashley says to his brother. I walk round the car, and see him pointing to something on the floor. There are two sets of parallel lines in the earth that lead back up to the road. Each line is about the width of someone's heel. I think about the 4x4, the chase, and come to the obvious conclusion. Frank laughs out loud and puts on a pirates voice.

"Ah ha. Looks like there's been some sort of villainy going on here. I wouldn't like to be in their shoes."

"Yeah, let's do one. There's fuck all here except coppers and questions." Ashley says as he mindlessly boots the only remaining window in.

We all walk away from the crash and head through the undergrowth to motorway, avoiding climbing back up the verge. As I swashbuckle through the dense foliage, I breathe a sigh of relief that we didn't come across some poor cunt with their brains spread all over the place. The fate of the occupants of the Capri is probably not too good. But fuck it – it's nothing to do with me, and it's best to stay that way. And it does. Right up until the point I stub my foot on the green duffel bag, lying hidden in the undergrowth at the side of the road.

The Reps Part 5 : Reckoning

There's a problem with the sound system. It sounds like Grainger's stuck on that fucking atrocious record that came out when mobile phones were in their infancy. That one that samples the interference bip-biddy-bip-bip-bip noise you get when you put a mobile near a stereo. Er, not on my watch. But Grainger would never play anything like that. His taste in music is far too good. I head over to the decks to find out what's going on. There is a girl sat on the floor of the DJ booth. She looks happy, if a little drunk. I step over her and am greeted with a confused looking Grainger.

"Sean, er, what's going on with the speakers? I'm not playing that!"

I nod, and start rummaging around the back of the decks, following the wires from the mixer round the back to the floor where the amp is resting on an upturned flight case. And right next to the amp, resting on the dirt is the reason for the interference – an iPhone. My fucking iPhone. Thank fucking God for that! My relief is short-lived though when I see the volume of missed calls and texts from Amy. Fucking hell. I look at the most recent text and it makes my stomach churn.

"If you don't get back to me immediately, you're FUCKING SACKED."

It was sent half an hour ago. Shit. That's not too good. She surely can't? Not when she sees the amount of cash I've made. I hope.

Still, it doesn't make for happy reading. A pang of guilt skewers me. Fuck. I know I've made a fucking packet, but I also know I've gone well beyond my remit with today's do. I just hope a profit close to five figures is enough to appease them. Whatever happens, I'm in for a bollocking at the very least. I hope she doesn't give me a slap. That would be the height of embarrassment. Fuck it. What's done is done. Not much I can do about it now. I switch my phone off and stick it in the side pocket of my combat shorts, the one with a zip. Jody emerges from the crowd with his phone in his hand.

"Joe's here with the beer, my man."

"Wicked. Let's grab Sweeney to help carry it and get it to the bar."

"Yeah cool. He's brought Laura and Kirstie with him."

Wicked. Reinforcements! I bounce through the trees to where the van is, grabbing Sweeney on the way. Joe opens up the back door and we are greeted with a wall made of 50 more cases of San Miguel. Perched on top of this beery throne are Laura and Kirstie. Sweet.

"Sean. That's a lot of fucking beer. Did they chuck in the girls as part of a promotion?" Sweeney quips. He picks up four cases and starts marching them back to the bar. It takes us a few trips, but we get them all behind the bar and into the bins just before the last of the original batch get pulled out of the ice. Fuck me, they are thirsty tonight.

I go over to the DJ booth where Kirstie and Laura have installed themselves. Kirstie has already stripped to her bikini and is dancing behind the decks with Grainger. She has her towel tied around her neck again. Like a cape, of course. Laura is jacking and grinding away, bumping her arse up against the other DJ's bum. It makes for quite a sight. Kirstie clocks me and grabs Laura by the wrist and they stumble over. She shouts in my ear.

"Fucking brilliant party Sean! Amy was not a happy bunny though. She's been like a super-secret sleuth today. I nearly made her a cape," she says, as she swigs from a two litre bottle of Fanta limon, which I suspect is more vodka than pop. "But I didn't. She's become such a killjoy this season. She isn't worthy of a cape."

"I wouldn't want to be in your shoes when Amy catches up with you," Laura chips in, peering over her sunglasses mischievously. I smile sarcastically and go off to find Joe and weigh him out some cash for driving up with the beer. He's chatting to Nicola at the bar. I go over and hold my hand up at him and rub my thumb and fingers together in the universal gesture of 'we have money matters to discuss.' I grab a couple of the older, colder beers and we stroll some of the way back to where he's parked the van, and take a seat under a tree. I take my top off, and remove my money belt, which by now is bulging. I peel off a hundred from the wad for Joe's trouble. He tells me to fuck off, and gives it straight back. As I said, he's a total fucking dude. There's no way he'd accept cash for helping a mate out. I know this, but I also know his flatmate, so I'll give him the money to stash in Joe's room for him to discover at a later date.

It's considerably calmer back here, and after the hectic day I've had, I think I'm entitled to have a breather for ten minutes. Joe's cracked open both the beers and hands one over as he raises the other towards me. We chink them together and both drain more than half our bottles in the first gulp.

"Well, mate, I'd say this is a resounding success," Joe says. "You should pat yourself on the back Sean. Amy should be fucking pleased with you. And she probably will be once she gets through kicking your arse all over San Antonio."

"Oh don't mate. I'm shitting it about that now. I found my phone, and aside from the 20 plus missed calls, the texts were pretty fucking harsh. The last one basically told me I'm fired."

"Mate, you're in for a bollocking definitely, but she won't fire you. You've made too much money for that.'"

"Yeah, I hope so."

He pulls a little baggie out of his sock and fishes out a swirl. He snaps it in two and presses half into my palm.

"Come on, I've got this left over from last night. I think you need to pop half and go and enjoy this wicked shindig you've created."

I eye the chalky white E and a little rush of excitement shoots up from my belly. Fuck it, why not? I might as well enjoy myself, regardless of the bollocking I'm in for.

"Cheers, bub," I say as I throw the pill into my mouth and wash it down with the rest of my beer.

"So what's the plan for the rest of the party then?"

"Well, we're getting picked up in a bit by the boat, and then going to head back to San An. And I've got about five workers coming up here in the morning – I'm bunging them 50 euros each to clear up the mess. Jody's going to take the decks back to the hotel in the motor tonight, and then we're both coming back here tomorrow morning to finish clearing up and make sure everything is as it was when we got here. But not before I get absolutely battered tonight. I think I've earned it!"

"You think you earn it every time you get out of bed, Sean!"

Our beers are spent, so we get up and head back towards the party. Everything seems to be going OK. The music is good, the bar is fully stocked, and everyone seems to be having a whale of a time. I think I feel the half an E fluttering away in my stomach, but know that it's probably 90% psychosomatic, seeing it only entered my mouth a few minutes ago. I leave Joe at the bar and circumnavigate the bowl, soaking up the party vibes and trying to push thoughts of the coming confrontation with Amy out of my head. I get to the crest of the hill directly opposite the bar and stand there, looking at the party playing out in front of me.

I see all the people having an amazing time. I see some of my best friends amongst them. They're grinning like Cheshire cats. The boss is going to be over the moon with me. She has to be, surely. Everything's come together. I feel elated. I know there will be few moments in life where I will feel like this and I let the positive energy flood through my body. It electrifies me. I'm living the dream. It's only temporary, my life here on the island, but its intensity will stay with me permanently. I know that as life goes on, triumphant moments like this will become fewer and farther between. Sure, there'll be other amazing moments, like getting married and having kids, stuff like that, but nothing as explosively ecstatic as this. I imagine this is a tiny bit what playing in the World Cup Final must be like. I feel lighter than air. I almost shed a tear. But you know what, fuck it, I'm 21 years old. I can carry this on for a few more years yet. And I'm fucking glad I can appreciate this for what it is now, and that I don't take it for granted.

    I stroll out to the centre of the clearing and slowly turn around in a circle and breathe it in. I see Jody up by the bar waving at me and gesticulating like a mad preacher. Or maybe it's just the way he's dancing. I wave back at him, just as a gap in the crowd opens up and I see Amy storming towards me. She looks possessed. I brace myself as she gets to within a couple of feet of me. She raises her arms as if to throttle me and I close my eyes. I feel her hands clamp the side of my head, just before fear gives way to total shock. Fucking hell. I did not see *that* coming.

The Resort Manager 5 : Caught In The Act

I peg it across the road to where the captain of the *Erebus* is tying up. He's an old ex-pat Yank I know from last year – we did a few boat parties with him last season.

"Hi Captain Hicks, how's it going?" I say. Nonchalantly, I follow up with: "Did you get Sean to his party OK? I've been held up all bloody day, and I got here just as you guys were chugging out of the harbour."

"Hey Amy, yeah I dropped them off alright. I'm just going for some dinner before I go and pick them up again in a bit."

Really. How interesting.

"Are you now. Brilliant. Tell you what, how about I bung you an extra hundred and we head back now – I want to see how it's going." I think about layering it on a bit more. "If it's going well, we might do a few more and that's more money for you isn't it! Haha."

He takes the bait.

"Yeah alright, you're the boss. Sean's paid for the boat for five hours, so whatever you want."

"Wicked."

He unties the rope he's holding and chucks it back onto the boat. Within five minutes we're heading out of the harbour again, taking a course towards Benirras. I take up a position on the bow, and spread out on the deck. The fine spray from the sea lands on me and it cools me down considerably. As we leave the port behind, it gets very dark very quickly, but I find the blackness calming. For a moment, I feel fucking amazing and remember what I loved about this island. Soon enough, we round a headland and approach a cliff. We begin to slow, heading towards an opening in the rocks at the back of a little cove. We come to rest by a little jetty in a cavern, mostly hidden from view from the main cove. It's lit up with blinking fairy lights and it looks magical. The boat's engine stops and I hear music off in the distance. Captain Hicks jumps onto the jetty and begins to tie up the boat. I disembark and take it in as I head towards some stairs that disappear into the rock. Flaming torches line the side of the path and lead the way into and up into a tunnel.

The music gets louder as I approach the back of the cave, the thump of the bass drum and the hubbub of the party is amplified by the cavern. It acts as a fuck off big speaker, and I can't even see the crowd, as it's all quite a way off. The torches lining the path make it look almost Glastonbury-esque. I follow the stone path to a wooden stairway that leads into the tunnel in the rocks. The beat of the drum gets louder as I ascend and soon darkness envelops me and I disappear into the tunnel. After a moment, my eyes adjust and I see an opening not far ahead. It opens out into a tree-lined clearing that resembles a bowl. It's bathed in light from more torches, fairy lights and some kind of rig that I think they have borrowed from the hotel. Any visible sky is completely black, with a smattering of starry pinpricks, and it's all framed by gorgeous green trees. It looks stunning. There is a shack resting atop the other side of the bowl with a soundsystem outside. The DJ is throwing out some wicked thumping tribal and techy beats that wouldn't sound out of place in Goa, and the crowd are loving it. There are fucking tons of people here. At least 150. There are girls on wooden podiums, stark-bollock naked and gyrating like porno-spinning-tops, as well as fire-eaters and stilt-walkers. It looks like the last days of Rome.

I'm shocked and flabbergasted. It's actually dazed me a little; the sensory overload, the epic scale of this little rave. It looks like the pictures I've seen of Ibiza back in the 1980s and 90s. Open air clubbing is something else. I'm so taken in by it all that I walk straight into Jody. He jumps out of his skin when he sees it's me.

"Amy. Fuck. Er. Hi. How you doing?"

"I've had a long day, Jody. How are you? Good? I think we should have a little chat about this." I turn and head back to the relative quiet of the stairway back to the dock. I get to the top of the stairs and let him go down first, giving me the higher ground. We get down to the jetty, but I stay on the second step, so I'm just above eye level with him.

"Start talking."

"Sean's made over ten grand for the company. He lost his phone, and only just found it. He hasn't been blanking you." He splutters.

Ten grand.

"Can you say that first bit again? I don't think I heard you correctly."

"He's made over ten grand. At least. For the company. For you."

I breathe out slowly, and try to suppress a giggle. I fail.

"Yeah, I know. Mental, isn't it? Is Sean going to get sacked for this then? Am I?"

I look at him. As if. I think a little bollocking is in order, and I'm going to tear Sean a new arsehole when we get back to the office, but there's no arguing with ten grand profit. The bosses will forget nearly everything if Sean is pulling that in on top of what he's already bringing in.

"I don't know about that, Jody, he's disobeyed direct orders, but fucking hell, ten large? Really? You're not guestimating?"

"Amy, I'm not bullshitting you. We've flogged about two vanloads of booze, on top of the tickets. Sean's actually shitting himself at all the cash he's carrying with him. But it's amazing. Come and see."

We head back up the stairs.

"Look around you. How fucking cool is this? We've got a ton of guests here, loads of workers, loads of people from outside the hotel. Everyone is taking pictures - we're going to stick them all online. It's all legit as well. Can you imagine the credibility and good PR this is doing for the company?"

I can't argue with him. It's brilliant. I can't help but feel a little turned on by all this. It makes me want to chuck an E down my throat and get involved. I turn to Jody and give him a massive hug. He tenses for a moment before I feel him relax and he picks me up and spins me round. We break off our embrace and he smiles at me.

"Good to have you back, Amy. Go and say hello to Sean." He motions over to where I can see Sean. I leave him and push my way through the crowd, a swirling mass of sweaty and ecstatic ravers, all having the time of their lives. A space clears and I see Sean. He clocks me and looks aghast, and as I get closer, I see fear in his eyes. I grab him by the head and plant the biggest kiss on his lips. I always liked this kid. He looks utterly shocked, and I am a bit. We both get caught up in the moment, and I swear we nearly snog, but we move away from each other and he leads me up to the bar, and grabs a couple of tins from a big dustbin. They're ice cold. We crack them open and a bit of froth erupts from each can. We crash them together and take a big swig. We make eye contact as we bring the beers down from our mouths, and it feels brilliant. It feels like it did last summer. It feels like we're friends again. I crack a big smile, just as I feel some arms drape something across my shoulders. Kirstie appears in front of me and ties two ends of a towel together around my neck, giving me a makeshift cape. She grins at me and gives me a big, pilled up cuddle. It feels great. I think I just fell a little bit back in love with this place.

The Shop Girl Part 3 : Gunfight At The OK Corrall

It's nearly half past two when we get to the West End and it's rammed. We circumnavigate the main strip and head down the side of the Ship, taking a right at Subway. Starkey wants to go in and get one, but the queue is out the door. I don't know how she can even think about food so soon after doing a line. Strange girl. We carry on past and head over the street to the bar. It looks like we're the first ones there.

"Shall we go upstairs?" I suggest to the girls.

"No stairs. Only chairs!" Lucy slurs as she drags a couple of empty seats around the table just outside. I love this girl, everything that comes out of her mouth is gold, especially when she's getting on it. We scoop a few more chairs over for when the others get here and I order a jug of sangria to quench the unbelievable thirst I've got. A bloke over by another table gives me the eye. He's wearing no top, is incredibly ripped, but his eyes look totally vacant. Same old story! Oh well, I'm not going to judge him on appearances. He might have something interesting to say. Maybe I'll say hello to him in a bit.

But first things first. The sangria is plonked on the table in front of us and I pour us out three glasses. We chink our glasses and take a large slurp each, just as Ryan and Jordan arrive. They're even more shitfaced than we are, and bundle over each other to take the remaining seats, even though there are enough chairs for everyone. They look like they're in a proper mischievous mood.

We get another pitcher of sangria in and Starkey points out the bloke who was giving me the eye.

"I think you might have a fan over there. Now all we need to do is find me one. Talking of fans, look who's here."

I look up and see Matt weaving through the crowd. His arrival is greeted with cheers. Ryan makes a smart-arse comment about him fleecing the tourists, and he laughs. A space opens up next to me and he sits down and flashes me a grin that makes me feel warm and cosy and safe. I smile back and ask him how his night has gone. He's had a good one, and I feel happy for him. I go back to talking to Starkey as he pours himself a drink and starts chatting to the boys. I notice he's got a bit of fag ash or some crud on his shirt, so I reach over and pinch it off him. I also refill his drink as it's empty. I'm so glad he's here. In spite of everyone's loaded comments today, I'm always pleased to see him – after all, we're fucking good mates. I'd feel like this about any of my best friends when I saw them. Wouldn't I?

The conversation between me and Starkey has shifted its focus to my lack of man. I swear I see Matt bristle when I bemoan the fact that I'm single, but I'm not sure. I think Nat's comment earlier has made me a little over-sensitive about it all. And when Matt asks me if there's anyone I like, it makes me think maybe it's all bollocks. I offhandedly say that the boy that was eyeing me up earlier is ok, and Matt prompts me to go and talk to him. Well, why would he be trying to set me up with someone else if there was anything between us? Exactly. We're mates. That's it. I still don't really fancy going over to talk to him though, so I stall by saying I'll have a cigarette first. As I reach for the packet, Matt grabs them and chucks them in his pint glass.

"What the fuck are you doing?"

"Well, now we've got no fags. You're going to have to go and ask him for one."

He then stands up and pulls me out of my chair, before manoeuvring me in the direction of the boy.

"Make sure you bring me one back too."

I go over to the guy, feeling a little despondent that Matt seemed so eager to get rid of me. I ask him for a cigarette. He gives me one. Upon closer inspection, I think he worked for Bar M last year – I saw him knocking around with Jody and Sean. He tells me his name and I immediately forget it. He asks me mine, makes the-oh-so-original Montana comment, and thus begins his clumsy attempt at wooing me. He will be called Himbo forthwith. We chat shit for a minute, he seems harmless enough, if a bit full of it. But he's also incredibly fit. He says he's heading off to Sean's party in the country in a minute, and asks me if I'd like to join him. I'm not that bothered either way, and was hoping to go with Matt, but I suppose there'll be time to hang with him once we are there. I mull this over and tell the Himbo to hang on a sec, and I head back to Matt and the others. Part of me screams out to say something to Matt about rescuing me from the brain-vacuum of a boy, but I decide against it and just say I'll meet them there later.

The PR Part 2 : Casting A Line

The rest of my shift passes pretty quickly – I drag more than 70 people into the bar, making for a very financially lucrative evening. I'm easily the best PR they have here, and that affords me a lot of leeway. Like being able to fuck off early occasionally, like tonight. I head into the bar just before 3, and find Don arguing with a couple of the other PRs. I butt in. I've done well enough tonight to be able to leave my manners outside.

"Right Don, I've filled this place and now I'm fucking off. I'll see you tomorrow night."

"Cheers Matt. Good work. I've got something for you."

And with that, he pulls out his wad of cash, and gives me a couple of 20s.

"That's a bonus. You've done fucking well this week." He turns back to the other PRs. "Why can't you useless cunts be more like him?"

What a prick. It's not fair to talk to them like that, and it's certainly not fair to use me as a bludgeoning tool to make them feel small. They've only started this week as well, replacing the previous fuckwitted PRs Don hired purely because he fancied them. I go outside and wait for the two PRs to come out. I give them a twenty each.

"Sorry about that – don't listen to Don. He's a fucking prick. You guys are doing OK."

They thank me. They're on their first season, these two, and they're trying their best. I was shit the first time out. It wasn't until my third year that I got really shit hot. Don should lay off them. There are better ways to inspire people than treating them like shit and scaring them. I leave them to it and head over to meet everyone else at the OK Corral, where they've colonised the big table out the front. She's there. As soon as I clock her, all the air rushes out of my chest. Every time I see her, my heart lurches, goes thud, and then explodes inside my chest and fills my entire body with euphoria. She's like an E, but without the gurning. But she's my best mate. And I love her. And she's oblivious to that. Well, either oblivious, or she's too polite to say anything to me. And I'm too scared to say anything to her.

It's doing my nut in. When I'm with her, I feel I don't have to put anything on. Not literally, obviously, but in terms of pretence. I can be me. I'm no shrinking violet, don't get me wrong, but I don't have the confidence to *really* be myself – I adjust to fit in. Like you do. Like everyone does. But when she's there, I feel like I have the strength and confidence to be the best me that I can be. She makes me feel 10 feet tall.

I push the thoughts to the back of my mind. The other day, I accepted that the feeling isn't going to be reciprocated. It put me on a right downer and I spent the rest of the night moping around like someone had died. Everyone was asking me what was wrong, and Hannah was really nice about it, not too intrusive, but obviously I didn't tell her why I had the hump that day. I just explained my foul mood away on mid-season blues and too many pills. And thank fuck I managed not to listen to the stupid voice in my head telling me to give the game away.

I stop short of the bar to pull myself together.

I take in a deep breath, steel myself and shake off any melancholia. After all, I'm about to go out and have a wicked time with people I love, so all will be well. I head round the corner to the OK Corral, and my arrival is greeted with a heart-warming cheer. They're all there: Ryan, Jordan, Lucy, Starkey….and her.

"Yay! So you've finished bullying holiday-makers into buying shit, watered-down drinks then?" Ryan says.

"Aye, got more than 70 of them in tonight. I'm on fucking fire." I boast.

I go round the table, kissing, fist-bumping and greeting everyone. I fucking love it. All the people I love in the same place, all looking forward to a great night. Without direction, or anyone saying anything, chairs are shuffled and dragged and a space opens up next to her and a chair is pinched from an adjacent table. I plonk myself down next to her. She grins and I melt.

"Hello, my love. How was your night?" She asks me. I glow inside.

I tell her I had a good night, made some cash, but now is when the night really starts for me. I feel like the King of the Fucking World sat next to her. That's the effect she has on me. Starkey leans over and they pick up on a conversation they were having before, about finding Starkey a good man. I light a fag and enjoy the warm, loved up sensation that covers me. There's a jug of sangria on the table, and an empty glass, so I half fill it and neck it in one. It tastes great, as the first drink after work always does.

I feel a delicate touch on my shoulder, and turn to see Hannah picking some ash off my t-shirt. She says nothing. She's mid-conversation with Starkey, but she also re-fills my drink for me, almost absent-mindedly. There's an unspoken intimacy between us which makes my insides feel liquid. Jordan gets up to get some drinks and asks who wants what. He returns moments later with a tray of pints, having ignored what everyone asked for. He smiles and says when it's someone else's round, they can have expensive drinks, but for now, it's pints all round. We all laugh, and graciously accept our jars.

I turn my attention back to Hannah's conversation with Starkey. Now she's complaining about not having a boyfriend. The urge to jump up and shout "I would LOVE to be your boyfriend" is very strong, so I just grip my pint as if my life depended on it and pour the beer into my mouth to stop the words on the tip of my tongue escaping. I can't let the cat out of the bag. It would ruin everything. So, instead, I ask her if there's anyone she fancies. I immediately regret saying it. Why the fuck would I want to know if there's anyone she fancies, unless it's me?

"Yeah, well, that boy over there is pretty hot."

"Well, if you like him, you should say something. Go on, seize the day and all that," I say, dying a little bit inside. Why don't I take my own fucking advice?

"Nah, I can't do that." She blushes, and my stomach spasms as I think how absolutely fucking gorgeous she is. I swallow hard and carry on encouraging her.

"Go on, don't be shy. Go and say hello."

"I'll have a fag first."

"No you won't."

I swiftly grab the pack of fags off the table and immerse them in my pint.

"What the fuck are you doing?"

"Well, now we've got no fags. You're going to have to go and ask him for one."

And with that, I stand up, grab her arm and pull her out of the chair. I gently shove her in the back in his general direction. All the while, my insides are shredding. In my haste to do the right thing, and set up a smokescreen for my own feelings, I've taken a course that is going to do nothing but break my heart. I am such a fuckwit.

"Make sure you bring me one back too."

She goes over to him and asks him for a fag. I feel sick, and it's taking a herculean effort to stop my eyes from leaking. I try and take some comfort from the fact that I'm being completely selfless. Maybe doing the right thing and holding it down when every sinew in my body is screaming at me to do the opposite will empower me. Hmm, chinny reckon. I can feel the smile on my face slipping, and find myself frowning. Luckily, no-one notices and I manage to stick my poker face on.

Starkey has been watching what's been going on and shuffles into Hannah's seat.

"What's up with you then? Not like you to be a grumpyguts, especially when I know you've got a pocketful of pills!"

"Nothing. I'm cool baby." I say with forced jollity.

"As I said before, I'm not stupid. And I'm not going to go into specifics, but this is something you need to deal with. And not by doing what you just did, you spacca. I see all. You should know that."

Hannah comes back over and reaches over to grab her bag. She looks at me for a second, and I swear I can see something in her eyes, and she goes to say something, but then thinks better of it.

"I'm gonna head over to the party with this guy. I'll meet you all there, yeah?!"

I feel a huge tear in my chest, going from my throat to my belly. I believe it to be my heart breaking. I go completely the other way in what I say though.

"Go get him, tiger!" And with that, she skips off to her new beau, some muscle-ridden twat who looks great, but probably has fuck-all going on upstairs. Anyone who pays that much attention to their physique has obviously been neglecting their mind.

As they go out of sight, I let out the biggest sigh and feel absolutely shite.

The Journalist Part 4 : West End Girls

We don't need to fuck around here too much, thank God. We got enough down the beach to satisfy the carnal cravings of our picture editor, so a few crowd shots will suffice. We push our way up into the heart of the West End. Hordes of lobster-pink 18-30 year old kids are swarming round us, desperate to keep up with their organised bar crawls and the prospect of getting a knee trembler off one of their fellow package holiday makers. It makes me feel old. Giles fires off shots all over the main drag, getting everything from every angle. Half way up the hill we stop outside Tropicanas and I go and get us more booze. I bring out two pints of vodka Red Bull and set them down, suggesting we have a little dab of the MDMA. So we do. We have a couple more pints and watch the night unfold, and have another dab before the din becomes a bit much and we get the fuck outta there to go and rendezvous with Kevin at the club. We go off down the side street and take a bearing towards the sea-front. We pass an alleyway that is crawling with police, and see someone getting loaded into an ambulance. We pick up our pace. San An can be a rough place.

    It's only a five minute walk to the club, and we get there just in time to see Kevin stumbling out of a cab with a bird in tow. One of the Big Brother birds. Ah ha. Right, I get it. I understand. It would appear I underestimated you, Kevin. My apologies. I can hear his seduction line now.... "I'll get you on the cover, darling...." Ugh. The thought of it makes my skin crawl.

He introduces us to the girl, who is cordial enough. We head to the front of the guest-list queue, where Kevin stands on tip-toes, peering over the top of the clipboard girl and waving for the attention of another girl who looks more senior. She sees him and comes forward and out to greet us. She's the promoter of the night, and is in charge of the whole thing. She dishes out a load of gold wristbands and takes us through a side door into an office. She leads us through the bowels of the club and we eventually emerge on a balcony that overlooks the dancefloor and is adjacent to the DJ booth. This is the VVIP. There are bottles of booze all ready on the tables, all comped. Nice. The other inhabitants are a couple of big name DJs and the other Big Brother housemate, and a couple of PR types, fussing and clucking over them. They're acting like they're looking after Hollywood A-listers, not some filler from a reality show. The PRs come over and introduce everyone, and tell us we can do the interview in the dressing room as soon as they come off stage, but right now they've got to go and get ready, and they take them off somewhere. Get ready for what, I wonder. What exactly is their turn going to be tonight? What are they going to perform? Some form of Avant Garde expressive dance? Some juggling? Capoeira?

I grab a drink from the table and go the edge of the balcony and rest against it, surveying the crowd. The music is the worst kind of housified chart twaddle, and even the tingle of the MDMA kicking in doesn't make it any the less offensive. I get handed another shot of hierbas by Giles. He's reeling, but still snapping away like a crocodile. One of the PRs comes back to join us and invites us to take a seat in a booth overlooking the stage.

The music fades out and the DJ gets on the mic, spouting the usual clichés about making some noise and giving a mahoosive (his word not mine) San An welcome to Julia and Georgina off Big Brother. The crowd hoots and hollers, and the two girls come out to a dodgy house remix of Hot Chocolate's "You Sexy Thing". Jesus wept. The DJ spits out some inane questions – what do they think of Ibiza, how long are they here for, what are their plans (they're releasing a single, do you know? Do you care?). The whole scene is fucking diabolical.

The DJ thanks them, calls for a cheer, and goes back to playing bad music, while the girls throw out a load of T-shirts. After the T-shirts run out, they stand around gawping and looking unsure as to what to do next. One of the PR girls runs on and shepherds them off the stage. The one who's babysitting me and Giles gets up and leads us off the balcony towards the dressing room.

"What a great show. I'm really glad you saw it." She purrs in the most sickly-sweet voice imaginable.

"Yeah, wasn't it?" What fucking show? They threw some T-shirts out and screamed into a microphone.

"Oh yeah, there's a couple of things you can't mention when you speak to Julia. Don't ask about the incident at the night-club, or the rumours concerning her and the footballer."

The ruck at the club happened earlier in the week, and was all over the gossip pages. Apparently she Tweedied the cloakroom attendant at Boujis. You couldn't make this shit up. As for the footballer, this is the first I've heard of it. Funny, telling a journo that. Call me cynical, but she wouldn't be planting a story would she?

"Of course. Remind me again what footballer I shouldn't talk about."

She half whispers the name of a high-profile premiership player, a notorious swordsman, and I nod sagely. This is so see-through, it's funny. Wise move on her part being linked to him, but it's just another example of the bullshit that mires this industry. I doubt they've even met yet – his club has been on a post-season tour of the Far East for the last week. Priceless.

I'm ushered into a store-room that is doubling as a dressing room. The two girls are there, being fussed over by their people, the handlers and hangers-on that their entourage consists of. There's a small table there that the PR clears, and the room is emptied, save for the girls and a couple of their press people.

"Right then. Fire away." The press officer says, before prompting the girls herself. "Why don't you tell him how much you enjoyed the show."

The girls look out of place. They've been "famous" and in the real world for less than a week. One of them is like a rabbit in some headlights, frozen, bewildered and startled. The other one has a gob and is spouting all manner of drivel, trying to sound intelligent but just using long words in the wrong places. I think she's called Julia. The fake sincerity and way she speaks with a forced determination makes me think of how Geri Halliwell would act on the celebrity version of The Apprentice. Wow, this MDMA is good. Yes, Sir Alan.

"So, did you enjoy being on stage chucking out T-shirts then girls? Has it given you a taste for the spotlight?" I say, completely deadpan.

"Oh yeah, it was amazing. It was so nice to see everyone turn out for us."

I have to bite my tongue and stop myself from pointing out the club is an attraction in itself, and if a potato was making a PA, it could expect a similar turn-out.

"It was really cool. But we were only throwing T-shirts off the stage!" The other one chimes in. I like her. "I'm just enjoying the ride for now. I know this won't last forever, so I'm making the most of my fifteen minutes."

"Nice. I like you. I think you're the brains in this outfit," I say, slurring a little. I fight off a gurn. "What are your plans for the future then girls? Ride the wave for a few weeks, then take a step back and retire from the cut-throat world of celebrity?"

"I'm going to be doing some modelling shoots for the lad's mags. Artistic stuff, nothing mucky. And I've had some offers to record a single. I've always loved singing. And I want to be rich and famous!" She whoops in insincere delight. The other girl – Georgina, I think – her reply is considerably less irritating and noxious.

"I have no idea. I didn't go on the show to get a career in the media, but I'm going to make hay while the sun shines and enjoy all the free parties while they last. I'm just going to see what happens."

I'm feeling a bit mischievous. I think it's time to misbehave a bit.

"Cool. So are you a little embarrassed by all this fame and attention? I saw you in the papers every day this week. I mean, it's not like you've done anything. Yet. You've only just arrived. Imagine the level of fame when you do something like release a record, or write a book, or even find a cure for cancer?"

"Oh, I love it. It's brilliant. Everyone's been so nice to us. I love all the attention, and I can't wait to do my record and show people what I'm really about."

"Some people are critical of the whole reality thing, and say you're not welcome and you're devoid of talent? What would you say to that?" I ask, ever so innocently.

"Don't answer that." The press girl snaps. She's out of her chair like a jack-in-the-box, and grabs my arm, pinching my bicep hard.

"Can I have a word outside?" She hisses. She practically drags me into the corridor, and slams the door behind her. She is apoplectic with rage, her face now the same colour as most of the sun-burned spotty-backs in San An. She leans right into me, and launches into a verbal assault of the ferocity I've not seen outside a gangster film. Her words come out like bursts of machine gun fire. Thank fuck the Dictaphone is still in my hand. And still switched on. I let her shout herself out before I offer an empty apology. She takes a deep breath and goes off again.

"I thought this was supposed to be friendly? Anything more like that and the interview's pulled. I'm going to be having a word with Kevin about this anyway. You're supposed to play ball, not be an arsehole. If you fuck us around with this, you won't get a sniff of any of our other clients. And believe me, they're a lot more important to your mag than you are. Now get back in there and stop acting like a cunt."

It never ceases to shock me when a girl uses that word. She's terrifying, but at the stage I'm at with the MDMA, I find the whole outburst incredibly amusing. I'm digging my nails into my palms trying to stop myself from laughing in her face. I splutter and choke on a giggle trying to escape, and manage to squeak out another apology. She holds the door open and I go back to the table. I say sorry to the girl, saying that I didn't mean to be rude to her. She haughtily accepts my apology. I stare at her, and slowly put the Dictaphone back on the table. I don't want to the PR snatching it, which is something I wouldn't put past her. I'm only going to have one more thing to say before I get chased out of here.

"OK. Let's talk about your being a role model."

"Alright then."

"Do you realise the responsibility that has been foisted on you as a role model?"

"What do you mean?"

"Well, for starters, the way you behave will be copied by kids."

The silence is heavy. I think they're trying to decide if I'm having another go. Of course I am, dummies!

"I think I'll be a good role model. I want to show kids that anyone can make it."

"I think you're a fucking terrible role model. You will inspire children to view success as something that will come about through their flashing at a camera or by twatting someone. You're contributing to a future that will be populated by nothing but mindless, attention seeking morons."

I'm amazed I've managed to say this much. I think the press girl has been temporarily turned into stone by my continued not-taking-this-seriously-at-all. She explodes into life, bellowing at me. She tries to grab at me, but I slide off my seat out of the way of her claws. The Dictaphone is in my hand and I'm out the door, running the opposite way from the VIP balcony and through a door into the main arena. I submerge into the crowd and head across to the huge toilet on the other side. I go to the end cubicle, bolt the door behind me and whip out my netbook.

It takes me less than 20 minutes to write the piece. I get on the club's wifi and upload it, along with an MP3 of the entire interview, to the mag's website and my own personal blog. It'll be taken down from the mag's site soon enough, but not before it's been seen by a bunch of people. It's a very public suicide note. I've savaged her, the mag, the show, the whole industry. But fuck it, I don't really care anymore. I don't want to do this anymore.

The Dealer Part 5 : Search and Rescue

"Um, Eddie, we've got a problem."

"Are the law after you?"

"No. We've been robbed."

Silence. For a good thirty seconds.

"Eddie?"

"Come to the club. Now."

And he hangs up.

The drive to the club is excruciating. I feel like I'm on acid, experiencing the most evil trip possible. I can feel the hot breath of Satan on the back of my neck. Everything is sharper, every noise is louder. I want to lie down in a hole and never come out. Perry is saying absolutely nothing. The veins on the side of his head are bulging out at the temple. His knuckles look bleached as he chokes the life out of the steering wheel. I'm fucked. Completely and utterly fucked.

We soon pull up round the back of the club and come to a stop in the loading bay. Eddie storms out of the back door, followed closely by Charlie, who yanks the shutter chain down behind us with some force. They clatter to the floor with a heart shattering crash, sealing us in. Eddie tears open the car door and pulls me out, flinging me to the ground. Charlie's giving Perry the same treatment. We are both shoved up against the shutters, on our knees, our faces pressed against the warm metal. I feel something hard shoved into the soft part at the base of my skull.

"Start fucking talking."

I'm crying like a baby, but I manage to bleat and blurt out what happened in between sobs. They let Perry go and I feel the pressure caused by the gun on head alleviate momentarily before Eddie cracks me across the top of the head with it. He then kicks me in the side and I end up on my arse, staring up the barrel of his gun.

"You fucking idiot. Thank your fucking lucky stars you're more use to us alive than dead right now. Right, you and Perry take a motor each and fuck off and go and find our fucking money. Talk to everyone we know we can trust. Put it out there there's a fucking large reward. You take Ibiza Town, Perry. You take San Antonio, Rocky, you stupid cunt. Leave these fuckers with us," he says, motioning to the two lifeless lumps slumped in the back of the 4x4. "Carry them into the bottle store and we'll take it from there. As soon as we've brought them round and got some information, we'll call you. Now fuck off and pray you find our fucking money."

Perry and I drag the still-comatose twats into the store room and dump them next to a pallet of blue WKDs. Within seconds the shutters are being swallowed up by the ceiling and Perry's backing the 4x4 out. Charlie gives me the keys to a Ford Ka they have. He grabs me by the arm as I start off, and mutters in my ear.

"Don't fucking come back empty handed, and don't even think about doing a runner."

He shoves me out onto the street. I head towards the car park and the Ka in a daze. I get in and drive off without looking back.

It helps to have something to focus on, but every sinew in my body is screaming at me to run as far away from these bastards as I can. But run where? I've not got anywhere to run to, and no way of getting off the island. So I concentrate on the job in hand and the only chance I have of saving my life. I rationalise how to go about looking for the bag. They wouldn't have chucked the money until they noticed us following them. That was at San Raf. So between there and the crash, they must've ditched the bag. So it could still be there, or there's a chance it could've been found by someone along that stretch of the road. I seem to remember nearly running over some clubbers by the tunnel. I turn the car towards San An, and head straight to the cab rank, where a friend of the firm works. I tell him that we've been robbed, and if anyone picks anyone up with a green duffel bag, to let us know immediately. I then drive back to San Raf and follow the route from the tunnel to the crash site, which is deserted. The car hasn't been discovered yet, but the sky is getting light and it's only a matter of time before it is. I pull up and get out. I go back to where the skid marks are and methodically search an area which I generously assume covers the throwing range of the inhabitants of the Capri. After 15 minutes, I've found nothing. I could be here for hours, but I've given the area a good going over and don't believe the bag is here. I go back to the Capri and examine it again. I'm sure the back window was intact when we pulled the boys from the car, but it's shattered now. I can't trust my mind 100% though.

I climb back up to the car and get back in. I feel faint. My eyes fall out of focus and I shudder. The acidity in my stomach is overwhelming and I feel like my guts are on fire. I turn the engine on and pull off slowly towards San An. I'll take the back routes and see if I get lucky.

I turn off the motorway and head through a sparsely populated yet tarmacked semi-industrial area. My eyes scan the road and the surrounding fields. The light is improving, but pretty much all I can see is just north of fuck-all. A wave of panic breaks on me, and I pull over again and try to calm my nerves.

I open the door of the car and swing my legs out and double up, placing my head between my knees and taking deep breaths. After a few minutes I begin to feel vaguely functional again, and I start the engine and drive through the back lanes towards the bay. There's absolutely no-one around. The place is deserted. I find myself willing someone to appear, with a green duffel bag dangling at their side. I've never wanted anything so much before in my entire existence. If sheer willpower alone could achieve anything, I'd have a hundred green duffel bags piled up on top of the car right now. But unfortunately, wishful thinking ain't worth shit.

I get into the bay proper and turn right towards the Egg. I'll try up around the hills near Pikes and up past Sa Capella. It turns out to be just as desolate and fruitless as the rest of my searching has been.

It's gone. There's no fucking way I'm going to find it. Someone else obviously has already and they've had enough time to get off the roads and go to ground. As if anyone with any sense would not go immediately into hiding if they found a bag of cash. The lucky new owners of that little sack are probably sat in their hotel room freaking out. They'll calm down and get over it, I'm sure. I don't think I will though. I'm in deep shit.

On autopilot, I turn the car around and head back towards San An. I cruise along the sea-front and park up near the ferry terminal, and get out of the car. I walk along the harbour wall, and look out at the bay. There are hundreds of boats. Some small, some large, some shitty fishing vessels and a lot of flashy yachts; all of them dwarfed by the massive ferry moored next to me.

As I look it up and down, a growl is emitted from its belly, and it shudders into life, beginning to belch ever-thickening acrid black smoke from its chimney. I look down at the sea, and contemplate throwing myself in. But only for a second. If I'm to die today, it's fucking well not going to be at my own hands.

I turn my attention to the ferry. It doesn't look like it would be too difficult to stow away. But what would I do at the other end? How would I get off Mallorca? And Eddie and Charlie aren't fucking idiots – by the time the ferry got to Palma, there would be a squad of their associates at the dock waiting for me to disembark before they disembowelled me.

I turn my back on the sea and head back along the harbour wall. I've just got back into the car when my mobile rings. It's Eddie. He says he wants me back at the villa.

The Holiday Makers Part 4 : Dancing In The Disco, Bumper To Bumper

I come round when I feel my face slap against cold concrete. I try to open my eyes, but can only see out of my left one, and what I see is a dark blur. After a couple of seconds, my vision sharpens and I can see I'm lying on the floor of some kind of storeroom. Next to me is a mountain of Smirnoff Ice, towering over me like a million menacing high street drunks ready to pounce. There's someone else in the room other than Kenny, but a sudden shaft of light appears and disappears along with the noise of a door slamming. It sounds like a deafening and terrifying death knell. The silence that comes next tells me we're alone now.

My head is feeling heavy, and I'm as groggy as fuck. I fondle my skull, and my fingers run over a large egg that has sprung up on my crown. It feels wet and sticky, but at least it's not gushing blood.

I try my eye again, and it adjusts to the little light that is seeping under the door. Along the back wall I can make out a worktop covered with all manner of rusty tools and a few more towers of bottled drinks and mixers. I think Kenny is curled into the foetal position next to me. I can hear muffled voices outside.

I try to calm myself down, but the panic is in control for now. I shiver. Where the fuck am I? What the fuck is going to happen to us? I roll over onto my side, and try to stand, but I can't. I don't think my legs are broken, but my god they hurt. The top of my thighs took a beating from the steering wheel when the car went over. I turn my head towards where I can hear Kenny's laboured breathing. I tentatively crawl over, and my hand soon touches against his arm. I gently rock it back and forth, trying to bring him round.

"Kenny. Wake up." I whisper at him. But before there is a response, I hear footsteps clunking towards the door. I roll back away from Kenny and pretend to be unconscious, burying my face in the hook of my elbow.

The door is yanked open, and someone flicks a switch and the light flickers on. Suddenly, my arse explodes in a maelstrom of pain as a steel toe-capped boot crashes into my coccyx with the power of a freight train. I leap forward and make myself into a ball in an attempt to protect myself from further kicks. From the crack and following yelp I hear next to me, I work out that Kenny has got the same treatment.

A strong pair of hands grabs me under the arms and hoists me up. I'm in too much pain to put up much of a fight beyond a token struggle, and I'm thrown into the wall. A rough hand clamps itself around my throat and I'm pinned up against the wall in an upright position. A second person shines a torch into my eyes, practically blinding me, and I feel the wind rush out of my lungs as a fist smashes into my chest.

"Where's our fucking money?" A calm, yet extremely menacing voice says.

I try to answer, but what with being winded and the hand around my throat, I can barely even croak. The grip loosens around my neck, and the same hand slaps me across the face.

"I'm not going to ask you again."

"We chucked it. It went out the car window just before we crashed." I manage to squeak. Tears are falling down my cheeks, and a big bubble of snot is slowly growing over my top lip. I get shoved to the ground, and I can see a shadowy figure pick up Kenny and throw him face first onto the work table. The same calm voice asks him the same question. In between sobs, Kenny manages to tell them the same answer.

"We threw it out of the car just before we crashed. Why would we lie? We don't want to die for the sake of a few grand."

Kenny is tossed back to the floor, landing next to me in a slump. A pair of hands roughly rifles through my pockets, and I feel the contents being removed and thrown against the wall. My wallet, my passport, and my roll of holiday scratch all end up in a little pile next to me. Shit. Now they're going to find out my name, where I live and anything they fucking want about me. Shit shit shit fucking shit.

Kenny's wailing and has turned into a gibbering wreck. I must admit I'm not far behind him. His green combat shorts have a dark patch in the groin area; he's obviously pissed himself. I wouldn't be surprised if he's shat himself too. I have a little bit.

My eyes are getting used to the dark now, and I can make out some sort of stick in the hand of one of our captors. I see him raise it above his head and bring it down hard towards the back of Kenny's legs. The noise as it makes contact is sickening, and I see Kenny slump to the floor, groaning in agony.

Just as he raises the bat above his head to rain a blow down on me, I hear his phone going off. He pulls it out and answers it, listening intently. He finishes the call, throws the bat on the ground and boots me in the small of the back before leaving the room. The door slams shut, and I hear it being locked from the other side.

I dry retch a couple of times, before realising how fucking cold my arms and legs are. Kenny's sobs are the only noise I can hear. At least he's conscious. I curl up and lay there shivering, and fighting the urge to drop my guts. I'm too scared and sick to talk, but I don't think there's anything I can say that would make any difference to mine and Kenny's predicament. It's not like we're the fucking A-Team. It's not like we're going to be able to formulate a plan to escape. All we can do is hope that they find the bag.

The Stags Part 6 : San Rafael

"What's that you've got there, Terry?"

I'm crouching down, fiddling with the tie around the top of the bag.

"I dunno yet."

The pair of them push through the brush to where I am. I manage to get the tie unravelled, and I open up the top of it and peer inside. Fuck me. Unbefuckinglievable The twins and I stare at wad upon wad of neatly bundled, high-denomination euro notes. 50s and 100s. I pull the bag shut quickly.

"Fuckin 'ell," Ashley says. "Good thing I got us chucked out of Amnesia."

We all burst out laughing, uncontrollably. This is fucking nuts.

"Yeah, mate. I think I might owe you a fucking pint. There's enough for us to split this three ways and we'll all be sorted for a long fucking time." I say, establishing what we're doing about this find. Don't want them getting any ideas.

"This is some serious fucking money right here." Frank airily whispers, before snapping into a business-like mode and issuing some commands. "Right, we've got to be a bit clever now, lads. We take the back roads from here on in. Anyone who is missing that amount of money will have no trouble finding out if any cabbies picked up anyone round here. It's too risky."

"Yeah, alright." I agree. It's the first sensible thing to come out of the Manc's mouth all night. "Let's get over the other side of the motorway and go cross-country."

From here, we can see San An off in the distance, and the motorway curves away from it before swerving back into the town. All we need to do is take a more direct path straight across this bit of country and we can get back to our hotel without every cunt using the motorway being able to identify the three blokes with a duffel bag strolling along the hard-shoulder. I pick up the loot and they follow me back up to the road. We crouch down at the side and wait for the coast to be clear, and then scurry across to the central reservation once a bus zooms past us. We climb over and peg it into the bushes on the other side of the road. We begin to follow a fence that runs roughly parallel with the motorway and provides cover from passing motors.

"How much do you reckon is there? How the fuck are we gonna get it off the island?" I ask, suppressing the need to get carried away and start babbling, the magnitude of our find only just sinking in.

"100 grand at least." Frank says. "We don't need to tell anyone else about this. So keep it fucking quiet, Terry."

"Yeah of course. Goes without saying."

Fucking prick. Telling me what to fucking do. I'm not soft in the head. We carry on marching through the field, which comes to an end soon next a roadside petrol station. The uneven surface combined with the weight of the bag conspires against me and I stumble over, crashing on top of the bag, awkwardly.

"Careful, you nob. That bag's worth a lot of money." Frank sneers, reducing him and his brother to hysterics. Fucking northerners. All of them think they're comedians. I get back to my feet and press on.

My mind is swimming. I'm suppressing the urge to panic, and start to focus my thoughts on how to ensure this situation turns out the way it should. There's more than enough to retire on here. You could start a new life anywhere in the world with this kind of cash. The thought of having to share it with these tossers makes me want to shit my ring through my mouth. It dawns on me that if I could somehow take them out of the equation, the money could be all mine, and I could bugger off and never be seen again. I'm sure these cunts wouldn't let it lie, and would try and hunt me down, but having money like this to hide behind can make a person very difficult to find.

So I decide to do it. I decide to fuck them.

I formulate a plan. Ideally, I'm going to need to get this sorted before we get back to the hotel. It'll be too hard with all the others around to do a runner. And killing them would be daft – I'd draw much more heat, the pigs would get involved, and probably that villain they work for. So I'm probably going to have to fight them for it. One on one, that wouldn't be a problem. But against the two of them, my chances are probably 50/50. I need an advantage. I rack my brains for an idea. It comes from an unlikely source as one of them suggests stopping off at the petrol station to get a drink. Remembering

I still have my gear left, tucked in my pants under my balls, I know exactly what it is I have to do.

We get to the end of the fence, which goes right up to the side of the petrol station. I say I'll go in, giving them some bollocks about the E making me want a shit. I emerge from behind the fence and jog across the forecourt and into the air conditioned shop. I grope around in my pockets for some change that didn't get swiped and find a few euros in shrapnel. I don't really want to dip into the bag here. I grab a litre bottle of San Miguel, pay the man and head to the bog. I lock myself inside the trap, and take a nice long swig of beer.

I retrieve the ket stashed in my pants and tip it into the beer. All of it – there's at least three grams left. I screw the lid back on tight, and rotate the bottle slowly to mix it up. I unlock the door, and head out of the bog and out of the petrol station. I unscrew the bottle top as I walk back to them, and put it to my lips, tilting my head back. I grit my teeth and purse my lips as I do so, ensuring none of the ket-infused beer goes into my system.

I get over to them and hand one of them the bottle.

"That's all I could afford, so don't drink it all," I say, knowing full well by saying that they'll deliberately finish it off between them. We start off round the back of the petrol station and head down a path away from the lightening sky behind us and towards the bright lights of San An. The bottle of grog is being passed between them, and after a minute it comes flying over me and smashes against some rocks.

"Sorry Tel, we finished it, mate." Frank sneers at me. I can tell he's challenging me, but I'm not rising to it just yet. I try to estimate how long it'll take before the K kicks in. We walk along in silence for about a mile, about 20 minutes I reckon, when we come across a small orchard, set back and down from the road, fenced off by some trees.

I hear him just before I see him in my peripheral vision. One of the twins shoulder barges me and shoves me through an opening in the tree line and away from the road. I drop the bag. Oh shit.

"What the fuck are you playing at, you cunt?" I say.

"Thing is Terry, we had a little chat while you were in the shop." The one who shoved me says.

"Oh yeah?" I reply. I don't like the sound of this.

"Yeah," Ashley continues. "We've decided we're keeping this money. And there's fuck all you can do about it. In fact, in a minute we're going to show you exactly what will happen if you try to do anything about it. And it ends here. You come after us on this, and you'll fucking die. Simple as."

"Sorry mate," Frank chimes in, his voice dripping in sarcasm. "We're taking it."

And with that, they fly at me.

I manage to get a couple of punches in, but they're ten years younger than me and ten years faster. They crack me in the side of the head and then my kidneys, moving in tandem and not getting in each other's way. You can tell they do this for a living. I grapple with them as best I can, and we all tumble down a verge and land in a pile at the bottom. They're up on their feet before I can even get my breath back. The blows rain down on my head with a ferocity that blurs my vision. They're alternating between booting me in the back and stomach, but then only the stomach. I'm slipping in and out of consciousness, but I'm aware the kicking has stopped when I feel something heavy fall on top of me. I try to open my eye and can just about make out the vague form of one of them stumbling to his knees in front of me, before he rolls over on his side and curls into a ball as I pass out.

The Shop Girl Part 4 – Disco Bombshell

We worm our way through the West End, turning onto the main drag at the junction by Trops and Upmarket, heading down towards the cab rank. We're buffeted from every direction, and I can't help but feel a little miffed that the Himbo isn't using his impressive bulk to even try and afford me some protection from the baying mobs. And who said chivalry was dead? Eventually we're spewed out of the crowd just beyond Koppas, and we take a left and slow our pace to a more relaxed stroll along the front.

I snatch a few glances up at my new friend, and listen to him waffle on about what clubs he's been to, is going to and how he can get list everywhere. Yawn!

We get to the cash-point just before Wips and stop. We've just got some money out when I hear a familiar voice call out my name and feel my face twitch into an involuntary smile. I turn to see a manic and bloodied face, and it takes me a moment to recognise it as Matt. He's got a different T-shirt on and looks like he's been in a fight. Panicked concern replaces the warm feeling in my tum that arrived when he called my name.

"Oh my God. Are you OK? What's happened to your face?"

"Um, I'm fine. I fell over. It looks worse than it actually is."

He looks fucked. Not on drugs, but physically and emotionally. He's in pain, I can see the turmoil and anguish plastered all over his face. And it makes me hurt. But it doesn't seem like the kind of pain that the gash on his head must be giving him.

"Um, Hannah, I need to talk to you." He says ominously.

I nod, tell Himbo to hang on, and I walk over to the minging fountain with Matt. He begins to speak, stumbling over his words at first, before he takes a deep breath and blurts it out. I can't believe what I'm hearing. The wind rushes out of me and I feel like I've just been punched in the stomach. He finishes talking, and looks as dazed as I feel. I'm completely lost for words. Total and utter confusion reign supreme in my heart and head. I give his hand a squeeze. I can't think of a thing to say, reeling as I am, so I just smile weakly and try to take it all in. Something changes on his face, and he stutters a lame apology. I'm on autopilot and say something along the lines of "Don't worry."

I'm vaguely aware of the Himbo shouting something over at me, and I release Matt's hand from mine.

"I better go."

The look on Matt's face almost crushes my already quite fragile heart, and I turn and head back over to the Himbo. I leave Matt behind, putting a lot of effort into not looking back at him, and walk away in total shock. The Himbo puts his arm back around me in a proprietary way, and I tense. Who is this twat? I can't think straight, my stomach is going loop the loop. I lock my face into a thousand yard stare, so as to not give anything away, but inside, I'm staggered.

The PR Part 3 : Biting

Starkey taps me on the shoulder.

"I fancy a Subway. Will you walk with me?"

"Yeah."

Once we're far away from the group, she stops me.

"Is there anything you want to get off your chest?"

I pause for about a second. Then it all comes spilling out. I'm having to fight hard to hold back the tears. I waffle on for a good five minutes, with her saying nothing, and then I finish off with a defeated analysis of how it's never going to happen, and how I need to move on.

Starkey looks at me, and slowly shakes her head.

"I love you to bits, Matt, and you're a fucking dude, but you have to be the stupidest person I know sometimes. How can you say you have no chance? How do you know? Man the fuck up and tell her. Just both get on with it. Whatever the outcome – you can't go on torturing yourself."

Starkey's words cut through the blackness surrounding my soul like the light of a hydrogen bomb. My breath rushes out of my lungs and my stomach tries to escape through my mouth. Something has just cracked in my brain. In the rush to put my pint down on the nearest table, I completely miss and it smashes on the floor, causing everyone to look round.

"I've gotta find her."

I sprint away from Starkey as she says something I can't make out, and I leg it into the hustle of the West End.

I barge my way through the crowd to the corner by Trops, and I jump onto a chair and scope the crowd to see if I can make her out. I look over the sea of heads to see if I can make her out – first, up towards Viva, and then down towards Koppas. I think I make out the back of her head turning the corner towards the Egg. I jump off the seat and peg it down the side street to head her off further down the promenade. Not looking where I'm going, my foot lands in a puddle of puke and I skid halfway down the pavement, before going arse over tit and cracking my head on a step. I'm vaguely aware of a chorus of laughter that greets my quite spectacular buckle, but to be honest, I don't give a fuck. I feel dizzy, even more so than before, and I'm sure I've given myself a concussion. I pick myself up, and stagger for a few steps before I lean against the wall and hurl my guts all over the street. A middle-aged Spanish couple walk past and glance at me with a look of abject disgust on their faces. I stop retching, and manage to pull myself together. I rummage in my pockets and stick a couple of tabs of Extra in my gob to get rid of the taste, but not before I clear my tubes by hocking all the residual vom onto the floor with a guttural growl. Nice and classy, I know, but I don't think my chances in what I'm about to do would be improved if I stank of sick.

I shake my head to clear the fuzziness, and feel some sweat spray off me. Oh well, sweaty is better than sick-encrusted. In the distance, I swear I see her walk past with him. Shit. I pick up the pace and dash round the corner, and there she is. Stood at the cash point. He's got his arm round her. She looks decidedly uninterested. I step back round the corner to check out my reflection in a shop window. I almost don't recognise myself. The entire left side of my face is covered in blood. It's like I'm staring at Terry Butcher after that England game against Sweden. I can't speak to her looking like this. I duck into the tourist shop next to where I am standing and buy a T-shirt. I tear mine off, and mop the blood from my face as best I can before putting the new one on and stuffing the soiled one in a bin. I take a deep breath and jog round the corner. They're just walking away from the cash-point. I call out her name. She turns round and looks at me, confusion scrawled across her face as she takes in my appearance.

"Oh my God. Are you OK? What's happened to your face?" She says, her voice tender, concerned and utterly gorgeous.

"Um, I'm fine. I fell over. It looks worse than it actually is."

Silence.

"Hannah. I need to talk to you."

"Er, yeah sure." She turns to her beau, who is looking at me like I've just shat on his shoes. "Gimme a second will you?"

We walk over to the piss-filled fountain. I take a deep breath.

"Don't go off with him. I'm sorry. I really don't know how to say this, but fuck it." I'm really making a balls-up of this. So I just blurt it out.

"I'm completely in love with you."

The silence hangs in the air like an anvil dangling on a thread, primed to come crashing down on me and squash my heart into a million pieces.

She reaches forward and holds my hand, squeezing it gently. Each second seems to last a year. I remember to breathe and take a long, steadying gulp of air. My intestines are wringing themselves into a tightrope.

The silence is deafening, and slowly I begin to realise what a massive fucking mistake I've made. She's looking at me with a mixture of shock and bemusement. The sense of regret at what I've just said is crippling. Shit. What have I fucking done?

"I'm sorry Hannah. I shouldn't have said that. I'm sorry. I'm sorry."

She smiles at me and says something about it being okay. The smile seems forced, and I can tell she's angry. Or something. I know for sure she's not happy with me.

Her new friend shouts over and asks if everything's alright. I look at him and want to punch his lights out. But I know that would be an even more stupid thing to do than what I've already done. Thankfully I have enough sense in me to know to quit when I'm not ahead.

She clears her throat, and looks over to him, before looking back to me.

"I better go."

I smile weakly and she goes back to him. He stares me out for a second, before exaggeratedly putting his arm around her again. I watch them walk away for a few moments, willing her to look back at me, or give me some kind of sign, but then I realise it's just not going to happen.

The Journalist Part 5 : Exit Strategy

I head back to the VIP to get Giles and tell Kevin to go fuck himself. I get up there and the twat is having his ear gnawed off by the press girl. Giles is lying on one of the day-beds surrounded by women and drinking from a bottle of champagne. The press girl sees me over Kevin's shoulder and goes berserk. The other PR girl has to restrain her, and Kevin comes marching over to me. He looks proper pissed off. If he was a cartoon, steam would be coming out of his ears. I smile at him.

"Jack, what the fuck are you doing? Do you know what you've done? Do you know how much trouble you've caused?"

"I do. I quit. Go fuck yourself, you fucking twat. You should be ashamed of that magazine you put out. You're making people stupid, you oxygen-thieving nob. Now fuck off."

And with that, I leave him open mouthed and go over to Giles.

"I say we dust off and nuke the site from orbit. It's the only way to be sure."

Giles immediately knows what I mean. He kisses his women goodbye and we peg it out of the VIP just as the PR tries to set the security on us. We rip off our wristbands as we walk past her, handing them to the PR.

"Thanks for a great night!" Giles shouts back at them as we go down the stairs two at a time.

We duck through the door next to the VIP and down one of the back corridors of the club. I have no fucking idea where we're going, but who gives a fuck. Nothing wrong with a bit of rampaging through the bowels of this shithole. I might even try and nick some booze! We wander down a brightly lit corridor, looking for a way out and trying every door on the way. Most are locked, but then there's a big metal one with an unlocked padlock. I pop off the lock and open it up. It's a storeroom. Haha! My eyes sweep around it for a couple of bottles of beer to pinch. Giles nudge me in the ribs and points to the floor.

"Christ, it looks like a fucking Guy Ritchie film in here," motioning to two dudes on the floor. I'd say it's more Pulp Fiction. One of the guys has clearly pissed himself, and the storeroom stinks of crap. I don't even want to know what the story is in here. I nudge Giles.

"No way. No interest in getting involved in this scene. Fuck this. Let's go."

We leave the door open and piss off down the corridor, but not before Giles takes a snap or two. Man, this is turning into one fucking weird night out.

We take a left and are greeted with a big door that says "Exit". We bounce through it and emerge into the street. I burst out laughing and then tell Giles what transpired with the story and how I no longer have a job. He smacks me on the back and cackles like a maniac.

"Oh, you are a silly cunt."

"Thank you!"

"Don't worry, I still love you. I'd say that could probably be the best club story you've ever done. Shame it won't ever get published."

"Haha. That's where you're wrong. It's already been published. I wrote the piece in the bog and uploaded it to the blog. And the MP3 of the interview, including the PR threatening me."

"Hahahah brilliant. Career Hari-kiri! I always thought you had style, Jack."

A cab pulls up beside us and we jump in and I tell the driver we want to go to Amnesia. I've got a date to keep.

The Holiday Makers Part 5 : Escape To Victory

After what seems like an eternity, but can't be more than a couple of hours, the panic has subsided. There's just an overwhelming and impending sense of doom, mixed with an evil hangover. It's sickening and debilitating and gnaws away at my insides. Thank God the physical pain from the beating has subsided.

I hear a commotion outside the door, but in amongst the hubbub I can hear laughing and giggling. Someone tries the door, and the lock turns, and two men I've not seen before come into the room. One is carrying a professional-looking camera.

"Fucking hell." The one with the camera wheezes.

"Shit." Says the other.

I twist my neck and look up to see the two men staring down at us with their mouths wide open. They don't look like villains. One of them looks like Dennis Hopper from Apocalypse Now, and the other looks fucked on pills. And they both look like they just might have saved our lives.

"Christ, it looks like a fucking Guy Ritchie film in here," the one without the camera says as he takes in the scene, and reels off a couple of shots. I try to speak, but just cough and splutter. I flob a massive globule of sick, blood and phlegm onto the floor next to me.

The guy with the camera says something to his friend I can't quite make out, and they step back through the door and disappear. Leaving the door wide open.

I roll over onto my side, and push myself upright. I ache all over, but I realise our window of opportunity is small.

"Ken, let's go. NOW!"

Kenny blubbers something, but pulls himself together enough to get to his feet. We scoop our passports, phones and belongings up off the floor, and stumble out of the room. The corridor is brightly lit, and in the distance, the low throb of a bass drum can be heard.

We cautiously move down the corridor, and come across a big door with "exit" emblazoned on it. We press down on the bar and it opens out into a deserted backstreet. At one end, it's bright, and there's a cacophony that only hoards of drunk Brits can create. At the other end is a car park and darkness. We head straight towards the light and immerse ourselves in the crowd of people. From what I've seen on the telly, I think we're bang in the middle of San Antonio.

We go round a corner, and walk down a hill past more bars, and I see a cab rank not too far away. As we move out of the mass of sweaty drunks, my knees give way and I collapse into the wall, managing to break my fall with my arms. Lowering myself to a sitting position, I take a deep breath, but my mouth fills with bile and I puke like a pissing racehorse. The look on Kenny's face when I look up at him after I've cleared my guts is something I'll never forget. His cheeks puff out like a blowfish and he turns and voms into the gutter. He looks just like the dude in the pie-eating contest in Stand By Me.

A group of passing English lads cheer at us.

"Looks like you're having a good night lads! Wahey!" one of them bellows at us.

You don't know the half of it, mate.

I feel a little more together, but I know I'm flirting with going into shock, so I pull myself up and steady Kenny by taking his forearm. My brain clicks into survival mode.

"Dude, we're not out of this yet. Let's get the fuck out of here. Cab rank. There."

I lead him towards the cab rank, which thankfully has about ten taxis lined up and fuck all people in the queue. I feel a smidgen of relief when I lean down and say the word "aeropuerto" to the driver. He nods in agreement and reaches for a switch that turns the green light off on top of the motor.

I open the back door and usher Kenny in. I slide in next to him so rapidly, we almost spoon for a second. The sound of the door clunking shut behind me makes me feel a little less scared and the tiniest bit safe. There's a nasty, unnatural smell in the car, but to be honest, it could be either of us responsible for that, or the cab itself. It doesn't really matter though. I get my iPhone out of my pocket and peck at the Safari icon with my middle finger. Navigating to the Ibiza Airport homepage, I check for the first flight out of Ibiza. It's 7 am, and it goes to Milan. I go to the carrier's website, and book 2 seats for us. I breathe a sigh of relief when I get the confirmation. I look at Kenny, who is as white as a tin of Dulux, and put my hand on his shoulder.

"This is going to be over soon, mate. It's going to be OK."

"I fucking don't know what the fuck is going on. What about the motor? They can trace you back home through the registration? What about our stuff in the boot? What are we going to say?"

"I don't fucking know. We'll report it stolen. I'll go on the lam. I really don't fucking know. What I do know though is, right now, we can get out of this place intact if we're lucky. Fuck all that shit, we'll deal with it when we get home. All I know is this island is not somewhere we should be if we want to continue living. We leave. Everything else is secondary."

I catch the driver's eyes in the rear view mirror. There is a magic tree in the shape of Jesus dangling from it. The source of the stench. I find it overbearing. After all we've been through tonight, I find it remarkable that this fucking magic tree is even registering on my radar right now. It fucking reeks.

I try and make myself comfortable on the back seat, but I'm aching like a bastard and something is digging into my arse. It feels like I'm sitting on a pea. I slowly reach underneath my bum and my hand brushes against something around the size of a small egg. I pinch it between my thumb and forefinger, and pull it out to see what it is. I hold up this pliable, squidgy lump of dark matter. I hold it to my nose, and the stench of the magic tree is replaced by the sweet hum that only very good, high-grade hash can emit. I nudge Kenny, and hold up what I've just found. We both stare at it, and then look at each other. I think it's a mixture of shock, relief and frayed nerves, but we start laughing like lunatics. When we eventually stop, Kenny tells the cab driver we need to stop at a shop for some fags and Rizla. Smart move – well, the plane's not until 7am, is it?

The Dealer Part 6 : Going For A Dip

I get to the villa just as Perry pulls into the complex in the 4x4. He still looks fucking pissed off and completely blanks me as we get out of the cars. We walk round the back of the house and meet Eddie on the terrace.

"Perry, you big cunt, get in the house," he barks. "Rocky, you fucking cretin. Charlie wants a word with you, so piss off and go and see him."

"Where is he?"

"He's down by the pool house."

I walk off the terrace and onto the lawn. The pool house is about 50 metres away, down a slight incline. The sun is up now and it's a really beautiful day. There isn't a cloud in the sky, and the sea just the other side of the pool is a deep blue colour, punctuated by little furry white lines splattered around on the crest of the waves. It looks fucking lovely.

I get down to the end of the garden to where the pool house is. For normal people, it would be a fucking massive house in its own right, but in this context, it's a posh changing room with sofas and a fuck-off big plasma screen. There's a new hot-tub/whirlpool being installed next week, so it's a bit of a building site at the moment. Charlie's having a poke around in amongst the materials, inspecting some tiles. I feel sick, my legs feel heavy and I realise I need the toilet more than I have ever before.

"You wanted to see me boss."

"Yes. Is there anything you want to say about tonight?"

"Sorry. It'll never happen again. I'll work off the money. I'll pay you it back. I promise"

"Yeah. I know you will. It's a real shame, because you've been doing a fucking good job for us down Playa D'en Bossa. And you fucked up all that good work with your cock-up tonight. I had you pegged for great things. You're going to have to work fucking hard to get me back onside."

"I'm sorry."

He doesn't respond. We stand there in silence for what seems like hours, but is probably no more than a minute. I'm wrestling against the urge to speak because the silence is unbearable. It's excruciating. I give in.

"So what's happened to those two lads, then?" I mutter, cringing when the words come out of my mouth. I really don't know when to shut the fuck up sometimes.

Charlie turns to me and stares at me. Another very long pause. He slowly walks up to me. As he walks around me, he leans into my ear and starts whispering.

"You don't need to worry about that. They've gone. It would have been messy. I don't need to bring any more heat on to us by snuffing out idiot tourists. They'd be missed."

I nod in agreement. His voice drops to a whisper.

"Unlike you, you stupid cunt."

It takes me all of a second to realise what's happening. I feel like an anvil has fallen on my head, and a resounding thud ricochets around my brain. I totter forward, seeing black circles in my peripheral vision, and sparkles of light dancing out of them. My back receives a gentle shove and I feel myself fall into a soft, lumpy liquid. It makes me think of porridge. The last thing I remember is how nice it feels as more of it pours down and covers me like a big wet blanket, making me snug as a bug in a rug.

The Shop Girl Part 5 : Rave-elation

We get into the taxi and I give the driver a piece of paper on which Sean scribbled out how to get to his party. Himbo starts rabbiting on about himself, saying how this is his third season, and blah blah how many drugs he's done this week, and how nice the villa he and his friends have. I'm barely listening. Matt's little revelation has spun me right out. His timing is impeccable. I'm pissed off with him for choosing to get that off his chest this evening, right in the middle of a night out we're both supposed to be enjoying. He'll probably not even bother coming down now. Twat.

The rest of the cab ride passes like a waking dream. I try my hardest to concentrate on anything but what Matt just told me. I ask the Himbo a few stock questions – where are you from, what do you do and so on, not really taking in the answers, but making the right noises at the right time so he thinks I'm listening. We get to Sean's party, which is in the middle of nowhere. I see my mate Belle, who takes our cab off us. As she gets in, she whispers a comment about a "what a spunk" as I go past, but I can't really hear her. I'm grateful when we enter the party proper, which is in a big clearing in the trees – any potential conversation is drowned out by the sound of thumping kick drums and sizzling electronic synth stabs.

We go up into the enclosure behind the DJ booth, and the Himbo offers to go and get some drinks. I nod and shout the words "Vodka" and "Red Bull" into his ear. And off he goes to the bar. I look around to see if there's anyone I know, but I'm on my own here at the moment. A couple of faces belong to people I know to nod hello to, but I can't see any of my proper mates yet. I hope Starkey and Lucy hurry the fuck up. I don't really want to be alone with this guy anymore. I'm sure he's nice, but right now, he feels like an imposter, an unwelcome one at a rather heavy and personal moment in my life. I hope he doesn't think I'm being a bitch, but to be honest, I don't really give that much of a shit at this exact moment in time. He comes back with the drinks, and flashes me a kind smile.

"Are you OK? What did that guy say to you?"

"Oh nothing, I'm fine. Don't worry about it. Thanks for the drink." I reply, probably a bit too tersely. I silence my gob by taking a long swig from my drink, the vodka making me gag a little. But I think I need a strong drink. I try and focus on the music. We're standing right next to the booth, and the DJ, Grainger, is mixing up some wicked 80s kitsch stuff. It sounds amazing, and goes some way to lightening my mood. The Himbo is gyrating next to me, completely out of time with the music. He keeps trying to grind his bum up against me and take my hand and pull me towards him, but I'm not having it at all. I breathe a sigh of relief when I see the others arrive. Starkey clocks me straight away and heads over. She can see there's something up with me, and smoothly moves herself between me and Himbo, leaning into my ear.

"Are you OK? Did Matt find you?"

I look at her. Does she know?

"Yeah. What do you know about it?"

"Not a great deal. Did he say what I think he said?"

"Yes."

"And how do you feel about it?"

How do I feel about it? I'm struggling to work it out myself.

"Completely shocked. I don't know what to think."

"Oh, for fuck's sake, sort it out. I've seen you together. There's obviously something there between you, and it's not just from him. I see you perk up every time his name is mentioned. When he walks in a room, something happens to you. I really don't know why you are wasting your time by not being together."

"And how long have you known?"

"It's been obvious for ages. But he only admitted it to me about half an hour ago. Don't for a moment think he's been talking about it behind your back to everyone. He's acted like a gent throughout."

"Fucking hell, Starkey. I don't know what to think. This is heavy." I say, feeling weighed down, drained and downright bemused.

"No it isn't. It's fucking wicked. Or it could be if the two of you stopped acting like 11 year olds at a school disco. Sort it out Hannah."

Starkey's words cut into me like a pneumatic drill, jarring me right to the core. I feel my eyes welling up. I walk away from the clearing, back to where the cab dropped us off, and sit under a tree. My thoughts crystallize and I know what it is I need to do. I slide open my phone and write the text. As I wander back towards the party, I get the delivery report on my phone, and my heart skips a beat.

The PR Part 4 : Reeling

I slink off home in tears. I feel like an utter cunt. She probably thinks our whole friendship is a farce. A lie. But it isn't. We were friends before I began to feel like this. Surely we can be friends after? But I suppose I've been extremely naive to have thought that it would survive the dropping of this truth bomb.

I circumnavigate the West End. The last thing I want is to bump into anyone I know, looking like this. I get back to my flat and Alan and Jason are sat on the sofa engrossed in a game of Fifa. Neither looks up at me, so I manage to get into my room with nothing more than an exchange of grunts.

I collapse onto my in bed, and let the snot and tears stream out. I've got to get out of here. I can't stay on the island now. Things with me and Han will never be the same. I've blown it. As a result of a moment of madness and lack of self-control, I've now lost my best friend. I'm such a fucking spastic. It'll be excruciatingly awkward. It'll be untenable.

I lift myself off my bed, and blow my nose and wipe the tears off my face using my sheet. I open my laptop and go to the easyjet homepage. I grapple around in the pockets of my trousers, and pull out my wallet. I fish out my credit card out and I'm just punching in the numbers when my phone tells me I've got a text message.

My stomach does a somersault as I reach over to it. I look at the name of the sender. It's her. I stare at the phone for a good ten seconds, willing with every atom of my being for the message to be something that will change everything.

I press the button to open it up and I very slowly read the four words on the screen. By the time I get to the last word, I'm crying all over again. I slam my laptop shut and jump into my clothes. I've got to find her. I grab my flatmate's scooter keys, and stumble out of the house and jump on his Vespa. It takes exactly seven minutes to get to my destination. I take the exit onto the dirt track, and soon pull up into a car park next to a van. I come to a stop and, illuminated by the headlights, I see her standing there. Her make-up is smudged. I get off the bike and go to her. She stares at me as I approach, saying nothing. Her bottom lip is quivering, her cheeks are flushed, but her eyes are sparkling and so brown and so beautiful. We just stand there looking at each other, as if we're seeing each other for the first time.

Her hand comes up to my face, and she lays her palm gently against my cheek. I put my arms around her and pull her towards me. She nuzzles into my neck and the smell of her hair wafts into my nostrils. Coupled with its softness caressing my face, it's like the most intoxicating drug I've ever taken. I'm completely overwhelmed and in a total emotional meltdown. We're trembling. Everything else outside of the two of us has ceased to exist. The din of the party going on in the background is gone, the glare from the headlights appears to have been extinguished. We break off our clenched embrace ever so slightly and look into each other's eyes. It's like we're peering into each other's souls. My heart explodes inside me as she repeats the same four words that she wrote in the text.

"I love you too."

The Hens Part 5 : Starting Again

I've lost myself in it completely. The music is coming at me like a tsunami from every direction and I'm just letting it spin me all over the dancefloor. E and house music have sent me deep into a trance and time has lost all meaning. I've never felt such a part of the music. Every tune the DJ plays hits the spot, and I even recognise some of them from my old clubbing days. A remix of Electric Dreams comes on and my insides soar and I feel like I'm floating on air. I feel completely free.

I look around me and see Jack and his photographer mate coming through the crowd towards me. Giles makes a beeline for the others, while Jack comes straight to me. I put my arms around him and pull him close to me, giving him a long and hard hug. It's great to be feeling someone else in my arms without any fear or anxiety. I know a lot of it's down to the E, but it's amazing to have some beautiful physical human contact. I let go and lead him by the hand through the crowd, away from the others, and we find room for the two of us to dance. We hold hands, we touch, we groove away with our arms round each other until they turn the lights on. I feel alive in a way that I haven't in years. We slowly shuffle out of the club, holding hands, and meet up with the others in the car park.

We turn to face each other. I say goodbye to him. He wishes me luck. And we kiss. Like, *properly* kiss. And it feels fucking great. I squeeze his bum and pull out of the snog and smile and walk away. There's a spring in my step, and I feel elated.

Then Keeley's face comes into my line of sight, and I feel a spasm of panic inside me. This is soon replaced by anger, and defiance. No more.

"Vicky! What the fuck are you doing? Paul will go mental!"

He already is mental.

"Fuck him."

Keeley's mouth drops open in shock. Only momentarily though, as it soon transforms into a grotesque mask of rage. She looks so much like her brother sometimes. I walk straight past her and into a waiting cab. Without waiting for them, I tell him to take me to the hotel. The flight back to London is in three hours, so I know they won't be far behind. But to be honest, I can't be bothered to share the same air as them any longer.

I get to the hotel and head to my room. Ten minutes later I get a tersely worded text from Keeley.

"Be in the lobby at 9. Don't make us wait."

I stretch out on the bed, and breathe out. It might still be the E running around my system, but I feel as if I don't have a care in the world. I'm lighter, taller, sharper and happier than I've been in years. I look at the time and see it's just coming up to nine o'clock. Right on the dot, my phone starts ringing. It's Keeley. I let it ring a few times before I answer.

"Where the fuck are you?"

"I'm sorry Keeley," I lie. "I fell asleep. I'll meet you at the airport."

"You stupid bitch."

She hangs up. I smile inside. I feel absolutely amazing. I prop myself up on my arms and work out my plan for the morning. The flight to London is at 11.30, so I've got at least an hour before I need to leave. I take off my dress and put my bikini on, not giving a shit if any bruises or marks are on display. I head down to the pool, toss my towel onto a sun-bed and dive in.

The water in the pool is deliciously cold, and the sensation as it hits my warm skin is almost orgasmic. I do a couple of lengths and climb out, feeling the residue of seven years of hell washing off me as I pull myself up the ladder and into the cool morning air. I retrieve my towel and go to get myself some breakfast. I fill up a plate with ham, cheese and croissants from the buffet, and pour myself a coffee. There's a table half in the shade just outside the door and I sit myself down. I wolf my breakfast down and guzzle my coffee. I haven't had an appetite like this for years. It's great. I'm ravenous. I go back for seconds on my coffee and grab another croissant, before heading back to my room. I throw on some jeans and a top and grab my passport. I bounce down the stairs and go to the scooter hire shop next door and get myself a purple Vespa. The ride to the airport doesn't take long. There is a moment of apprehension when I see them walking away from the easyjet check-in, but they're far enough away to not pick me out of the crowd and are soon disappearing up the escalator to the departure lounge. I don't really fancy a scene down here. This isn't where I want to do it.

I check the board, and head over to the correct desk to check-in. The queue is short and I'm processed quickly and given a boarding card I have no intention of using. I head up to the first floor. I'm getting a few butterflies now, but my resolve is cast-iron and I'm well up for this. I go through the security check and hear the last call for their flight. I walk over to the gate, and see the three of them looking flustered. Everyone else has boarded the plane, and it's just them waiting to get on now. Sharon sees me and nudges Keeley and points. Keeley's face is scarlet and she looks more pissed off than her brother is going to be. I feel the air rush out of me, but not through fear. It's exhilaration I'm feeling. As I get close, Keeley's mouth springs open and she spews a torrent of swearwords at me.

"Where the fuck have you been? What the fucking hell are you playing at? What's got into you? First you cheat on my brother, and now you've nearly made us miss our plane. You're a selfish fucking cow, Vicky."

The others stand behind her casting disapproving looks, their arms folded across their chests. They all look like they're sucking on lemons, but I know they're actually enjoying the intoxicating and unfamiliar feeling of self-righteousness coursing through their veins. They all look at me like I'm a piece of shit, and pick up their bags and walk through the gate, handing their boarding cards in to be scanned. I stand completely still on the other side of the gate.

Keeley stops and turns round.

"Are you coming or what?"

"Um, no I'm not coming with you."

"Come again?"

"I'm leaving Paul, I'm leaving Liverpool, and I'm not coming back. And while I'm saying goodbye, I'd just like to tell you all to fuck off. You've all been fully aware of what Paul has been like to me over the last few years, and not once have any of you stepped in to offer me support. Not once have any of you asked if I needed help. Not once. You're not my friends. You're a shit collection of self-obsessed bitches. Have a nice life."

And with that, I leave them at the gate, gawping like the group of fishwives they are destined to become. I feel liberated. I strut out of the departure lounge and out of the terminal building. I stand outside, basking in the blue sky and think about what I'm about to do. I'm not heading back to England at all. I'm actually going in the opposite direction. I'm flying to Frankfurt this evening, where I'm picking up a flight to Japan. From there, I'm flying to Australia. I'm starting again. I've already got a second interview for a job in Sydney. I did the phone interview from work last week, and it went really well. I'm going in for a face to face on Friday. I'll have been there for four days then, the jet-lag will have gone, and hopefully the panic will have subsided. When I focus on what I'm doing, I feel abject fear. But at the same time, there is hope. A voice inside me, long since muffled and crushed, but one that I recognise as my soul, my being, my true self; that voice tells me I'm doing the best thing I'm ever going to have done in my life. And I seize upon that voice. It gives me the strength and the courage to do what I've got to do. And I know I can pull this off. I'm going to be Me again. I'm getting my life back. I start up the scooter and head off, gleefully looking forward to a day at Benirras and a life free of fear.

Epilogue

The sun pokes its forehead over the horizon, casting long shadows and refracting off the moisture in the air. The resulting half-light and haze shimmers and gives the world a brief appearance of a dream sequence, or at least a soft-focus effect. Like a 1980s pop video. It looks fucking magic.

At the side of the road sits a bag. A green duffel bag. Just next to it, bushes cover the verge, beyond which lies a steep incline. One of the bushes has been disturbed, and is a little fucked up – broken twigs, branches stripped of their leaves. But it's hardly noticeable; no-one would really clock it. Blink and you'd miss the only evidence of someone having tumbled down the incline, grabbing at any bushes in the way to unsuccessfully help break their fall. Well, not the only evidence. The bag might hint at something.

In the distance, a low rasping put-put-put sound appears. It grows louder, and soon, a little purple scooter comes into view. It carries on its back a young woman. She looks like she doesn't have a care in the world. She sees the bag in the road ahead, and brings her bike to a halt next to it.

Acknowledgements

Massive love to everyone who politely smiled and nodded when I bleated about writing this for so long, and even more love to those who read it.

Special thanks to Matt Cogger for getting this whole ball rolling. Gutted you couldn't hang around to see this come out.

On the island, thanks to Jordan, Ryan, Lucy, Amy, Vikki, Jill Canney, Jasmin, Joe, Newton, Hedden, Aimee, Bear, Brown, Harry, Grainger, Cov, Jack, Cliff, Chloe, Jason, Macca, Alice, Mike B, Mike D, Griff, Laura, Kirstie, Jill Collins, Rachel, Sexual Harassment Panda, Katie and Jesus, Sweeney, Lauren and James, Dec, Cila, Fish, Little Dave, Jo and Darren, Toby, Andy, Dawn and all the Ibiza Rocks crew.

Back home, thanks to John Perry, Zoe, Chas, Punk Workie, Jon Bills, Chris, Green, Phil, Jo K, Lottie, Towelie, Swin, Jamie, Cath, Max, Lee, PB Rex, Mum, Dad, Emma and Jason and LME. And Piggy Smalls.

And most thanks go to Hannah. For everything.

Printed in Great Britain
by Amazon